# IN THE CREASE

## CONNECTICUT COMMODORES
### BOOK 3

## SKYE MCDONALD

*For Winston*
*The World's Greatest Corgi*

# 1

## NICA

My husband just got married.

I sat in the back of a limo in a long line of luxury cars while it happened. Just when I couldn't check my phone again without it being a tic, we started to roll forward. The driver turned onto a lane that wound up to the biggest freaking house I'd ever seen in my life. The double red doors stood open. White wreaths and roses welcomed guests inside. Butlers and security guards stood at the ready. Once I showed my invitation, they offered me canapes and pointed to the backyard.

I smoothed the black cocktail dress over my chest. An online boutique gifted it to me when they learned I had a coveted invitation to this event. But fancy clothes didn't stop the screaming in my head that said I had no freaking business at a place this swanky. Out of my league didn't begin to cover it.

Not only that, I was a creep. A "stalker." I was *her*. As in, "Can you believe they invited *her* to this wedding?"

For a girl whose momma taught her to lay low, blend in, and take just enough to get by, I felt way too out of place.

A waiter walked up with champagne, and I had to resist the urge to swipe two off the tray. Sucking down the delicious bubbly, I flowed with the river of people heading to the party at the massive tent on the rolling lawn. Once we were out on the patio, I stepped aside and let others hurry along the path.

*Is that a little rink?* I did a double-take. Sure enough, a pair of ice dancers performed for onlookers. The tuxedoed men and gown-clad women applauded while the band played. I boggled at the opulence, even though it couldn't have been more appropriate for a hockey goalie's wedding.

But I wasn't there to gawk. I was there to work. To be *her.* Sick of the schtick as I was, it was this or go back to waiting tables in a casino. And that was not an option. Not now that I knew what working for myself felt like.

I whipped out my phone and panned a slow video of the grounds. My voice became gravelly with a lift at the end of each sentence. It was my trademark tone to make me sound cool but committed to what I was saying.

"It's wedding day, besties. You'll have to wait for photos of my Quentin in his tux. Keep the drool in your mouths, babes. It'll be well worth it when I finally show you. For now, dig this party. *So* nice of my new mom to host us, don't you think?"

I flipped the camera to me and winked. As soon as it posted, notifications flowed in. Meanwhile, I hurried to set up a video I'd taken before leaving my apartment. The gorgeous peach metallic suitcase sat on my bed with a pair of panties and a toothbrush inside. In the video, I open the case to show its contents and say, "Leaving for honeymoon, anyone? Quentin's season starts Monday, but I bet you're ready to travel! With Elsewhere's latest colors, you'll stay in style no matter where you go. Don't forget your Bellini panties, of course!" I scheduled that post to drop in half an hour to optimize the algorithm.

Once that was done, I looked up to find I'd emptied the champagne and hadn't gotten any closer to the actual party. Guests and staff strolled by without a sideways glance. I slipped a little bit further off the path and opened my phone again, this time for a call.

"I thought you were at the wedding."

"I am," I said softly into the speaker. "It's... fancy."

Vinny laughed. "No shit it's fancy. It's in the Hamptons." He affected a snooty accent that made me smile at last.

"Well, exactly. I feel so out of place. Like, if I'm not in a waiter's uniform, holding a tray of prosciutto-wrapped figs and sneaking rolls into my purse, what am I even doing?"

"Aw, sis. You're not Mom, and you know it. Chin up. You've made a name for yourself. Walk around that party like the loudmouth influencer you've shown the world you can be. They ain't gotta know you come from a trailer park in the woods of Connecticut. As far as they're concerned, you go to the Hamptons every weekend."

I took a deep breath and nodded. "Thanks, Vin. I got this."

"You got this."

I said goodbye and dropped the phone in my bag. After rolling my shoulders and stealing another flute from a passing tray, I made myself go to the tent.

People tossed glances when I stepped into the receiving line, but just as quickly, most turned away again. Better than the lip curls of disgust that a few of them flashed to say they knew exactly who I was. At least there weren't many of those so far. It didn't surprise me that most of Quentin Paris's friends and family didn't recognize *Mrs. Quentin Paris*.

I sipped the champagne and shuffled forward. Quentin

and Audrey's ceremony had been intimate, but the reception was a VIP soiree. Everyone who hadn't been there for the "I dos" wanted to congratulate the family. I shook hands with the parents of the bride and groom, Quentin's brother and sister-in-law, and finally got to the happy couple. Audrey looked radiant in her wedding gown. She smiled to see me.

"Nica. Thank you for coming."

I clasped her hands. "Congrats, girl."

She breathed a laugh. "I'm ready to hide from so many people already."

"You got this." I grinned to echo the phrase again. Audrey was the coolest. The fact that she invited me to her wedding blew my mind. I still marveled that she let me anywhere near her or her man. My social media handle had started as a goof but became my whole career. I never imagined so many people would want to watch me fangirl over Quentin Paris, the smoking hot hockey goalie. Almost from the start, though, my online persona had become a massive hit.

As the Connecticut Commodores' head of PR and Quentin's bride, Audrey had decided that the best way to handle me was for us to work together. Once she seemed sure I wasn't going to single white female her and steal her life, that is. She respected branding and image and had no desire to put her relationship in the spotlight. At the start of last season, Audrey began sending me press passes to team events with strict orders to stay in my lane.

Ever since then, publicly lusting over her boyfriend felt weirder and weirder. I'd shifted a lot of my focus to the team as a whole, even though Paris posts always got the biggest reaction. She clearly understood, but it made me feel like a creep sometimes.

Still, having her as a connection gave me content gold. I was over the moon last week when she sent me front-row, center-ice tickets to the first preseason game of the year—only to find out about the surprise wedding that took place before the game. Ethan Rivera marrying his bride on the ice was fairytale fodder that kept my fans talking for days.

But to get an invite to *her* wedding? That had put my stomach on the floor.

I gave her another squeeze and stepped face-to-face with my "husband." His blue eyes sparked with a bit of mischief. "Bonsoir, Mademoiselle," he murmured as he kissed my hand.

*Damn. There's a reason I've gotten thousands of people to swoon with me over this guy.* I forced a cool smile. "Congratulations, Mr. Paris."

"Oh, but you must call me Quinn. I feel like we have known of each other too long for formalities, don't you?"

"Well, if you insist—Quinn."

"Lovely. Enjoy the party, Nica." He winked, and I nearly fainted.

I hurried to a corner and pulled out my phone to go live for a short blurb. "Oh-em-gee, besties. Quentin is in top form tonight. Y'all aren't gonna believe my stories when I tell them!" I fanned my face and cut the feed. Even though he'd just told me to call him Quinn, I always called him Quentin online.

*You've been at this whole schtick for too long. He's freaking married now. How can I stop being a rabid fangirl and keep supporting myself? Can I be more than that and be worth anything?*

I wasn't sure if I could. But I was sure that there could be more champagne. I located my table on the seating chart and took a detour to the bar.

In my periphery, I saw a gray blazer approaching the empty spot I was aiming for. We arrived at the same time and bumped arms. Immediately, he stepped back, gesturing me forward. "Sorry about that."

"My fault. You can go first." The urge to slide through this party unnoticed kept my gaze lowered. I was more than fine to let him order and move on.

"I cannot, actually, because I have manners. Ladies first."

His soft laugh drew my eyes upward against my will. *Holy crap. Don't stare, but damn.* That jawline and those green eyes demanded a lot of self-discipline on my part. He wore an amused smile that dimmed to a little curve of his lips as he studied me. But he didn't frown. He just nodded toward the bar.

I fumbled out a champagne order. The bartender nodded and looked at the guy. "And you, buddy?"

"Uh, you can take care of her first."

"I've got her. What do you need?"

He didn't answer for long enough that I looked back at him. He glanced down at me, jaw sliding side to side, and then blew out a breath. "One throw me down and fuck me, a cherry popper, a blow job, and two blue balls, please. Oh, and a beer. I don't care what kind."

The bartender stared at him. So did I. Then, we both burst out laughing. "What'd you do, man? Lose a bet?" the bartender asked.

"Bingo," he muttered. Bless him, his ears had turned bright red.

"Five ridiculous drinks coming up. Let me get you the beer and champagne first."

Two glasses appeared on the bar in under a minute. We reached for them. Another giggle escaped me, and he heaved another sigh.

"Well, um, cheers. Enjoy all your sex drinks."

Those green eyes hit me again. This time, his lips were pressed into a line. "I'd swear they weren't for me, but the impression has already been made, hasn't it?"

*Do not flirt at this party. That is the worst idea in the world, no matter how cute he is.* "It was a memorable one. I'll give you that." I clinked my glass to his. "Have fun."

It took a lot not to turn around and see if he was watching me while I found my seat. But as soon as I sat down, I was back in work mode. Unsurprisingly, I was at a table of journalists. Only a few of us had been granted access with very strict contracts about what we could and could not reveal and photograph during and after the event. They talked stories and players over dinner. I gave my usual "freelancer" response when they asked who I worked for. And, as usual, they largely ignored me.

*Who cares if no one talks to you? Bruce said this would kick some life into my platform. Maybe I should've brought him as my plus one...*

I winced and smacked the back of my left hand with my right under the table. *You don't need a toxic jerk, no matter how lonely or overwhelmed you might be. Besides, you have a meeting with him next week.*

The bride and groom cut the cake, and dancing began. I watched my "husband" absolutely own the floor. The way he held Audrey and moved her with effortless confidence. The way he and his brother laughed together even while they danced with their wives. I wasn't the only one appreciating the scene. Everyone seemed delighted by the party's energy.

It was great, no doubt. But it also made me feel kind of... empty.

I wasn't jealous of Audrey *at all*. Quinn was a fox, sure.

My celebrity crush on him had started the page, but by now my whole focus was on algorithms and sponsorships. He was my content, not my obsession. No matter what anyone thought.

The emptiness came from feeling so out of my element here. So on the outside of this situation. Not only because of the rich-as-hell vibe. Because this was family. This was fun, frivolous, and free. And I didn't have time for that stuff.

I didn't dance. I drank another champagne. I took all the B-roll footage I could without capturing anyone's face. When I'd sat politely and collected enough content, I excused myself. As soon as I stood up, the booze hit me hard.

Damn, champagne was a sneaky fucker. It went down like water and then hit you like a frying pan to the head.

I weaved my way through the tables to the edge of the tent and looked around. The cute guy was leaning against the bar, watching the dance floor. He must've sensed my gaze because he looked over. I wiggled my fingers, and he lifted his glass my way.

Even with the alcohol in my system, I didn't have the guts to go talk to him again. Instead, I stepped out into the grass. My heels wobbled, so I kicked my shoes off and held them in my hand. The late September night on Long Island was cool but refreshing. A path cut through the grass, leading me away from the party. I followed it all the way to the beach and nearly fell down the wooden steps to the sand. As I steadied my feet, the shushing waves and salty air hit my senses.

"Oh, wow," I breathed, dropping my shoes and hopping down the steps. A fingernail moon hung in the sky. It was so peaceful. So easy to just be me for a second without all the hashtags and hustle.

Tipsy tears pricked my eyes. I sucked in a wobbly breath and wished on the moon. "I'm not asking for a fairytale. Just that someday, maybe, things could be a little... sweeter."

I pressed the heels of my hands into my eyes and groaned. My head spun with how very *mid* even my wishes could be. With a huff, I dropped my hands. But my champagne brain kept spinning and spinning...

Just in time, I ran to the nearest sand dune and puked. Champagne, wedding cake, and all my sappy hopes were lost to the dark.

# 2

# RYAN

*Don't follow her. That's fucking creepy.*

I watched the dark-haired woman from the bar turn and wander down the path to the beach. No way would I follow a woman I didn't know, not even to explain how my goofball teammates had put me on the spot in front of her earlier.

Instead, I leaned on the bar and put my attention on the scene on the dance floor. Ethan "Twinkle Toes" Rivera had created a flash mob. At least thirty people gleefully followed his moves. He shouted and gestured with his iced tea glass, clearly delighted at the crowd's efforts.

When the song ended, Dustin and Yuri, two more of my teammates, hurried toward the bar with their partners in tow. They were all flushed and grinning as they surrounded me.

"You should've gotten out there, Molls," Dustin said while they waited on their drinks—actual drinks this time, not the goofy-ass bullshit they'd made me order earlier. They'd pissed themselves laughing coming up with that list. Damn me for not remembering which hockey players had ever worn sixty-nine as their number. To be fair, they weren't goalies.

I sipped my beer and shook my head. "Why would I be out there? I can laugh at you just fine from here."

"It's a hell of a party for sure," Yuri said after we clinked glasses.

Everyone agreed.

Yuri's wife, Tanya, looked around. "The house is exquisite. And it seems as if an arena full of people are here! The guest list must be three hundred at least. They invited everyone."

Dustin's girlfriend snorted. "No kidding they did. Even a few reporters got in. They're over there." Jazzlynne nodded at the table and then frowned. "Hm. I don't see her now, but did y'all notice they let *her* in, too?"

"Who?" Yuri asked, echoing the question in my head.

"Mrs. Quentin Paris."

"Ohh." The collective murmur only furthered my confusion.

"Audrey and her publicity stunts," Dustin chuckled.

"Mm, more like keep your enemies closer," Tanya said with a headshake.

"*Who*?" I asked.

Jazzlynne tossed me a patient smile. "Quinn's superfan. She goes by Mrs. Quentin Paris on social media and has a huge following."

"Oh. How, uh, weird that she's here."

"She's press."

We all turned at Audrey's voice. Jazzlynne and Tanya shouted and kissed her cheeks in congratulations yet again, as if they hadn't already done so. Audrey laughed and thanked them while her friend, Stella, stood nearby. Audrey and Stella had both become players' wives within the week, but their places in the Commodores' community had been cemented long ago. Well before I'd joined the team. Audrey was the first person I'd met after Coach Delgato.

Audrey nodded toward the press table again. "I wanted her to have the inside story. It's good for the team's image. That's why I put her front row for your wedding, too." She smiled at Stella.

"You're a bigger person than I could be," Jazzlynne said. "I'd sharpen my nails and take out my earrings if someone showed up calling themselves Mrs. Dustin Simmons."

Audrey shrugged. "It's not just about Quinn. She promotes the whole team. I figured working with her was easier than making her an enemy. Plus, she's nice."

"Like I said, girl. Bigger person." Jazzlynne smiled and hugged Dustin's neck.

I absorbed the conversation with almost no interest. Yes, it seemed odd to invite a social media personality to a wedding, but what did I know about such things? Audrey was head of the team's PR for a reason. If she decided it was right, then why should the rest of us care?

By the time Quinn and Audrey made their exit, I was more than ready for the night to be over. Going solo to a wedding, even a teammate's wedding, drained me. There was only so much small talk I could endure and only so many beers I could consume until I felt like shit. So I beat the crowd out of the driveway and rode to the inn where several of us were staying for the night. I found a handful of my teammates and their partners in the lobby when I walked in. They greeted me as they headed for the stairs.

"Anyone want to hit the bar for a nightcap?" I asked, not quite ready to be alone with my thoughts.

But the women frowned, prompting the guys to shake their heads no. Even Max, who was my fellow single guy on the team, yawned and said he was done for the night. So, I followed them upstairs and unlocked my room. I sat down on the bed with a sigh and pulled off my glasses.

The room was too quiet, I was too awake, and I had nothing to put my mind on. Preseason was over. The regular season didn't start for a week. I could've reviewed stats or gamed on my laptop, but I wasn't in the mood. Something about the wedding left me feeling restless. Wanting something different. Routines were my friend, but not that night.

I shucked the suit jacket, dropped my tie on the bed, snatched my glasses, and went to the bar by myself. The old bartender slid a whiskey my way while I climbed on the stool. We chit-chatted about the weather and the ESPN highlights running on the TV behind him for a moment. Then he went back to washing dishes while I stared into my glass.

The inn's front door opened, sending a chilly breeze straight into the bar. High heels softly tapped the hardwood floor several moments later. From my periphery, I saw a woman with black hair and a black dress slide onto the stool one down from me. She ordered a water and sat motionless while it was poured.

My stomach dropped. *What were the odds? What do I say? How do I start a conversation with—*

"Where's your blow job?"

A laugh burst out of me. The bartender dropped a spoon with a clatter. Turning my head, I found her smirking with a wicked glint in those blue-gray eyes.

"I swear on this whiskey, those weren't for me."

"Yeah, right. They always say that."

"You'll never let me live this down, will you?"

"Afraid that's impossible. You'll forever be the sex drinks guy. Cheers again, sex drinks guy."

I shook my head. "Cheers."

Her lips fit around the straw. I looked down at the whiskey in front of me, fully prepared to return to my thoughts. But with another sip, I heard myself say, "Can I buy you a drink? Um, a sex drink or... whatever your pleasure?"

Inwardly, I groaned at my awkwardness. *Who do you think you are, trying to sound cool? Leave that to Quinn, Ethan —hell, even Dustin.*

But when I glanced over, she wore a little smile. "Thank you, but I've had enough for tonight."

I frowned. "Then why are you in a bar?"

# 3

# NICA

I suppressed a snort. "Fair question."

The limo had just dropped me at this boutique inn. My car was parked in the lot, but I'd thanked the driver and walked inside like I could afford a room here. Even with the gifted dress and wedding-provided local chauffeur, my wallet had sobbed when I'd researched hotels on Long Island. So I sucked it up and prepared for a long night of driving. Good thing I'd vomited out all the booze and was sober again.

But while I was brushing my teeth in the hotel restroom, I double-checked the ferry schedule back to Connecticut. A cold stone settled in my stomach as I refreshed the page twice, sure I was mistaken. No way had I missed the *weekend* schedule that ended two hours earlier than on weekdays.

The answer to the guy's question of why I was in a bar was simple: I had to sleep in my car and was in no hurry to do so. Why not stay warm and have a moment in this cozy inn before facing reality?

He, of course, did not need to know that. Finding him on

the barstool down from me was either a blessing or a fateful trap. I wasn't sure yet which.

I tossed my hair and looked him over. Yet again, my stomach dropped at how cute he was. Strawberry-blond hair combed back off his face. Those glasses gave him a serious, trustworthy look. Broad-as-hell shoulders stretched a white dress shirt despite the fact that the sleeves were too big on him.

Instead of explaining why I was in the bar, I redirected. "Did you have fun at the wedding?"

He didn't fight it. "It was a great party, yeah. Did you? I saw you disappear."

"Just went to get a breath of air."

"Are you a friend of Audrey's?"

"Uh. Yeah." *No, I made a career out of lusting over her husband.* No way did this guy need to know that. Time to redirect again. "Did you dance?"

He snorted. "Yeah. I drank all those shooters and then did the Lindy Hop."

That made me laugh. "Well, why not? You could have."

One shoulder shrugged. "Could've, but you were nowhere to be found."

I loved the cautious glance he tossed me. As if he was assessing whether his line was cute or corny. *Both. Definitely both.* "You would *not* have wanted to be seen with me. We'd have caused a scandal." I said it all flirty. Like I was joking.

I was not at all joking.

But, ooh, his grin. I tried not to blush at the flutter in my gut when his teeth flashed. "In that case, good thing for the wedding that we didn't."

"Mm. Mm-hm."

"Sure you don't want a drink?"

I ordered a club soda with lime. When I'd thanked the

bartender, I slid off the stool to my feet and jerked my head toward the booth in the corner. "No booze, thanks. But it's drafty in here, and I'm cold. That spot looks warm. Want to join me?"

He seemed startled at the suggestion but nodded after a beat. I led us over with my shoulders back and my chin up.

*Biding a little time won't kill you. He's cute. He seems into you. You've spent the last four hours lonely, out of your league, and awkward. All you do is hustle. Let yourself feel something different for a hot second.*

I slid to the inside corner of the rounded leather bench. He joined me, sitting close enough that we were properly cozy. "Here's to having no one around to scandalize."

He smiled again. "Cheers to that. Although..."

"Yes?" I drawled. It was nice to flirt. I hadn't flirted with anything but a camera in ages.

"Although I'm less concerned with scandal and more concerned with whether or not you're enjoying this."

I raised my eyebrow. "Does it seem like I'm not?"

He looked down and shrugged. "I don't normally talk to women in bars. Doesn't seem smart to presume."

"You wouldn't have offered me a drink if I hadn't talked to you just now?"

"Nope."

"Even though we kind of met earlier?"

"Nope."

"How un-single-guy-in-a-bar of you."

That earned me a soft laugh. "Maybe so. I tend to assume people prefer privacy."

"I tend to prefer privacy, for what it's worth." I nudged his shoulder to get his gaze on me. "But this is nice."

He studied me in a way that should've made me uncomfortable but didn't. I had on my classic Mrs. Quentin Paris look of dramatic makeup and long, luscious hair. Even without the filters I used on every post, I knew that, outwardly, I seemed classy enough to belong in a place like this. Even if I never really felt it.

So his gaze didn't make me cringe. It made me lean closer. "Well? Do you agree, stranger?"

"Do I... what?" he murmured.

"Is this nice or not?"

He nodded slowly.

"Let's make a bet. I'm going to guess your name. If I'm wrong, I have to go order a blow job from that poor bartender."

"And if you're right?"

"You have to kiss me."

His face froze except for his brows. They hit his hairline.

My pulse raced at my audacity, but dammit. I wanted something, anything, so long as it was different. I didn't want to video anything or tell the world how hot someone was that I barely knew. I didn't want to promote a product, think about metrics, or create new content. I didn't want to pay rent, and I sure as shit didn't want to sleep in my car.

For just a few moments, I wanted to be irresponsible and free.

"Go for it," he whispered at last.

I grinned. "I bet your name is..."

"Yep, that's it." His words tumbled out as he leaned closer, one hand sliding to my cheek. He dusted a soft kiss on me while I wrapped my hand around his thick-as-hell bicep. I opened my eyes to see him pull back an inch and blink at me, clearly assessing my reaction.

My answer was to fit my mouth against his for a proper kiss. His jaw clenched for a brief moment before I heard him inhale sharply. Electricity shot through my body when he cradled my head and kissed me with a soft, wicked tease of his lips and tongue. My sober brain spun and then went silent, totally unprepared for the raw sexiness of this moment. I tried to keep up and kiss him back, but he had taken control. Instead, I moaned. The needy sound vibrated in my throat as my tongue tangled with his. It made his fingers tighten against my scalp just before he broke us apart.

"Jesus. *Fuck.*" His ragged hiss hit my ears over my own shameless panting.

"Uh-huh," I managed to agree.

We stared at each other. Simultaneously, we leaned in again for another series of searing kisses. He had me pinned against the booth, alternating between kissing my mouth and skimming his lips along my jaw. My fingers twined in his hair, tugging desperately to keep myself from climbing into his lap.

The old bartender's subtle cough snapped the moment. I swallowed a moan as he threw himself against the booth. The nearly feral look in his eyes was certainly a mirror of my own. *Holy shit, when was the last time I was so turned on?*

My guy's jaw slid side to side. "Um. I... I don't know if I should ask this, but... Do you want to get out of here? We could go to my room for a while. Only if you want," he hurried to add.

"I... uh, I need the restroom." Not the most logical response, but I was completely unprepared for how he'd short-circuited me.

He nodded quickly. "Of course. Take your time. I'll go upstairs. My room is two-twelve. If you decide you want to."

I pressed my lips in a line and nodded. "Okay."

He slid out of the booth, signed the bill at the bar, and glanced at me once more as he headed out. I didn't move until I heard his feet on the stairs, but then I raced to the lobby bathroom to pee. My panties were soaked from his kiss. I cringed to hitch them back up but then hurried to wash my hands and stare at myself in the mirror.

*Sleep in your car, or go upstairs and...*

*Sleep with a stranger. To avoid sleeping in your car. And then explain to him in the morning that you don't have a room here. No room, no change of clothes, nothing but a beat-up little sedan in the parking lot. Oh, and not to mention that you don't have your makeup with you, and you can't sleep in your hair. In the light of day, you'll look like an urchin in a rumpled designer dress. Like your momma's daughter. A good-for-nothing from the wrong side of the tracks. He'll probably check his wallet to make sure I didn't steal from him. Not that I would. I am* not *my mother and never, ever will be.*

I sighed. No way. I couldn't do it. Not even for a kiss that good.

"I didn't need the fairytale anyway," I whispered to the mirror before grabbing my purse and damn near running to my car.

The ferry terminal was dark and silent when I pulled into the parking lot. I gazed at the building for a long moment and then reached behind me to undo my pushup bra and unclip the extensions that gave me my glorious dark mane. Then, I lowered my seat all the way down. Using my flimsy wrap as a blanket and my arm as a pillow, I shut my eyes and prayed for an early boat.

At least I had the memory of those few moments in the bar to keep me warm.

The long, low bleat of the ferry's arrival jerked me from

fitful sleep. I jolted upright to see people queuing up for the first ride of the day. My skin was clammy with the early autumn chill, so I fired the ignition and blasted the heat as I rolled forward onto the boat.

Coffee was essential but getting that bra back on without stripping down was impossible. For once, not having much of a rack came in handy. I fixed my raccoon eyes as best I could, hugged the wrap around me, and prayed everyone on board was too sleepy or hungover to notice my ghoulish ass skulking around.

No amount of ferryboat coffee could warm my bones once I stepped out into the breezy morning. I bought a large and clutched it tight. Huddled in a seat inside and trying not to shiver, I pulled out my phone.

Metrics from last night's posts were strong. Summer was my slow season, so this was the most traffic I'd had in a while. I just wished it didn't feel quite this slow. At least I had content from two hockey weddings to push for a few days. That ought to boost interest while the season got started.

"Mrs. Quentin Paris" had been a goof fueled by a night of drinking with my girlfriends two years ago. We'd gone to a Commodores game and wound up Googling players at the bar afterward. How could I have known that my posts would go viral as the new goalie proved to be a superstar?

I barely knew anything about algorithms or branding before. Now, it was my whole life—a little too much so. My girls didn't call anymore. We'd all waitressed together at the casino. Their lives went on while mine took a different track. We were all too busy working to make time anymore.

It was nothing new. Friends had come and gone with jobs before. Especially when I'd left home and moved to Hartford. Even growing up, friends didn't stick around long.

Thank goodness for Vinny. My brother had been my best friend through long nights when Momma was either out doing god-knows-what or stoned off her ass in the trailer.

I stared into the coffee. Feeling this small and cold brought me back to being a teenager. Momma had gotten me a job as a catering waiter with her. She trained me for weeks. Not only on how to serve and blend into the background, but also how to fill our purses with leftover food before anyone noticed.

She knew how to lift a lot more than food from the patrons. I left home when she tried to teach me that trick.

My mother had addictions to feed on top of my brother and me. Once, when I was in elementary school, she came home with her bag nearly bursting after a catered event. But the leftovers weren't that great, and they didn't feed us more than a day or so. The next night, I heard her in her bedroom. When I peeked in, she was counting a stack of cash. Her eyes widened when she saw me, but she smiled.

"Tips were good, baby. Go play with your brother."

So, I shuffled down the hall to Vinny's room. He never minded much when I'd sneak in and sit on the floor, so long as I didn't ask questions while the game was on. Through the years, we watched the Commodores like it was our job. On many long, lonely nights, it was.

I sucked in a deep breath and shook myself out of those ancient memories. *You are not that girl. You are a self-made woman who just spent her Saturday schmoozing at a Hamptons wedding. You fit in just fine. None of them know shit about you.*

My heavy eyelids closed. *You'll be home soon. Hot bath, curtains drawn, long sleep. Last night was important. The season is starting. You'll figure out a way to stop fangirling Quentin and do something bigger. You'll be fine. Meet with Bruce soon, get some fresh ideas, and keep going. You're golden, babes.*

My eyes stayed closed while I sipped again. Somewhere between dozing and dreaming about the bathtub in my little apartment, I pictured my fella from last night. Despite the perma-chill, my cheeks warmed.

*My god, he was cute. My god, you were bold to hit on him!*

*... My god, you were a dick to ghost him like that.*

Oh, but my toes curled when I recalled his fireball of a kiss.

*Who cares? You'll never see him again. He said it was my decision. So yeah, I kind of ghosted him. He'll be fine. He'll move on by tomorrow. And you have work to do.*

# 4

# RYAN

"Good game, man. Good game... good game..."

I mumbled the phrase nineteen times and then joined the end of the line to the ice. While the guys skated a circle, I went straight to the end of the bench. Even though I was in full gear, my helmet sat at my feet. As usual, I kept a ballcap pulled low on my head. For the next few hours, my main duty was to cheer on the team and keep an eye out for holes in our defense.

Our first game of the season was much grittier than expected. We eked out a win against Philly with a last-minute goal, but Paris gave up three in the first two periods. For him, that was a terrible night.

But a win was a win, and especially since it was game one, we showered and all headed to the local bar to celebrate. The Pub, a very on-the-nose name for the only bar in Seacrest, was basically a second home to the team. We gathered there after most home games, especially if we'd won. The bartenders knew us and had established long ago that fans were welcome before and during games. But about two hours after the final buzzer sounded, the only patrons besides the team and our pals were locals who knew how to be cool. I'd always wondered how they kept the space so chill for us, but anytime I'd tried to ask, I just got a knowing grin from the owner.

As expected, Quinn sat at the end of the table, staring at his beer like it held the answer to life. I dropped down beside him.

"Your right leg bothering you?" It was all I needed to say. I knew he knew damn well that all three goals had gone in on his lower right side.

He stirred. "I don't know. I felt... tight? Was not a problem at practice yesterday."

"Here's to it not being a problem tomorrow."

We clinked beers.

I let Quinn do his usual introspective thing. I had my quirks, but that man had a tunnel vision for the game that was unparalleled. While he pondered, I fell into a conversation with Dustin and Gene.

"You were on the ice for all three of Philly's goals," I said to our captain.

"Don't I know it. Our D was wobbly." Gene flinched. He'd turned thirty-eight this summer and knew he was slowing down. Still had a hell of a slapshot, though.

"Do me." Dustin chuckled.

"You didn't score a single goal. And you allowed two turnovers, one of which became a goal."

His grin fell. "Fuck. I like your notes better when we play well."

I shrugged. "Keep your head up, Simsy. They get you every time when your head's down."

He nodded, and we moved to another topic. I didn't like giving critical feedback, but my teammates looked to me to analyze their performance. Sitting on the bench gave me a great POV to collect data and notice little details. Two things I was naturally good at. I was so good at it that when I went home, I would scrape hockey stats websites and populate a running spreadsheet that I kept on the team. It was fascinating work that made a big difference in our season.

Wild and sexy, it was not. But then, I'd never pretended to be the coolest guy on the team.

As usual, most of the guys had already left by the time I threw cash on the table. Max and I were often the last to leave since we didn't have partners to go home to. But eventually the bartenders started washing up. Time to shuffle to my car and call goodnight. The drive took ten minutes. As always, my thoughts got quieter with every minute that passed.

But the sound of scrabbling feet behind the front door *always* gave me a smile.

I tapped the numeric code to unlock and stepped into the dark foyer. Immediately, my feet and ankles were assaulted by frantic paws and little nips. Henrik danced around, welcoming me home, so I crouched down and scratched his ears. "Hey, buddy. How you doing? Did the kiddos look after you today?"

Of course, I knew my neighbor's kids had pet-sat him. I saw the alert from the front-door camera when they came over in the afternoon. If it weren't for them, I might've had to rehome Henrik. A hockey player's lifestyle isn't great for pets, certainly not without someone else to help. But the family next door loved Henrik and kept him whenever I was away. They didn't know it yet, but I'd started college funds for both children as a thank-you. Knowing my best buddy was looked after and still waiting when I got home was priceless.

Henrik hurried outside to do his business. I hung up my

coat and shut the door. He would run around the house and enter through his dog door into the kitchen, so I headed there.

This house's ultramodern amenities and rustic Cape Cod design screamed architectural showcase. Probably because I'd had an architect create it and a decorator furnish it to create my dream home.

Our dream home. Or so I'd assumed.

I called to the automation to turn on the lights in the kitchen. The globes above the marble island glowed at thirty percent, exactly to my specifications for this time of night. My footsteps sounded on the tile as I filled a glass of water and wandered to my office. Henrik beat me to it. He was already curled in his bed beside my desk when I walked in. I scratched his ears again and sat down with a sigh.

Over the two years since the Connecticut Commodores had signed me as their backup goalie, I'd carved out a niche as the stats guy. For as much as I loved to play hockey, I realized soon after we'd inked the contract that plentiful ice time wasn't in my future. Not with Paris in net.

Amanda had realized it, too. And when she did, our dream home became my oversized house for one and a half. Henrik was a puppy then. She never even suggested wanting to take him with her. She was too focused on what a disappointment my job turned out to be.

I played one game out of five or six, usually. Some backup goalies in the league had a more even split, but with a superstar like Quinn around, I wasn't needed as much. Of course, I practiced with the team and worked out on the same schedule. I had to be ready to play at a moment's notice should the need arise. But the last time Paris hadn't finished a game was in a brawl with Atlanta two seasons ago.

So while I remained alert and ready, I took the bench each night knowing to get comfortable.

I didn't mind. I had my place on the team, and I loved it.

But when I opened the new season's spreadsheet, I wound up staring into space instead. It was Saturday night. Precisely one week ago, I was on Long Island for Quinn and Audrey's wedding. That wasn't what had me distracted, though.

*She* did.

With a week's worth of practices and prep, I'd put her out of my mind. Mostly. After I'd stayed up for three foolish hours in case she knocked on my door, of course. After spending Sunday replaying that whole series of events. How the hell had I wound up kissing a stranger in a bar? Who the *hell* was I to ask her to my room? Since when was that my style?

I should've been relieved she didn't show. Should've known better than to invite a stranger to my room. And I certainly shouldn't have been embarrassed when she vanished.

But then, Quinn *should* have had at least two more saves tonight. And yet.

Shoulds meant nothing in hockey or life, apparently. Because although that half an hour—and that kiss— shouldn't have stayed with me, they did. One week later, I knew I should let it go.

And yet.

*Audrey. She's friends with Audrey. Maybe I can ask her... what, exactly? I didn't even get a name. What a shitbag I'll sound like if I even try to ask. If only I'd gotten some detail that told me who the hell she was. That's the problem. She was a mystery. An unsolvable puzzle. If not for that, I definitely could let it go.*

I laughed at myself in the silent room. "Bullshit. Get to work."

Good advice.

$\sim$

"Come on, give me that deke, Rivera," I muttered under my breath as I tracked Ethan racing in on me. As predicted, he feinted left and then shot right.

"Kick save!" I shouted while the puck rolled away.

Ethan plowed to a hockey stop in front of me and groaned. "Dammit, how'd you see that coming, Sieve?"

"A, fuck off. B, that's your signature move. Better start changing it up if you want to try and get inside these pipes."

I shot Gatorade into my mouth and smirked. Ethan loved calling me Sieve. The none-too-flattering nickname had become an old joke over the past year, as had my consistent "fuck off" in reply.

"Hmm, gauntlet thrown. Just you wait." Ethan laughed and danced away per his team nickname.

But practice had an edge to it that morning. We had another game tomorrow night, so this was meant to be a light skills drill. Apparently, the rough opener had the guys tense. Pucks rained on my net from every conceivable direction. I developed a rhythm of blocking that had me more sensing where the next shot was coming from than looking for it.

My own personal goalie Force.

Coach Bowman, the goalie coach, shuffled across the ice to me. "Hey, buddy. Looks like summer training did you right."

"Yeah, Coach, thanks. Feeling good so far." I'd spent the summer in Alberta, Canada, working on my style. Bowman and Delgato, our head coach, wanted me more athletic in net versus using my body to block all the shots. It wasn't like I'd completely changed how I worked, but I'd learned a lot and enjoyed the new challenge.

Anything that gave me a puzzle to solve, I was for it. Anything that demanded I focus and understand all the details got me going. It was how my brain worked and why I was so good with numbers *and* goaltending. A strange combination, maybe, but I'd quit trying to be something I wasn't just to please people a long time ago.

It had ended me up alone, sure. But that didn't matter when the season was in front of us.

# 5

## NICA

"Not gonna lie to you, sweetheart. The numbers are slipping." Bruce did an impersonation of a sympathetic frown. It made him look like he was holding in a fart.

Arms crossed, chin high, I refused to flinch. "My wedding videos were a huge hit."

"Mm, yeah, but that was the biggest spike you've had in weeks. And the season opener was rocky. Face it. The schtick is getting old."

*No joke.* Two years of showing the world how in love I was with someone I barely knew had more than worn thin. Working for myself, however, did not get old. I never wanted to go back to slinging drinks in a casino and answering to a dickhead boss again.

But as I stared at my ex-boyfriend-slash-manager, I wondered if I'd traded one ball and chain for another. Bruce and I had been dating for about a month when I created the profile. He was the one who had suggested I monetize my brand and had done a lot to show me how. I wouldn't have been this successful without him, but our personal relationship had only lasted a few months before I called out how obviously incompatible we were.

Bruce had the kind of ego that let him rationalize our breakup as my flighty personality. No way was any fault his. He indulged me and kept the door open for whenever I, little bird that I was, might want to return. Hearing him call me *baby* or *sweetheart* at our meetings barely registered anymore. He talked business but had never quite let go of the idea that I would come running back to him one day.

Probably because I had come running back to him before. More than once.

Damn fits of loneliness. Damn a persona based on lusting after someone. Damn me for all the times I asked myself, *who else would even want you?*

And damn him for the subtle, constant suggestion that the answer was, *not a single soul.*

I dropped my arms to my sides and shrugged. "I'm ready to do something different. It's weird going on about him all the time. How do I get out of it and make a new profile?"

Bruce rubbed his beard. "I can't guarantee you'll be as successful on a second profile, but I can scout some ideas for you. If I do that, if we launch a new brand—I'm gonna want a bigger cut."

My fist hit the table. "Are you joking?"

Bruce looked at me like I'd spoken backward. "Why would I be? If I'm doing market research, I think I'm entitled to—"

"You already get forty percent of everything I earn!"

"So fifty would be reasonable."

I blinked twice.

"You're the face. I'm the brains. Half and half, yeah?"

"I... I'm going to have to think about this."

He shrugged. "I'll do some preliminary research and draft an amendment to our contract. You let me know when you're ready. In the meantime, good luck with the metrics."

I stood to leave. As I walked past, Bruce clasped my wrist. "And, uh, I don't have plans next weekend. Just FYI."

He winked, and I had to force down my gag reflex. "Later, Bruce."

In my car, I cranked up the stereo to drown out my primal scream. My fists pummeled the seat on either side of my hips as tears spilled down my cheeks. When my lungs were empty, I put my forehead on the steering wheel.

*Your only hope for not crawling back to your old job is a lizard who wants half of all your paychecks.*

*A lizard who knows what you look like naked but couldn't find your pleasure spots to save his life.*

*A lizard who could at least keep you from waiting tables in a casino until you're a grandma.*

*A grandma to baby lizards. Oh, god, I'm fucked.*

I groaned again.

If only sleeping in my car to save money was a low point. Far from it. All I could see were dead-end streets no matter which way I turned. Just when I thought I'd gotten my big break, I was back in a corner.

*I need something new, and I need it yesterday.*

A month into the season, the Commodores were off to a mixed start, and my followers dwindled daily. The team lost three games back-to-back, one at home and two on the road. Quentin grew more rattled with each puck that flew past him.

Even so, I let out a gasp when Coach Delgato announced that Ryan Molloy would start on the road against Cincinnati.

Molloy games were nothing. He usually played when we faced low-ranking teams where the win was nearly guaranteed. He was decent, but he wasn't Quentin. And Cincinnati had become a serious rival since the Commodores acquired their former player, Ethan Rivera, last year.

Time to make a statement.

I pulled on my Commodores Jersey—with PARIS 26 on the back, of course—and got camera-ready. No one wanted to see plain old Nica. And plain old Nica didn't want to be seen.

Glamorous and full of energy, I hopped in my car and drove out to Seacrest. Technically, Seacrest was a remote suburb of Hartford, but I always thought a forty-five minute drive made the word *suburb* a stretch. Why they put the state's hockey team out in the sticks instead of downtown, I never understood. It would be so much easier to get to games if I could take the bus or walk. But no.

While I drove, I called my brother. "I'm coming to Seacrest to watch this game at The Pub. You practically live at that bar. Come watch with me?"

Vinny groaned. "I wasn't planning on it tonight. We were slammed at the garage today... fine. I'll meet you there."

I squealed and hung up. When I pulled into the pub's gravel driveway, his F-150 was already in a spot. I hurried inside and spied him at the bar right away. Same black hair and blue eyes as me, just like Momma. He'd saved me a seat, so I climbed on and turned to him.

"Can you believe they're putting Molloy in against Cincy?" I asked in greeting.

He laughed. "Yes, actually. Paris needs a break. He's in his head."

I hummed. "I still think he's amazing, but the fangirl thing is old. Bruce says I need a new schtick."

Vinny scowled. "You're still hanging out with that douchebag?"

"He's my manager, Vin. Not my boyfriend."

"Not much better. Are you thinking of quitting the profile?"

I gestured to my face. "Not tonight, obviously. But I don't know. I'd have to find something good as a replacement. Speaking of, one moment, please."

I opened my video app and made sure the filters were set just like I wanted. Even with the makeup, I had to have my trademark look. I angled the camera to catch the crowd behind me and pursed my lips.

"What is going on in Connecticut? How *dare* they bench my husband? Are you as pissed as I am that Molloy is in net tonight? Comment below. Let's tell them we want Quentin!"

Vinny took a pull on his Budweiser and laughed at me. "Sis is pissed. Watch out, Ryan Molloy."

I wiggled my shoulders in agreement. Meanwhile, I could feel my phone vibrating with notifications. *People had something to say about that video. Yes!* My smile grew wider as I ordered a beer.

Before I could lift it to my lips, Vinny tapped his bottle against mine. "Here's to more than twenty years of Commodores games together."

A lump formed in my throat. "Cheers to that."

We traded a secret smile. Just as quickly, though, my tough-as-nails brother cleared his throat and redirected. "So, you doubt Delgato's decision, even though Paris is clearly having a rough start."

"I mean, do you really think we stand a chance tonight without him?"

He gestured toward the screen. "Let's find out."

We turned our attention to the opening puck drop. I grabbed my phone and made a bunch of short clips and pics of myself making faces and flashing a thumbs-down. By the time I had posted a little collage, we were almost through the first period.

And we were up 1-0.

I sipped the beer and focused on the game. Cincinnati stole the puck and raced into our zone. Molloy batted away a shot. It rolled into the corner, where Yuri Ivanov, our star defenseman, tried to take possession. The puck squirted out straight to an Ohio forward waiting at the net. He flipped it up and over Molloy's shoulder.

The light went red, the crowd on the TV went wild, and the bar let out a collective groan. Molloy dropped to his knees in a classic defeated posture while the Cincinnati players celebrated. But just as quickly, play continued. The clock wound down, and our boys went to the locker room.

"Paris would've had that save," I said with a smug smirk.

Vinny laughed. "Probably, yeah. Even with how he's been lately."

"Molloy sucks."

"Hey. Hang on, sis. Molloy is good. Bro has to warm the bench for so many games on end. Give him some credit. He made three saves that period."

It wasn't that I hated Ryan Molloy or anything. I really didn't know anything about him. And I wanted us to win, of course. But my whole brand was built on Paris. Based on the traffic these posts were generating, my followers agreed. I had tons of comments supporting my pro-Paris stance. But a lot of other haters and trolls were calling me names and saying I didn't know what I was talking about.

Controversy was even better than agreement on social media. I didn't care what they called me. All I cared about was that they were talking.

"Look him up," Vinny said while I replied to a few top comments. "His stats are strong. Molloy plays a smart game."

"Blah, blah, blah." I poked my tongue at him just to make him groan. Little sister privileges.

Vinny opened his phone. A moment later, I had an AirDrop alert that opened to Molloy's team page. "What the hell is this profile pic? An evil leprechaun?" I exclaimed while I examined the little icon where his photo should've been.

My brother laughed as he thumbed his phone's screen. "Halloween's this weekend. Looks like a little publicity stunt. All the players have some kind of monster or ghost as their avatar."

"Audrey doing her thing yet again." I shook my head in admiration. She really was a queen of marketing. *She could probably teach you a lot. Not that she has any reason to, stalker that I am. She's already been cool enough. Can't press that luck.*

"But to my point, I told you his stats were good."

"Mm, yeah, yeah. That's not what I need, though." I flipped away from Molloy's page and tried to find some images of him that I could repost. The only shots I could find were of him in net, full facemask and gear on. If candid photos of this guy existed, they weren't on social media. I gave up and went back to the TV for the next period.

By the end of the game, Molloy had blocked twelve shots, and Gene Valentine had managed to nab us a goal. I put my cheek in my hand and turned on the camera. "We won. Go Commodores! But can we please bring back my boo for the next game? K, thanks, bye!" I blew a kiss and ended the video.

Vinny laughed. "You and your hustle."

"You know how it is."

"I do. Speaking of, I gotta get going. Work starts early tomorrow." He arched his brows. "But tomorrow's also a home game. Think I could get you to grace a barstool again?"

I tapped my finger on my chin. "I feel pretty good about that."

Vinny grinned. "I'd love it."

We walked out together and hugged goodbye. Back at my apartment, my phone glowed with notifications. I did a little dance. Best night in a while, that was for sure.

Even better was when Coach Delgato confirmed that Quentin would start the next game. I geared up for another night in Seacrest. Vinny waved to me from the same spot as yesterday. There were no free chairs, but he stood up and let me take his seat. I accepted, ordered a beer, and settled in. The team warmed up on screen while I filmed a Let's-Go-Quentin video.

Unfortunately, the notifications didn't roll in. I had a few, but nothing like last night. While I gazed at the stats, a text came through.

BRUCE:

Bash Molloy again. It gets people talking.

I made a face but had to admit he was probably right. Quickly, I created a side-by-side image of the two goalies in their full gear and used it as my background. "Even with the masks on, it's clear that there is one true BAE here. Quentin Paris, you are our goalie no matter what. Ryan Molloy, thank you for your service. Now, get back to the bench, baby. Buh-bye." I blew a kiss and changed the photo to one of my favorites of Quentin before closing out.

And cue the reaction. My phone lit up within seconds. Again I had haters calling me a fool and lauding Molloy's skills. Even better.

Halfway through the second period, I checked my phone. Some dude had stitched my video to explain how dim I was. He recited stats from both goalies while his comments blew up. Some defended me, and some agreed with him. Either way, I had gained one hundred new followers since I walked into the bar. *And* I had an email from an athleisure company wanting to do a sponsorship. I cackled at the screen.

All around me, a collective gasp rang out.

My head snapped up.

Onscreen, Paris lay on his stomach. His legs were sprawled out in a weird, twisted position that looked anything but natural. One knee bent around the goal post, but his body was mostly behind the net. A Nashville player was climbing off of him from a dogpile.

My hands flew to my mouth. Our goalie didn't move.

Gene Valentine stood close by while the goalie coach and a medic ran out onto the ice. "Turn up the volume, Tony!" Vinny shouted at the bartender.

The commentator's voice blared through the speaker in the hushed bar. "Trying to discern whether this is... yeah, no, I think this might be serious. Let's go to the replay..."

We watched in slo-mo as two Nashville players flew toward the net. One of our guys came in hot behind them and reached for the puck. The blade end of his stick tangled in the Nashville player's skates, causing him to launch forward into Paris, who'd come out to defend. Paris went flying backward as the Nashville player crashed down on him.

"Fuck, that's bad."

I wasn't sure who said what we were all thinking, but they were right.

The TV went back to live feed after about five replays of the crash. Quentin had sat up while they examined him. He put one knee to the ice to stand, but when he planted his right skate under him, his leg gave out. I joined in the groans as he tried—and failed—to stand again.

"Oh, this is bad, Bob..."

"I know, Al. Quentin Paris is indomitable, but it seems like the giant might have fallen tonight..."

The commentators rambled on and on while Valentine and the team doctor lifted Quentin to his feet. On one skate, he glided to the hallway off the ice while the arena cheered for him. Even with his helmet still on, it was clear how much pain he was in.

"Fuck," Vinny whispered. "I hope he's okay."

"Me, too," I said with my hands still at my mouth.

I did, and it had nothing to do with business. Despite attending his wedding, I didn't know Quentin Paris, not really. But the last thing I wanted was for someone to be hurt. I loved the Commodores and had cheered for them since I was a little girl. Players gave their all for the team. This was bad.

My phone vibrated.

BRUCE:

Here comes Molloy. Now's a good moment to post.

I dumped the phone in my purse. He might've been right, but I wasn't going to be that person. I watched along with the rest of the bar while Ryan Molloy warmed up in front of the net. Finally, the whistle blew for play to resume.

Only after the game, which we lost in a shootout, did I open my phone again. I started a video and glared at the screen.

"Ryan Molloy, you better pray our Quentin is back tomorrow night. Because you, buddy, are no substitute."

# 6

# RYAN

The silent locker room had nothing to do with losing in a shootout. We all showered and sat waiting for news. Quinn's gear was piled in his locker, but we'd heard nothing about how he was doing.

Hunter Cathcart himself walked in. The team owner was heavily involved in operations, but something about his presence made the moment even more grave. I held my breath.

"Paris is at Hartford Memorial Hospital. It's a broken tibia."

"Shit. *Broken*?" Gene murmured.

Cathcart nodded. "Doctor says based on the way it broke, he's likely been developing a stress fracture before this event. The collision looked worse than it was, but the bone just snapped."

We all hissed, but no one asked the obvious question.

Cathcart looked around until his gaze landed on me. "French is out for at least four months. Molloy, you're our starting goalie now. We're recalling Jimmy Osborne from the minors as your backup."

His words reverberated through my body. My heart pounded. Whether it was excitement or dread, I wasn't sure. Both, maybe.

"Get home, guys. We've got a rest day tomorrow, and then we'll regroup. This is still the best damn team in the league. Don't forget it. Molloy, be here for a press conference tomorrow morning. Meet us upstairs at Audrey's desk at nine."

He walked out, but we all stayed motionless, staring at the door.

"Fuck," Yuri muttered.

"He's going to freak the fuck out," Gene said through his teeth.

"Oh, god. Poor Audrey." Ethan shook his head and pinched his nose.

Poor Audrey indeed. Quinn Paris was one of the most superstitious goalies I knew, and that was saying a lot. The fact that he got married days before the regular season started, then had all this happen? Good god. Even I would struggle with that kind of luck.

"Fuck going home, and fuck it being an L tonight. I need a damn drink." Gene slapped his knees and stood up. "Who's coming?"

Every single one of us stood up.

We filed into The Pub and nodded at Tony, the bartender. A few loyal regulars raised their glasses as we entered, but no one tried to talk to us. They never did. Tony's rules were sacred.

When we'd drank to Paris, everyone slumped into a thoughtful quiet. A few guys murmured as they watched the highlight reels on TV. Most of them were on their phones.

"Oh, shit, Molls."

I looked up at Dustin's chuckle. He rolled his eyes and waved his phone. "Don't check social media."

"I never do." I hesitated, trying not to care, but finally heard myself say, "Why?"

"French's superfan is coming for you with her nails out."

*She's... what?* I squinted as I sorted through his words.

Dustin slid his phone toward me. I picked it up—and nearly dropped it again.

Her. It was *her*.

Wasn't it her? The sharply angular face and wide eyes on the screen looked more like an AI rendering of a person than the woman I'd met that night. She clearly used filters. No human being looked that flawless or contoured.

Still. It was definitely her.

I hit play, and her thick lashes narrowed into a glare. Pouty lips pursed. "Ryan Molloy, you better pray our Quentin is back tomorrow night. Because you, buddy, are no substitute."

I ruffled my hair and watched her again before sliding the phone back to Dustin. "In that case, I guess I shouldn't try and be a substitute. I'll just be myself instead."

"Hell yeah, man!" Dustin's exclamation jolted the table. He grinned and reached across Max to high-five me. "That's the energy we need."

I knew it was. I knew the guys relied on Quinn in a whole different way than they did me. But I didn't want to be his substitute. I wanted to do things my way. And I knew I would.

Still. That video stung a little. I didn't give a damn about social clout. Algorithms were only interesting from a data standpoint. But no one wanted to hear that they're not even second best. Certainly not from the woman who'd ghosted me the one and only time I'd tried to flirt with a stranger.

*Second best... ghosted... Oh, god. Ghosted by Quinn's fucking superfan. Did she know who I was? Did she realize it? Is that why she didn't come to my room?*

*Was it all just a media stunt??*

My stomach rolled. Queasy humiliation prickled in my gut. Quietly, I opened my phone under the table and googled Mrs. Quentin Paris.

I moved backward through her timeline with the volume on low. She'd posted a few things recently, calling me out for starting last night and praising Quinn's performance. My breath caught when I found clips from the wedding.

*Please, please, please. Do not let there be a post about the loser backup goalie who ordered stupid fucking shooters.*

No such post. Nothing but footage of the wedding and some product placements. I went forward again, just to be sure. Nope. No reference to our run-ins.

With a hard exhale, I shoved the phone into my pocket and went to take a piss. Adrenaline was still abating as I washed my hands, hauled open the door—

And collided with the woman exiting the restroom opposite me.

She let out a little cry that got muffled by my chest. Her face bumped square between my ribcage. I heard the unmistakable sound of a phone clattering to the ground.

"Whoa, sorry." Instinctively, my hands landed on her shoulders to steady us both.

"My fault." She bent to get the phone and then tilted her face up to look at me.

*Of all the fucking odds.*

I had been right about the filters changing her look. Her cheeks were fuller in real life, but her jawline was delicately sharp. I studied the cat-eye makeup she wore as anger, surprise, and a base urge to kiss her again bubbled in my chest.

Meanwhile, her face morphed through three distinct emotions. A blank stare narrowed into a suspicious glare. Blue-gray eyes scanned my face, clearly searching for the connection. To be fair, I likely looked a good bit different than I had that night. I wore a hoodie, my hair was towel-dried, and I still had my contacts in from the game.

But I saw when recognition hit. It looked a lot like dread.

Her jaw fell open, eyes widening. "Oh. Oh, um... hi."

I ignored the cringe in her tone. My turn to glare. "Is that hi for ghosting me—or for *roasting* me?"

Her brows knitted. "What?"

"Tony kicks nearly everyone out before we get here. I might belong on the bench in your estimation, but I'm quite sure *you* have no business in this bar right now."

The color drained from her face. "Hold on. H-hold on. You're... wait. *You're*—"

"No. *You're* the one who shouldn't be here."

But she grabbed my arm and hauled me into the single-use bathroom. The door slammed shut, and she slammed me into it. She pressed both hands into my chest to keep me still. Her cheeks had gone pink, and she seemed to struggle for breath.

I realized I was having the same problem. This bathroom was far from romantic. I had met her once, a month ago. She'd rejected the hell out of me and left me sitting alone for hours. Then she'd dissed me to the whole world.

And yet, my heart hammered. *Dammit.*

"What is your name?" she whisper-hissed.

I rolled my eyes. "Ryan. My name is Ryan, *Mrs. Paris.*"

Saying her "name" gave me a sour taste in my mouth. It

helped calm my pulse. She'd spared me public humiliation
—personally, that is. Professionally, I was clearly fair game.
So I had absolutely no business thinking about the way she
moaned when I'd kissed her.

Her hands went slack, resting on my chest. Eyes fluttered
shut as an anguished groan vibrated in her throat.
"Fuck. Me."

*I wanted to.* The useless thought hit me, but I kicked it
away like an errant puck. I kept my mouth shut and refused
to notice how warm her hands were.

But then she peeked at me through her lashes. Her
tongue darted out to wet her lips as those eyes opened
wider, gazing at my face. Both hands on my chest closed into
fists around my shirt.

*Goddammit, man. Don't fall for it. Don't you dare. She's
nothing but trouble.*

I fell for it. Or she did. Or we did. It didn't matter. Even
my super-sharp goalie reflexes couldn't keep up with the
flurry of motion that had us staring at each other one
moment and locked in a kiss the next. My tongue lashed
hers, so angry at her for duping me. So fucking hungry to
taste her again.

*You total fool.*

Her teeth scraped my lips, just as rough as me. I heard a
little growl in her throat. *Oh, I don't think so. You don't get to be
angry, you loud-mouthed, rude... delicious... sexy as hell...*

Blind, I grabbed her waist, spun her around, and pinned
her to the bathroom wall. She let out a grunt, but her nails
sank into my shoulders as her chest pressed against mine.
Her leg wrapped around my thigh. On instinct, I hoisted her
higher.

Damn that woman for the audacity to wrap both legs

around my back. How dare she feel so goddamn good grinding on me like that? The fucking nerve.

"Jesus Christ," I hissed.

"Shut up." Her breathless command came just before she plunged her tongue back into my mouth. Her nails raked my scalp, and my eyes rolled back in my head. I hated her. I was humiliated by her. And I wanted to absolutely devour her.

"Mmohmygod, what am I doing?" Her lips tore away from mine with an anguished cry.

I jerked my head back and tried to stop my spinning head. "I don't fucking know," I damn near panted.

Fear and dread returned to her gaze. I set her down immediately and stepped backward to put space between us. "We... that wasn't... that shouldn't have happened," I muttered at last.

She huffed a laugh. "No shit."

I glared. "I don't want anything to do with you. I can't believe you have the nerve to roast me to the whole world and then kiss me like that."

One eyebrow rose. "Uh, buddy? Hate to tell you, but I wasn't the only one kissing just now. And, ha. I was definitely not the only one enjoying it."

My ears heated, but at least her cheeks colored, too. I knew I shouldn't stay in that room with her for another minute. "Forget it. This never happened—any of it. Okay?"

"Freaking perfect by me."

"Good. Let's just steer clear of each other. You need to leave before Tony kicks you out."

She cut her eyes to me. "I could. But you could give me a quick interview first."

My brows hit my hairline. "So you can abuse me live for all your followers?"

Her lips tugged into a sassy smile that made me want to groan. "I mean, if you're into that kind of thing, I sure can."

I shook my head. "I'm not into it."

*Fuck.* The way her smirk turned into a pout tested all my discipline. One nod of her head, and I was sure I would snap. Thankfully, she opened her mouth to protest. That let me pull myself together. I squared my shoulders and reached around her to open the door. "I'm serious. Disappear before you get into trouble."

She slung her purse onto her shoulder and strolled out when I gestured. "It would be worth it."

"What would?" I instantly kicked myself for asking, for engaging her more.

"The trouble."

Before I could respond, she flashed a quick smile, looked left and right, and then hurried to the exit, head down. Something about the way she moved let her avoid all attention. Even Tony behind the bar barely glanced at her. Only when the door closed behind her did I return to our table to frown at my beer.

Ethan's laugh hit my ears. "Oh, god. Watch out, guys. Molls has been starting goalie for about ten minutes, and already he's glaring into his drink."

I glanced up and twisted my lips into a smile. "Cue requisite brooding. Actually, ah, I think I'll head home."

"You?" Max asked. Max and I were usually some of the last ones at the bar. Single dude life and all that.

"Press conference tomorrow. Lots to think about. See y'all at practice."

I barely gave Henrik his hello pets when I walked in. For the first time in two years, the quiet house didn't bother me. My mind was too full. If anything, there was comfort in familiarity that night. I could count on Henrik's patterns, the dark kitchen, the softly glowing computer screen, and the silence. God alone knew what my life was about to become. At least some things stayed the same.

In my office, I blew out a breath and shook my head. The stats that usually gave me comfort swam in front of my eyes. Yet again, I couldn't stop thinking about *her*. Worse, I was certain there was a better way to handle it than I'd done. I just wasn't sure what that was. How do you navigate running into the woman who ghosted you when you've just found out she's your teammate's professional fan?

Making out like the world was ending was surely not the optimal strategy.

Like in a game, this was an error I had to shake off. Goalies more than anyone else needed to have amnesia about mistakes. If we carried that shit with us, we'd crumble. Standing alone between the pipes, it was always just me and my thoughts. Those thoughts were either my friends or my career's end. A few minutes of awkwardness with a stranger wasn't either of those things.

*Damn. I hope this isn't Quinn's end, though.*

I shoved back from the computer and went to crash. My head was too full for anything else.

Check that. *Both* heads were too full. As soon as I was in bed, her vicious kisses and frantic grunts filled my mind. I was hard again in an instant thinking about her legs around my back and the way she rocked her hips. *Fuck, she's a nightmare. She humiliated you and then did it again for the whole fucking world to see.*

*Why does she have to be so sexy, too?*

I gripped my cock and clenched my teeth. My fantasies were weird and jumbled. Nothing like what I usually got off to. I pictured her embarrassing the shit out of me in a post—

and then begging me to spank her ass red. Telling the whole world how I belonged on the bench—while she rode my face and held back her orgasm.

I unloaded to that image with a loud groan. When I quit spasming, I opened my eyes in the dark.

"What the fuck, man? Forget about her. She isn't part of your world. No more of this bullshit. Mrs. Quentin Paris is nothing to you. If you ever see her again, remember. She is a stranger."

Early the next morning, I pulled up to the rink and entered through the office door. Joey, the team's media manager, greeted me with a bottle of water and a grim smile. "The press is already chomping at the bit. How are you, Ryan?"

"Can't complain." I followed him to the elevator. "How's Paris?"

"He's..." Joey trailed off.

"Paris?" I supplied with a brief smile.

Joey nodded. "Exactly. He's not thrilled about this press conference, no surprise."

The bottle froze halfway to my mouth. "Wait. He's here?"

"Mm-hm. Audrey's putting Coach, Doc, you, and him all up together. Bold move. Classic Audrey."

Audrey Cathcart—sorry, Audrey *Paris*—had been promoted to head of PR for the team this season. She deserved it. Even though she was the owner's daughter, Audrey worked her ass off. She was brilliant with marketing and not afraid to take risks.

Joey ushered me into a conference room where Audrey, Quinn, Hunter, Coach Delgato, and Doc were all gathered.

Quinn was in a wheelchair, his leg in a cast straight out in front of him. I gave him a sympathetic cringe.

"How you doing, man?"

His left eye twitched. "I think I am not yet accepting what has happened. I think I am in shock. Or it is the painkillers."

I chuckled. "Both seem reasonable. Fuck, French, I'm sorry. I hate this for you."

"I should have listened to you," he said while the others talked to each other. His eyes squeezed shut. "I was not wanting to admit something was wrong beyond a little ache. You kept saying my lower right was weak. Foolish of me to ignore it."

I swallowed the instinct to keep digging into details and shook my head. "It wasn't knowable. We move on."

"Oui. We move on. And I... spend the season on my ass. Is too bad Audrey was just promoted. Otherwise, I would rehab in the Bahamas."

"Tell her Doc ordered it." I grinned and fist-bumped him just as the others called us over.

Audrey's eyes were ringed with dark circles. Her mouth pulled down in a worried frown, and I guessed she hadn't slept much last night. Despite Quinn's calm, I hoped this wasn't a problem for them personally. The last thing Quinn needed was to let a career setback hurt his relationship.

"Okay, fellas," Audrey said with an attempted smile. "We're going to go in there and give the updates. You guys will answer some questions, and then we all go home. Ryan, here. I prepared a few notes for you. Got it?"

We got it. Hunter led the parade down to the largest press room we had. The place was standing room only with reporters packed in. Quinn hissed and muttered something in French. When he caught my glance, he shook his head.

"I loathe interviews."

Well, that made two of us.

Worse than the crowd for Quinn was the dramatic gasp when Audrey pushed his wheelchair into the room. The gasp was followed instantly by shouted questions and bedlam.

"Stop that," Audrey snapped into a mic. "Be quiet and listen. We'll answer questions in a bit."

I sat at the end of the table beside Quinn and stared at the flashbulbs and people while Doc gave the prognosis. Another gasp went up. Coach cut in with the logistics and to reassure them that Paris would recover and resume his position as soon as possible. "In the meantime, Ryan Molloy is an incredible goaltender. I know we're going to have another stellar season here in Seacrest."

The silence in the room suggested that the press had their doubts.

My palms began to sweat. Partially from the blinding cameras and spotlights. Mostly because the weight of the situation was sinking in. I had to carry the team. I hadn't been a starting goaltender in years, and that was in the minors. Connecticut had signed me to back Paris up. That was always my role. I knew, of course, that I had to be ready to step in at any moment. That a Paris injury was possible. I'd just never imagined that it would actually happen.

Beside me, Quinn spoke softly and calmly, answering a question that had been thrown at him. "... Molloy is a first-class goaltender. While I am absolutely devastated to miss most of the season, I am confident in his abilities and..."

*Are you? Am I?* Imposter syndrome wrapped around my neck until I cleared my throat. It was only a soft cough, but it flipped the spotlight right onto me. Thirty people began calling my name at once.

Audrey managed to silence them all with a stern glare and then said, "Ryan has prepared a statement."

*She* had prepared my statement. My job was to read it. So I slipped my glasses out of my blazer pocket, pushed them on, and unfolded the paper. One more throat-clear, and I opened my mouth to finally address the press.

# 7

# NICA

*What is this guy's story? He looks like he should be building websites, not playing pro hockey. How would I have even guessed he was an athlete that night?*

"... will stand in for Quentin with every ounce of dedication and talent that I have. I assure you, this season will..."

I listened to Ryan Molloy damn near whisper his way through a statement from the back corner of the press room. Those black-framed glasses slipped down his nose more than once, making me wonder just how hard he was sweating under all this attention. But every time, he pushed them back up and soldiered on.

It reminded me of how he played hockey. Steady, reliable, and safe.

But it was the opposite of how he kissed. Deep, teasing, and hungry.

*Shut up, Nica! You don't know how he kisses because that never freaking happened. Focus!*

My thoughts snapped back to the podium when he folded the paper and looked up. The lights reflected off his glasses as he managed a half-smile. "All that to say, I know

I'm not Quinn Paris. And I'm very well aware that I'm not nearly as popular with the fans as he is. I've seen some of the commentary already."

He chuckled, and my cheeks warmed. Absentmindedly, I rubbed the bridge of my nose from where I'd straight up plowed into him last night as I stared at my phone. Was it worse that I didn't recognize him immediately or that he knew exactly who I was?

Was it worse that I had, as he said, ghosted him or roasted him?

No. It was definitely worse that I kissed him. Again.

*Leave it alone, woman. Focus, focus, focus! You can't mess up anymore!*

While I struggled to stay in the moment, Molloy went on. "But my dedication to the Commodores is unwavering, and I have a hell of a team surrounding me. We've got this, guys. I promise."

His quiet oath seemed to settle everyone down. Even my skeptical heart cheered him on. I suddenly wanted him to succeed, regardless of the likes I got for talking smack about him.

The conference broke up. Journalists filed out, murmuring to each other and making notes on their phones. I pushed my shoulders off the wall and checked my messages. Several social responses and a text.

> BRUCE:
>
> I have some thoughts about your platform. You can lean into Molloy and win. Ready to talk more—if you're ready to discuss my cut?

I dumped the phone into my purse. When I looked up, the room was nearly empty. Resolving to mute Bruce's texts from now on, I hurried to trail behind the last reporters headed for the door. I held my breath until I was safely in the hallway, where I saw security escorting people to the exit.

Leaving me alone.

Alone and unsupervised. In the Commodores' arena.

A wicked little smile curled my lips. The angel on my shoulder shut up quickly. I spun around and scurried down the hall, unsure where I was going but ready for anything.

Navy and maroon stripes on the walls gave a sense of leading me somewhere. Where, I wasn't sure—until I got to a T in the path. A sign said *To the ice* with an arrow to the right. To the left, *Locker Rooms*.

I went left.

A short way down was a huge door. The iconic *C* in the Commodores' signature font was emblazoned in the center. Further on was a door marked *Visitors*, so of course I tried the one in front of me. It swung open easily. With my heart in my throat, I stepped inside.

"Wow."

The oval-shaped room was gorgeous. It was done in light wood, navy, and maroon with ambient lighting. Along the walls stood each player's locker. *Rivera, Simmons, Valentine, Ivanov...* the roster went on. At the very back, side-by-side, were *Paris* and *Molloy*.

The temptation to shoot video overtook me. I knew Audrey would kill me for this if she saw it, so I'd just have to be super careful how I used the footage. I shot several slow pans of the place, ending every time on the goalies' names.

When I had enough, I walked down for a closer view. Paris had nothing but gear in his locker, but Molloy had a little Yoda figurine on his top shelf. *Huh.* I went up on tiptoe and plucked it for a closer look.

"Now, I am damn sure that you're not supposed to be *here*."

My stomach crashed to the floor at the voice behind me. I whirled around to see the backup goalie himself standing with his arms crossed.

I resisted the urge to double over in a cringe. I'd done enough of that the second I got to my car last night. Jesus Christ, what a mess. How had I hit on a fucking Connecticut Commodore and not had a clue? How did I miss that entirely?

Why, oh why, oh *why* had I then launched myself at him like the world was ending?

Foolishness. That's how. On that late night in that lonely bar on Long Island, I should've asked more questions. Thought with my head. Not been so damn vulnerable. Then I would've put the pieces together. I was careless and sloppy, and now I had a mess on my hands.

Instead of a cringe, I forced myself to face him. His expression was a neutral mask, giving nothing away about how angry he might be to find me snooping in his locker. In a panic, I hid the figurine behind my back.

His gaze followed the sudden movement. "What do you have?"

"N-nothing. I'll go. Sorry, I was just…"

"Trespassing again."

"No! Well. I mean, no. Looking."

"Funny thing about looking in places you're prohibited from being. It's generally called trespassing."

"Forget it. I'm going." I huffed out a breath like this was all one big inconvenience.

But he stepped in my path when I tried to make for the door. One palm rose to stop me. "Not with my Yoda, you're not."

His voice was low, firm, and... amused? I looked from his palm to his face. He stared down at me, eyes narrowed but not angry. No emotion. Just waiting. Patient.

Since he seemed content to wait me out, I took a long moment to study him. To understand how I'd not instantly recognized him last night. To figure out how the hell I'd hit on him without a single inkling of who he was.

The more I gazed at him, the more it made sense.

He looked like a man trying to look like a hockey player and not quite succeeding. His clothes were slightly too big. His hair had some length to it but wasn't styled like it was at the wedding. The rusty-blond mop ruffled on his forehead and over his ears.

Plus, he wore his glasses again, just like at the wedding. I couldn't picture another player who wore glasses. He wore them well, even if they did distract from his fucking gorgeous green eyes. *Damn, my memory was right. Those are the greenest eyes I've ever seen.*

Usually green eyes were hazel. Ryan Molloy's eyes were moss green and objectively striking. I found myself itching to pull off those glasses, comb his hair, and see if I could glam him up.

*Definitely not itching to rake my fingers through that hair like I did last night. Nope. Not even a little bit.*

"Give me the Yoda, please." He broke the silence at last, flipping his wrist so his palm was outstretched.

I wet my lips. My career had been built on audacity. No reason to be meek now. "Or else what?"

His brows arched over the glasses. "It wasn't a threat. I want my property. If you want a consequence, I guess... I'll call security and have them arrest you for theft and trespassing? Sounds like a scandal that'll be hard to spin to your fans."

I clasped both hands behind my back and twisted side to side like a cheeky child. "You don't know that. It could cement my legend status among my followers."

"Only if you say it's Quinn's Yoda. Otherwise, you'll look like you're in cahoots with the enemy."

"You're not the enemy. You're just..."

"Better on the bench?" His eyes narrowed. "Not good enough to warrant saying no to my face? No *substitute* for your precious Quinn, professionally or personally?"

Horror rashed over me at the implication in his words. My empty hand shot out to shove his chest. "How dare you? Paris is my *job*. My content is my paycheck. I know I fucked up big time by not recognizing you. I'm kicking myself for that so damn hard. But how dare you suggest I flirted with you as some kind of stand-in?"

That narrow gaze scanned me. "Then why the hell did you?"

I shoved him again. "Why the hell did *you*? Why didn't *you* recognize *me*?"

"I don't use social media."

"Obviously, you don't! When would I have seen a photo of you without your helmet on? Why would I recognize you with no context any more than you would me? And it's not like you *look* like a hockey player."

"So you didn't flirt with me because you were upset about Quinn getting married?"

"I flirted with you because I thought you were cute, okay?" My tone made it anything but a compliment.

We both took deep breaths. Our glares didn't abate.

At last, I spoke again softly. "Can we please just do what you said last night? Forget it ever happened. Pretend we're total strangers?"

He blinked but then nodded. "Strangers. Yes. It's forgotten."

"Good."

"Are you going to give me the Yoda or not?"

"Of course I am. I'm not an asshole."

*You sure about that?* He didn't open his mouth. The question flashed clear as day on his face.

"Hey. Don't give me that look. I'm not. I swear."

"You're snooping in my locker and stealing my shit after bad-mouthing me to the entire planet—after... uh, forget it. Forgive me if I'm not enchanted."

"At least I'm not asking for an interview."

He exhaled hard. "Miss... whatever your real name is. Can we end this, please? I need to go. You may have heard, but I'm suddenly a little busy."

I brought Yoda out from behind my back and held it to my chest. His jaw flexed. "Only if I get to know the story behind Yoda here."

Brows lifted above the glasses again. "A fan made it for me a long time ago. A kid in the local hospital had his dad three-D print it for me. The kid painted it."

*Well, damn.* My eyes burned at that story. "Oh, wow. That's so sweet."

But he glared. "Yeah. Yoda is my talisman."

"Your what?"

"My good luck charm. He sits on my shelf all the time for luck." He stepped closer and bent so we were face-to-face. "And you, ma'am, have now fucked with it."

"I... oh. I didn't know you were superstitious."

That got me a sly smile. "I'm a goalie. What did you expect?"

Now I *really* wanted to pull those glasses off and kiss him again. The urge slapped me upside the head so hard that my breath caught. *You literally just agreed to be strangers. What the hell, Nica?*

*Calm down. It's just goalie core. You know you can't resist their quirks. That this guy has them is... inconvenient, sure. But pull yourself together, woman.*

"How... how can I un-fuck with it?"

He held his palm between us. I glanced down, sighed, and surrendered the toy. With a sharp inhale, he spun for his locker and put Yoda back in the exact spot he'd been before. His back was still to me when he said, "You can't. You've fucked with it. The question will now be, for good or for ill?"

"How will you know?"

Ryan Molloy turned around and crossed his arms over his broad chest. He tilted his head and studied me head to foot. "I guess we'll find out on game night."

I opened my mouth to respond but snapped it shut when my phone vibrated in my pocket. I recognized the double buzz of a text and whipped it out to check. In the corner of my eye, I saw him doing the same on his.

"Excuse me. I have somewhere to be."

"Same." He pocketed the phone and fell in step beside me.

I tried not to look at him as I strode down the hall, back toward the conference room and around to the elevators. By the time I stabbed the button, my heart was in my throat. *Why are you following me?*

"I promise I'm not trespassing," I said under my breath.

"I promise I don't believe you."

I breathed a little laugh at the smile that threatened his face. The elevator arrived, and that smile vanished. We stepped in. He beat me to pressing the third floor. As we walked down the hall, I could feel his side-eye on me.

Audrey blinked in surprise when we both stopped in her doorway. "Oh, wow. I didn't think you'd be here at the same time. Ah, Ryan, can you hang out in the conference room for a minute, please? I'll text you to join us."

He strode away, and I slipped into the office chair like I'd snuck in despite being invited. Audrey flashed me a tired smile.

"Hey, girl. How are you doing?" I asked to break the ice.

Her eyes shimmered. "It's, ah, not easy. Quinn is so sweet, but it's obvious this is killing him. He's ready to climb the walls already. I think he may go spend some time with his mom on Long Island. Just for a change of scenery."

My nose wrinkled. "Shit. I'm so sorry. This is supposed to be your honeymoon."

"Yeah. That's definitely been postponed for now. I knew the season would keep us busy, but I didn't imagine... anyway. We'll get through it. It's not a problem *between* us, but it's still hard. You know?"

I didn't, but I nodded anyway.

She pressed her hands to her cheeks and drew in a breath. "Sorry. I didn't ask you here to hear all my woes. How's business?"

I pressed my lips into a line, trying to dam all the words threatening to spill. *She doesn't need to know you're struggling. She's got her problems. You're lucky she gives you what she does... fuck it.*

The dam broke. "I'm so tired of it, Audrey. He's your husband. He seems so nice, but *god*. Who'd have thought I would still be posting thirst trap videos two years later? Do you know how old this whole thing is? But I can't let it go because it's my job now. If I have to close it without something else, I'm gonna wind up... up... sorry."

I dropped my forehead into my hands. Heat rushed my

face at my pitiful word vomit. "I'm so sorry. I know you have your own shit to handle," I mumbled, face to the floor.

Audrey cleared her throat. "Wow, Nica. I... had no idea you felt that way."

I peeked up at her and rolled my eyes. "Not quite the stalker you thought, hm?"

She flickered a smile. "That's part of it, I'll admit. But also, it's kind of nice to hear you're looking for something else. You'd say you're looking for work, then?"

I sat up straight again. "I definitely would say that."

She sat back in her chair and gestured to the door. "Molloy is the man of the moment, but he has no platform. He's too young and filling too big a gap to stay unnoticed. The Commodores have become one of the most popular teams in the league, and fans want content. Even Gene has his own profiles.

"I'd like to hire you to write a bio on him. *Puck Drop Daily* has agreed to publish a freelance article. They'll have editorial privileges, of course. They'll pay you per word. I'll pay you per day and cover any expenses—gas, food, whatever. You'll come to practice and training. Attend a few home games where you'll shadow me to get a sense of how the team operates.

"And, of course, you'll spend time with Ryan for one-on-one Q and A. I can't promise how fruitful that'll be, but he's obligated to do interviews. I'd *love* if you could go really in-depth and find some click-worthy angles, but I'm not asking for a miracle. Just a feature."

"A real news story? You think I'm the right person for this?"

She shrugged. "Honestly, I don't know. But also honestly, I don't have time to interview freelancers. The press wants news on Quinn right now, and I want them looking at

Molloy. Quinn needs privacy. Molloy needs an image. You make people listen. I don't have the mental real estate to think too hard on this. Are you in?"

I blew out a breath. Ryan Molloy was the last person I would've picked to try and "go really in-depth with" at the moment. Or he was the first but for all the wrong reasons. Either way, this golden opportunity was also a minefield.

*You can make something out of literally nothing, girlie. This is a chance. This is money on the table. We might not lift from pockets like Momma, but we do not leave money on the table.*

"Of course. I'll do my best."

She picked up her phone and typed before I finished speaking. When she set it down, her eyes shimmered again. "Thanks, Nica. I appreciate it. I, ah, also appreciate your honesty."

"Sure... Um, I'm not really a hugger, but do you need a hug?"

Audrey laughed and rubbed her eyes under her glasses. "Yes. I do."

I ran around the desk while she stood up. This was awkward as hell, but it also wasn't. She was a woman in a hard spot. I knew about being in hard spots. Why wouldn't I support her? I squeezed her hard and let her squeeze me right back.

The door opened. Ryan cleared his throat. Audrey and I stepped apart, trading a smile, and I went back to the chair.

"Have a seat, Molls." Audrey gestured to the second chair.

He perched like it might be booby-trapped. "What's up?"

"Ryan Molloy, this is Nica Solance. She's best known as her online handle, uh, Mrs. Quentin Paris." Audrey breathed a laugh that made me blush and smile.

His jaw flexed. "I know who she is."

"Nica is going to do a feature on you for *Puck Drop Daily*."

"What?" The question burst out of him, jolting Audrey and me.

Audrey's cheeks colored. "She's going to write a feature on you. She'll shadow you—and me—for a few weeks. You'll need to schedule at least three interviews with her in that time, too. I know you're not used to talking to the press, but it is part of your contract."

Molloy's breath came in short puffs through his nose. "I... Audrey, I don't want her."

*Ouch.*

But Audrey pursed her lips and lifted her chin. "Ryan, there's a lot I don't want right now. But we can't always have our way, now can we? Too damn bad, buddy. She's doing this."

He sighed and nodded once. Audrey dismissed us, and I followed him back to the elevators. In the lift, he gazed straight ahead and sighed again. "Totally fucked," he said softly.

I didn't dare reply in case I jinxed him even more.

Two nights later, I stood in front of the arena while fans streamed inside. My thumb tapped record, and I tossed my hair and puckered my lips. "It's night one of the Molloy era. Are we going to survive, besties? Do we dare cheer for the *other* goalie? My darling Quentin says he's confident in his backup's skills. I guess if the GOAT himself says so, maybe we can give him a chance. What do you think? Is it cheating if I say 'Go Ryan'? Comment below!"

By the time security escorted me to the owner's box, I

had twenty comments to the effect of #goRyango and #CommodoresForLife. I also had twenty comments chastising me for being disloyal to Quentin. My favorite was, "If u r really his wife, you'd never dream of supporting someone else."

"Ouch." I laughed as I typed a reply. *Thanks, hun. Xoxo.* No point reminding everyone of the glaring truth—that I was not, in fact, Quentin Paris's wife. Besides, three people replied to the comment saying just that before I could even post.

I smiled at the phone, pleased at the buzz. It was good for my platform, it got people talking about Ryan, and it kept me from fixating on the game.

Which I may or may not have been fixated on for the past day or so.

Not that the butterflies in my stomach had anything to do with that silly Yoda. I was just curious how this game would go was all. Definitely didn't think for a second that I might've fucked the whole team over between snooping and getting this gig. Nope, that was absurd.

I gulped while the door swung open. *It's fine. It's just a game. It's just the owner's box. Fake it till you make it, girlie.*

Audrey greeted me with a smile. "Come on in. We'll watch from up here and then go down to the ice at the end. Want a drink?"

I let her lead me inside. She introduced me to Hunter Cathcart, the freaking owner of the freaking Commodores. Fair, I'd shook hands with him at the wedding, too. But this was different. This was game night.

*You're supposed to be here, Nica. You don't have to hide. You don't have to sneak food into your bag. You don't have to do anything but relax. So, freaking relax!*

The team stormed the ice, and we all took seats. I chose

a front-row chair and watched while they skated laps in their zone. Ryan left the formation and glided to his net. He dropped down, legs spread wide to stretch on the ice.

I didn't blink until he stood up. Then, I shut my eyes and sucked in a breath. *He's a goalie. Of course you're gonna crush a little. You thirst scroll goalie footage for crying out loud. Shake this one off. It's no big deal.*

*God, I hope I didn't ruin our season.*

# 8

# RYAN

The buzzer sounded. For an eternal second, the whole world paused, and it was just me, alone in my crease, slowly realizing what had happened. What I'd done.

The moment broke. Before I could snap my helmet off, the guys jumped over the boards and raced to me. A group hug squeezed me so tight that I lost my balance and fell backward onto the ice. They crashed on me in a dogpile, stealing my breath and making everything real somehow.

I'd gotten a shutout.

My first as a Commodore. My first in the league.

A grin split my face while they slowly disentangled. Someone reached down to help me up. I got to my feet and focused on Ethan's wide grin.

"Goddamn, Molls. Hell of a game!"

It was the first time in my memory he didn't call me Sieve. I stared for a moment and then burst out laughing. Ethan chuckled, clapped my back, and danced toward the boards. I removed my helmet and followed him to the hallway.

Audrey was there—with *her* hovering right behind. I nodded and kept walking, but Audrey grabbed my sleeve.

"Uh-uh, buddy. You're the star of the game. Get over here."

"What?" I understood the words. I just couldn't believe they applied to me.

Dustin punched my arm. He, too, was waiting to skate the victory circle. "That's what happens when you stonewall twenty shots, dude. Killer game. *Killer*." He held up a gloved hand for a fist-bump.

*Is this happening? What were the odds? How the fuck did I do that?*

I mean, I knew how. Practice yesterday had gone well. I wasn't trying for Quinn's acrobatics, but it felt good to keep working on this new approach. At warmup, I tried to shut off my brain and get in the zone. The imposter syndrome that kicked off at the press conference finally quieted. Without it, I was just me, doing the thing I loved best.

Again, my own personal goalie Force.

The thought made me smile as I took a quick breath and hopped back onto the ice. I waved, and the fans answered with a deafening cheer. When I got back to the door, I hurried down the hall, deliberately not glancing over at Audrey or her wide-eyed companion.

In the locker room, though, my gaze landed on Yoda while I stripped out of my gear. Adrenaline that had nothing to do with the game spiked my pulse. How dare she touch my things? How could she possibly say yes to Audrey's request for an interview? Her gall knew no bounds.

"Still smiling over your shutout, Molloy? Can't blame you."

My head jerked at Max's comment. "Hm? Oh, yeah. Thanks, man."

He clapped my back and went for the shower. Impulsively, I grabbed my phone. It took two seconds to find her latest post: "Is it cheating if I say go Ryan?"

*Don't read this crap. It's bad for your focus. And she is not your good luck charm.* I couldn't help myself. I also knew I shouldn't like hearing her say my name, and yet.

I slid the phone on the shelf beside Yoda and headed to shower. As I toweled off and pulled on my jeans and flannel shirt, Gene shouted over the chitchat. "Ana's mother is visiting, or I'd say party at my house. But every one of you better get your ass to The Pub to toast Molloy, you understand?"

"Yes, Captain!" came the collective shout.

Gene pointed at me. "See you there, man."

I lagged behind the guys to the bar. My feet crunched the gravel parking lot, hands in jacket pockets, mind very much split between replaying the game and ridiculously fixated on that whole Yoda exchange yesterday.

I stepped onto the porch to find the door open. Tony stood with his arms crossed, barricading the way. He pointed out into the night. "Closed party, sweetheart. Can't have someone like you in here right now."

"No, but I'm Vinny's sister. And-and Audrey said I could..."

"Do. Not. Care."

A laugh slipped out of me as I approached. She had balls, I had to admit. Part of me hated that she was here now. That she was going to interview me. That she had gone from a foolish, fleeting memory to damn near *everywhere* I went.

Part of me couldn't stop wondering at the odds.

And a larger part of me than I wanted to admit fucking loved the way she'd suddenly stumbled into my life. I knew I shouldn't love it, that I should let her be a stranger.

Yet again, shoulds seemed quite irrelevant.

"Oh, look. You found more trouble," I said when I reached the doorway. "Why am I not shocked?"

Her black hair whipped across her face, attention snapping from Tony to me. Dread filled her eyes, even in the low light. "Well, uh. Kind of, yeah."

I quirked a brow and looked at Tony. With a gesture to her, I nodded. "She's with me, Tony."

His jaw dropped. "Ryan, buddy, that's—"

"Mm-hm, I know who she is. Trouble. But I've got an eye on her. Promise."

He shrugged. "Anything for the man of the night."

"Come on." I walked inside without looking back. My goalie senses let me track her even though she trailed behind. Once we were near the bar, I turned to her. "Find Audrey and Stella or whoever told you to come here. Don't do anything like start filming us or whatever else you'd scheme up."

Her lips pursed. "Can I interview you yet?"

"No way. I'm here to celebrate."

"Well, can I at least congratulate you?"

My grin damn near broke my face. It surprised the hell out of me. *It's okay to celebrate, man. You got a fucking shutout. You* should *be thrilled.* "You? Congratulate me? Figured I'd ruined your night by winning. Rude of me, I know."

Humor sparked despite her tense shoulders, just as I'd hoped. "You really were kind of gross out there. It was almost as if luck was on your side."

*Dammit. Stop flirting with her.* Every time we talked felt like foreplay. I hadn't flirted with anyone in years and was rusty as hell at it, but she kept me smirking and ready to tease. "Wonder how that could've happened?"

Her lashes fluttered as she dropped her gaze to the floor and then peeked back up at me. "I'm sure I don't know," she drawled. "But I think we both have to start remembering that I'm not your enemy, Ryan Molloy."

My smile slipped. "Right. You're a *journalist*."

Hurt flashed in her eyes, but she hid it fast. "Exactly. So before you go celebrate your incredible luck, can we schedule an interview?"

"Ugh, fine. I can meet you at the diner tomorrow. Good enough?"

"Tomorrow is good, but we can't go to the diner in Seacrest. People will talk."

I shrugged. "You want to just go to Audrey's office? She can get us a conference room or something."

Nica bit her lip. "If we have to. But I think this will go better if you're more relaxed. Is there somewhere not as public as a restaurant where we could hang out? Maybe then it'll just feel like a conversation."

"With someone I don't want to talk to," I added, knowing full well it was a lie. I wanted to talk to her. Wanted to stand there all night talking so I could know her better. So I could feel the rush she inexplicably gave me.

Lie or not, hurt flashed in her eyes again. "Fine. Audrey's office. Whatever."

She turned to walk away, and my Goalie Force kicked in. I snagged her fingers before I realized what I'd done. Nica froze. Her gaze hit our hands and then my face, clearly asking what the hell I was doing.

I wet my lips and spoke fast, releasing her as I did. "I didn't mean that. I'm sorry."

That got me the daring spark I wanted. She pursed her lips. "Then why did you say it?"

"I, ah, figured you'd call out my bullshit." My ears heated to admit it.

Nica didn't laugh, though. She gazed at me and shook

her head. "I wouldn't assume it was bullshit that you wanted nothing to do with me."

I ruffled my hair. "I just... Never mind. Meet me at the practice rink tomorrow, okay? I'm sorry I was rude."

At last, at fucking last, I got a little smile. "Between the shutout and now, you've been insulting me all night."

I breathed a laugh. "I'll be nicer. Promise."

"Oh, don't worry about being *nice*. I can handle the insults. But you better atone for it. I expect good coffee, two milks no sugar, when I see you tomorrow. Got it?"

"Got it."

Her blue-gray eyes rolled. "Obviously, I'm joking. See you tomorrow."

"Stay out of trouble, okay?"

"Promise to sort of try."

I nodded and turned to the table where the guys had gathered. I allowed myself a glance back at her as I did. She watched me, but when our eyes connected, she blinked several times. With a toss of her long hair, she strolled over to where Audrey and Stella were sitting at a high-top.

I nearly collided with the table because I was so busy watching her. My hand grabbed the chair just in time. I pulled it out with a loud scrape on the wood floors and dropped down to sit.

Max and Yuri gaped at me. Dustin's gaze bounced from me to her several times.

Max cleared his throat. "Dude. That girl you're checking out. Do you have any idea who that is?"

"I do."

"Do you know the shit she's given you?"

I cut him a glare.

All three of them exchanged a look. Yuri laughed. "Damn, man. I didn't know you were into punishment."

"I hang around you guys all the time. What did you think that was?"

Gene stood up with a glass in hand, ready to make his speech. I fixed my gaze on him and smiled. For the rest of the night, I refused to allow myself another glance her way.

But as soon as I got home, I jumped on my laptop to see what I could learn about *Mrs. Quentin Paris.*

# 9

## NICA

Connecticut was colder than normal for early November. Even with a puffy vest over my long-sleeved top and jeans, I shivered in my boots outside the practice rink. It was definitely warmer in Hartford when I left my apartment an hour ago.

A sleek silver Tesla hummed into the parking space in front of me right at ten. Ryan stepped out wearing a beanie with the team logo on it and another flannel shirt. More importantly, he carried two large coffees. I refused to stare at the second steaming cup. Refused to think he'd actually—

"Two milks, no sugar." He held the cup toward me.

"You really brought me coffee?"

"You told me to."

I hurried to accept the cup. "I said I was joking."

"Who jokes about wanting coffee?"

*Fair point.* I didn't have anything good in reply, so I sipped and sighed. "Thank you so much."

"No big deal."

It was a big deal to me, but he didn't have to know that.

Not every day a guy who ostensibly hated my guts was considerate enough to bring me coffee. Not everyday guys who ostensibly liked me did so, either.

Ryan gave me a hesitant look that pulled me out of my thoughts. "Can you skate? I should've asked."

I hitched the duffle bag on my shoulder. "Yep. Nothing fancy, but I have my own and go sometimes with my brother."

"Cool. So, second question. Do you like dogs?"

"I think I do. I've never really been around them, but they're cute. Why?"

"You said I should be as relaxed as possible. So I brought a friend." He kept his gaze on me as he reached to open the backseat door.

A long-bodied dog with stumpy legs and big ears hopped out and wiggled his butt in a little circle. He looked like an animated ottoman in the best way. He was red and white with a nub tail and the cutest face I'd ever seen. A delighted squeal bubbled in my throat. The pup noticed and came over to sniff my shoes.

"Oh, my god, what kind of dog is this? It looks like a cartoon!"

Ryan flashed a smile. "It's a Corgi. This is Henrik."

"Henrik?"

"As in Lundqvist. My goalie idol."

I whipped out my phone to make that note. Then I looked back at the dog. "Can... Can I touch him? Will he bite me?"

"No." Ryan's expression confirmed that I sounded like a paranoid weirdo.

"When I said I've never really been around them, I meant that I've only seen them in parks and on the street.

I've never actually met a dog." As expected, my explanation didn't dispel his confusion.

"Seriously? Never ever?"

I shrugged and looked away. In my periphery, I saw Ryan bend down and then stand up again. Chills ran down my spine as a wet nose sniffed my cheek. I squealed again, and Henrik licked me.

"That tickles!"

Ryan laughed. "Pet him. He won't bite you. Promise."

"If he does, can I bite him back?"

"No, but you can bite me."

We both froze. Heat rushed my face despite the chilly morning. At least he blushed, too. I tamped down the urge to lean in and suck on his neck and instead turned to the dog. "Hello, Mister Doggy. You are a cute little thing. You know it? I bet you do."

His head was soft when I hesitantly skimmed my fingers between those big ears. Henrik panted and tried to lick my face again. I scratched one ear, and his eyes closed.

"What do you think?" Ryan asked, drawing my attention back to him.

"He's sweet. This is cool."

I stepped back and admired the sweetly sexy sight of Ryan Molloy cradling a dog. *I get now why they make calendars of content like this.* He murmured to Henrik and set him back on the ground. The dog sat staring up at us, but as soon as Ryan grabbed his skates, the pup went nuts. He sprinted to the rink's doors. We walked together to catch up.

"I figured today's interview would be about your professional life," I said on the way. "Next, we can do one about your personal life. And the last one, I guess, will be to hit anything we might've missed. Cool?"

"We can't just do it all at once and be done?"

"Audrey said at least three."

"We could tell her we did three."

I turned to him at the doors. "Look. This is my first time writing an article, okay? Can you please just suck it up and give me the time? I don't want to miss anything. And I don't want to piss you off by asking for more if I do."

He sipped his coffee and gazed at me. "Fine."

"If it helps, your disdain for the situation has been noted and logged."

That got me a twitch of his lips. "Thank you."

Ryan keyed in a code on the pin pad by the door. The lock hissed, and he pushed the door open. Henrik hurried inside. A grin tugged at me as I walked through the silent, cavernous rink. Only the efficiency lights were on, but gray sunlight filtered in through frosted panes on the domed roof.

The door's click behind me froze my smile, though. *Oh, god. We're the only two people here.* My heart fluttered as I turned to him.

He stopped several feet away from me. His expression tensed. "I, uh... is this okay? I didn't think about being the only ones here. Should we go? We can go. We should go... right?"

Of all the wild places I'd wound up. Of all the times I'd been in a tight spot and wondered if I was going to make it out unscathed. Of so many moments from a life lived on a shoestring and sheer determination, this one was somehow uniquely odd and yet not at all scary. *He* wasn't scary, which of course was a fool's logic.

I toyed with my skate bag. "That depends. Will we get in trouble for being here?"

"Not at all. I can come anytime."

"Promise not to murder me?"

His shoulders dropped with a soft laugh. "I promise not to murder you, Nica."

My scalp prickled. "That's the first time you've used my name."

He adjusted his beanie. "I... did you prefer I call you Mrs—"

"God, no!" I clamped my mouth shut too late. The words burst out of me. Henrik let out a little woof. Ryan flinched, so I tried again. "That is not my name. You should call me Nica."

"I promise not to murder you, Nica Solance. But if this is uncomfortable, we can leave."

*Before we go, can you whisper my name in my ear for about ten minutes?* Good lord, the ache his voice gave me made no sense.

"You're not getting out of this interview that easily, buster."

My throat felt dusty as I said it, but he laughed and sat on the bench to lace his skates. My smile returned as I did the same.

"Appropriate color palette," he said with a nod to my maroon top and navy vest. Commodores' team colors.

I shimmied my shoulders. "That was no accident. I like your beanie."

"Fun trivia for you: Quinn calls it a toque." He stood up and walked to the door to the ice.

But I leaned on the boards with my phone. "I don't care what Quinn calls it. This is about you. Now, go do hockey things. I'm gonna film you."

"I didn't consent to that."

My finger froze over the record button. "It's part of the journalistic process."

Ryan opened and closed his mouth, then shrugged and opened the door. Before he could step onto the ice, Henrik beat him to it. I yelped, delighted at the sight of this little loaf-shaped dog skittering around on the ice. He slipped, and his little legs splooted out in all directions. Just as quickly, he was up and running again.

"Oh, my gosh. He loves it. I guess I don't have to ask if he's done this before." My face hurt from smiling.

Ryan glanced over his shoulder at me, and my breath caught. *Dear lord.* The way his hair peeked out of that hat. The broad, pure smile that creased his face. Those green eyes dancing with amusement. *Focus, Nica. Focus... Stop focusing on him, I mean!*

Impossible. He was too gorgeous.

"He's done it before, yeah. Ever since he was a puppy. Henrik loves the ice. Just like his dad," he added with an eye roll that only made me warmer.

I needed this man's gaze off of me. I wanted to sit on the boards and wrap my legs around his back again. The internal war just would not quit. It took tremendous effort to shoo him onto the ice, but Ryan nodded and skated away backward, still gazing at me.

Henrik chased him. His little legs worked frantically to keep up, but he was no match for Ryan's long strides. Instead, he took to playing angles in order to cut him off. Excited barks echoed through the rink while Ryan picked up speed, spun around to skate forward, and fell into doing laps on the ice.

It took me several minutes to close my jaw and remember my job. Between the dog-dad vibes and the effortless power in his movements, staring was required.

*Hello, doofus. You have seen hockey players skate before. It's literally his job. No big deal.*

But I hadn't skated *with* a hockey player before. This wasn't a front-row seat to a game. This was something much, much cooler.

No.

Something hotter. Much, *much* hotter.

"Are you going to join us or stand there all day?"

His shout jolted me out of my thoughts. I stepped onto the ice, phone in my pocket. Henrik ran up to sniff me, but Ryan dumped out a bag of pucks while I got my legs under me. As soon as the rubber hit the ice, the dog zoomed to investigate. I coasted around and watched Ryan egg him on with some stick handling. It was a game of keep-away that had Henrik barking and trying to bite the puck, even though Ryan's moves were lightning-fast. I leaned on the boards and videoed the game for several moments. Ryan finally noticed. He shook his head and shot the puck down the ice so that Henrik ran for it. Then, he skated over to where I stood.

I shook myself out of a trance and started a voice note. "I'm here with Ryan Molloy. It's Thursday morning, and..."

"Why are you talking like that?"

I blinked. "Like what?"

"In that weird, gravelly voice."

"I—oh. I guess that's how I talk in posts."

"Yeah, I noticed. What's that about?"

"Branding?"

He leaned on the boards. "Well, this isn't a post, so could you please talk like Nica?"

*Ouch. Good point.* If I was going to be a serious journalist, I needed to act like it. I nodded once and dropped the affect. "Who's your favorite teammate?"

"All of them. I don't pick favorites."

"What's your favorite meal before a game?"

"Steak and eggs. Gosh, you know. I gotta tell you. I didn't realize you'd be hitting me with these heavy questions today. I'm not sure I'm prepared to be probed so deeply."

Heat rushed my face. I tried to glare, but he held me with a patient look. He didn't seem mad. He seemed playful. Daring.

"What do you love about being a goalie?" I asked softly.

"My sex symbol status. Obviously." Green eyes rolled behind those glasses.

"You mean your sex drink guy status."

I wanted to crow when his ears went pink. "I thought we'd forgotten about that."

My chin lifted, but I kept my gaze on his. "Then answer the question, Molloy."

With a nod, he said, "I stand alone. The last line of defense for the team. If I can play better than my absolute best, then we will win. If I don't, then no matter how many goals Simmons chips in, or slapshots Rivera rockets, it won't matter. Because, as the goalie, I'm out there to keep us in the game. I'm tied to the team, but I don't move with the team. It's unique, which suits me well. It's demanding, which also fits for me. And it makes me part of something but also an individual. That's why I love it."

"Then what do you hate about it?"

His lip curled on the left side. "See my previous answer."

My breath had gone shallow. This man had just beautifully summed up why I loved goalies. I loved the way they carried the weight of their role. My heart broke for them when they had bad nights, especially when they lost a playoff game. The pressure they voluntarily bore made me admire the hell out of them.

Plus, the way they could move was sexy as hell.

An inconvenient detail for sure when it came to *this* goalie. This goalie, who I'd been thisclose to having a night of random, anonymous sex with. *You could've bagged a fucking goalie, Nica. You could've known exactly how he...*

"Next?"

"Right." I shook myself out of the trance his words put on me. "So, what's it like to be a backup goalie?"

His brow twitched. "Good question. It is never a kid's dream to be the backup goalie. You don't give your life to the game hoping to play one in five or six. You don't dream of inking your contract so you can sit on the bench night after night."

He gazed down the ice to where Henrik was trying to pick up a puck. "But I still fucking love it," he said softly.

I arched a brow. "The reality is better than the dream?"

"So much, but for a reason. I love to play. I also love data and stats. Sitting backup for one of the greatest goalies in our era, on one of the best teams in the league, gives me all the data to analyze I could want. My job isn't to warm the bench. My job is to support the guys by watching their game performance, tracking it with historical data, and helping them notice weaknesses and strengths as they develop."

"Wow. You are the biggest nerd in hockey."

A laugh burst out of him, just like I wanted. Cheeks flushed pink, but he shook his head and didn't answer. Warm pride spread through my chest at the way I'd made him laugh. He'd laughed easily the night we met. Since then, in each of our disaster meetings, I'd longed to have him drop the tension for a second. His laugh felt like a victory.

I cleared my throat to return us to the subject. "Describe your goaltending style. Are you making any changes as the starting goalie?"

"Skate with me, and I'll tell you."

We pushed off, and he launched into a long explanation of how his style had changed thanks to his coaches and some off-season training. He spoke in a lot of technical goaltending terms like *positional, athletic, butterfly,* and *blocking.* I held the phone out to catch everything until he took it from me and spoke into the mic.

When he slowed down, I blinked hard and said, "That was a lot of detail."

"Told you details are my thing. That's how I think about the game."

"Tell me more."

Shrug. "I'm a data nerd, to use your term. Statistics, percentages. Data tells the story of a player. The more you track it, the more precise you can be with your focus and how you play."

"I have two questions."

"Okay."

"First, is the nerd vibe why you reject the typical hockey player's attention to style?"

He whipped his head to me. "What does that mean?"

I gestured to him. "Your clothes. Your hair."

"What's wrong with them?"

A little laugh slipped out. "Seriously, Ryan?"

He huffed. "Yes, Nica, *seriously.* What am I rejecting?"

"Fashion? Style? Call it what you want, but it seems clear you're not about your physical image."

"Fuck's sake," he mumbled. "You're harsh."

"What? No! I didn't mean to be." I turned to him—too fast. My skates tangled, and I pitched straight into him.

Ryan didn't lose his footing in the least. He might as well have been wearing rubber-soled shoes on carpet for how sturdily he took the crash. A little grunt of surprise hit my ears as he gripped me by the arms.

"Sorry, fuck, what a klutz," I babbled, my fingers digging into his biceps to keep me from eating ice. My skates slipped out from underneath me, but he tightened his grip.

"Shh. Relax. You're not gonna fall. Henrik, go play." His voice went from soft to stern, and the pup quit sniffing us and jogged away.

I looked up at him while I planted my feet. "I am so sorry," I whispered.

He bit his lips in a line, clearly suppressing a laugh. "For your poor skating skills or for insulting me *again*?"

"Oh, come on!" I stood up straight but didn't release my grip on him. He still held me, too, so I ignored the voice in my head that screamed to back up. Instead, I rubbed his flannel between my thumb and forefinger. "You can't be insulted about the truth."

He looked down at my hand. "What's wrong with my clothes? It's just a shirt and jeans."

"They don't fit you, honey." I used the epithet teasingly, but it snapped his attention to me.

"They fit fine."

"They're too big!" I grinned and shook my head. "Look at all this fabric. And your hair doesn't look like it's seen gel since—uh... since Long Island."

His pupils dilated. Suddenly, I noticed that he'd shifted his hold on me. Instead of my shoulders, Ryan held my waist. Meanwhile, my wrists rested on his forearms. My neck craned back to hold eye contact since he was so damn tall, but we were definitely hugging right there on the ice.

And, my god, did it feel good.

His clothes might've been big, but they smelled divine.

And his hair might've been fluffy, but I wanted my hands in it again so fucking bad.

I gazed at him and wondered if he knew how often he blushed. Then I wondered if he blushed more around me than others. *Then* I kicked that silly thought away.

*You blew your chance with him, girlie. He would never want you in real life. Nerd or no, this man is a pro athlete—who you shit-talked and ghosted. He is so far out of your league it's not even the same game.*

## 10

## RYAN

I hated the way my face heated so easily around her. Damn being pale as fuck. Normally, it just meant turning bright red after a hard skate. With her, it meant I blushed like a schoolgirl too damn often.

But, god, why did holding her feel so fucking good?

She was shit-talking my clothes and calling me a nerd, and all I could concentrate on was how she smelled. Sweet and floral but without the heavy perfume I'd almost expected from someone who wore so much makeup. She smelled like she had that night. It overrode all the good reasons I had to release her and back away.

"I, uh... Long Island? Did we meet on Long Island?" I said at last in a desperate attempt to draw some kind of line between us.

She flinched. "Oh, uh, no. No, that's my mistake. I just meant you don't seem to own hair gel."

"I feel attacked." I managed a half-smile.

She squeezed my arms. "Then our second interview can be a shopping trip. You should get some clothes that fit."

"Nothing fits. Too big in some places, too tight in others."

Blue eyes rolled. "Not off the rack, silly. You're a hockey player. Go get some bespoke shit."

"I'll consider it."

Nica wet her lips. "Ryan?"

"Yeah?"

"My other question?"

My cue to release her. I nodded and eased backward. Nica's fingers slid down my arms, holding me until I was out of reach. I noticed. I also noticed how she balled her hands into fists once we had space between us.

*She doesn't want you. Nothing about this woman says green light. Certainly not the way she absolutely rejected your ass already.*

"Your other question." I pushed off in a slow skate so she could follow.

"My what? Oh. I wondered if you, like, hacked other teams to find their weaknesses?"

I laughed and shook my head. It helped take my mind off having her in my arms. "No. I focus on our team to help us improve."

"But could you?"

"Could I what?"

"Hack another team's... I don't know... system?"

"A, it doesn't really work that way. There's not a main-frame holding each franchise's secrets. And B... if there was, I guess I could. Maybe. Depending on the security level. But I wouldn't really need to... shit. I don't want this in the interview."

She hit stop on the phone. "Off the record. Keep talking."

I shrugged. "It's not hard to get info on someone if you want to. There are ways that don't require illegal moves."

Her gaze narrowed. "Sneaky. I like it."

"I bet you do, Nica Allison Solance."

I laughed at her unhinged jaw. "Oh, my god. You stalked me?" she hissed.

"No. Not at all. That was an easy one to find. Felt like digging deeper would be ... invasive."

"Damn right it would. *Damn*, you are sneaky."

"Swear I'm not. If I was, I'd be texting you this conversation."

She pointed at me. "Don't snoop, Goalie. Just ask me what you want to know. If you want my number, all you have to do is say, 'Nica, may I please have your number?'"

I bit back a smile. "I'll bear that in mind."

She gazed at me, clearly waiting to see if I'd ask. When I didn't, she rolled her eyes and skated away. Henrik barked and hurried to herd her along. Nica looked down and cooed at him, and I tensed. "Hey. Don't talk to him unless you want him to herd you."

"Huh? I think he heard me fine. Didn't you, Mister Puppy?"

"No, herd. Corgis are bred to herd sheep and cattle. He'll chase you if you—"

As if on cue, Henrik sped up. He ran close beside Nica's skates until she sped up, too. I heard her laugh at first, but then Henrik started nipping her laces. "Hey!" she cried.

"Just slow down."

But she didn't. Henrik saw it as a game. He ran beside her, barking. I hurried to get to them, picking up a puck along the way for distraction, but Nica was skating too fast. Henrik tugged her laces undone, and she hit the ice.

"Fuck." I kicked it into gear to get to her.

Her phone clattered to the ground as her palms shot out to break the fall. Her knees hit and buckled so that she was flat on her stomach. "Ungh," she groaned.

"Hen, get back," I commanded as he scurried around, trying to lick her face. I flung the puck, and he raced for it.

Nica lifted her head when I dropped onto the ice in a lunge and then twisted to sit down. She groaned again and scowled. "How'd you make that look so smooth?"

I sat facing her on the ice. "I play hockey."

"Ungh." She managed to roll over and sit up.

I slid closer to grasp her wrists and examine her hands. Both were bright red with ice burn. Tiny scrapes stood out, but nothing seemed too serious.

"Does it hurt?" I asked.

"Stings like a motherfucker."

That blunt-as-hell reply made me snort. I shook my head and blew gently on her tender skin. Since teasing seemed to be our most effective form of communication, I tried a little levity. "I'm sorry. Should've been on hand to break your fall again. You're a terrible skater, by the way. Shocked you said yes to it."

Her impish smirk flickered, but her gaze drifted to my lips while I blew on her hands again. "I'm a very good skater," she said at last.

"Sure, tell yourself that."

"Piss off, Goalie."

"Thanks a lot. Your hands are freezing."

"No shit. They just felt up the ice."

I laughed again and wrapped my hands around hers to warm them up. Her hands fit entirely into mine. She was small-boned, but from everything I'd seen, Nica Solance was anything but fragile.

She watched our hands. "We, uh, well. That's nice. But if I keep sitting here, my ass is going to freeze, too."

Wicked fire flashed through me. "Not sure I can help with that one." *I can. I absolutely would.*

Before she could answer, I helped her to her feet, scooped up her phone, and guided her off the ice. We sat down side by side on the bench while Henrik lay nearby, panting like crazy.

Nica stood up and shouldered her skate bag. "I think we're done for now."

"I have some questions for you."

"Not sure that's how this works. But fine. Hit me."

We ambled toward the exit. "You used the phrase, 'Paris is my job.' What does that mean?"

She explained how she'd started the profile as a goof that had gone viral. I listened, trying to imagine how strange a journey that must've been, and then said as much. "That must've been so bizarre to have your page go from a crush to a career."

"No joke." She laughed softly. "But it's been fun. And it's so much better than my old job."

"Which was?"

"Waitress."

I nodded and opened the door for her. In as casual and neutral a tone as possible, I asked, "Do you still crush on Quinn?"

*Not that I care. Nope. Could not be less interested in who you're interested in.*

She waited until we were out on the sidewalk. "I think he's amazing. But knowing Audrey makes him a person, not a hockey god that I see on TV. Audrey's been awesome to me. Crushing on her husband would be creepy. Besides," she added with a light laugh, "I get the feeling he's not my type in real life."

*Do not ask her what her type is. Do. Not.* "Would you quit doing the profile if you could?"

"Absolutely," she whispered. "But I can't. Not at this time."

"Why?"

"Well, I mean, I could. But you try slinging drinks in a casino wearing a miniskirt. Then tell me if I have a lot of a choice. Run a social media page that pays, or get your ass felt up by drunk douchebags over and over for shit tips."

"What? They don't. Not really. I mean, security takes care of that. Right?"

She rasped a humorless laugh. "You're cute. Naïve as hell, but cute. At the place I worked, security would stop major breaches—probably. Hopefully. But patrons who are gambling but a little too friendly? Come on, Ryan. It's part of the job."

"You've been groped?"

Her gaze dropped . "I'm the one doing the interview, Goalie."

It was a clear yes. Anger flared in my chest. An irrational desire to hunt down scumbags who did shit like that rashed over me. I clenched my hands into fists. "Well, if you have any names, I can hack their email and send their colleagues a bunch of weird shit that'd get them fired."

I loved her real laugh. She clapped a hand over her mouth at the sudden giggles that burst out of her, but it only made me grin. "And you criticize what *I* do online?"

"Only because it's directly related to me."

I put my skates in the trunk and opened the back door for Henrik. "So what happens next? With the interview, I mean."

"I guess we'll schedule another meeting. Can we go shopping? Puh-leese?"

I groaned. "Fine. I'll figure out where I should go. I'm on the road for four days starting tomorrow, so it'll have to wait until I'm back. We can get this wrapped up then. It'll make Audrey happy, and I'll get you out of my hair."

"With that mad scientist look you've got going, lord knows you don't need anything else in your hair."

I palmed my eyes, but my smile flashed as I peeked at her through my fingers. "Fuck's sake, woman. You are hateful."

Nica hesitated. Then, in a flurry of motion, she reached up, snatched the beanie off my head, and ran to her car. I took off after her, slow enough that she had her door open before I caught up.

"Excuse me. That's mine."

She jammed it onto her head and grinned up at me. "Collateral. You'll have to see me again to get it back."

I bent so we were eye-to-eye. "You are nothing but trouble."

"You like it."

"I definitely probably like it more than I should."

Her lips parted. Mine did, too. We stared at each other. Breaths mingled. Mouths nudged closer and closer. I swallowed hard. "Fuck. I can't."

"We can't," she whispered.

Neither of us backed up. It was an endurance test unlike any skate drill or workout I'd ever known. I ached to snap the barrier and knew damn well I wasn't going to.

At last, we both pulled back and traded a glance that agreed that we'd passed the test.

"I'll see you soon," she said softly.

"Yeah."

And then, she was gone.

# 11

## NICA

"Molloy's doing well. That shutout last night was awesome."

"Hm? Oh. I know."

Bruce tapped his water glass. "Am I boring you? Because if you feel like you don't need—"

I ignored his pissy expression and waved that off. "Of course not. But I know they won again. What I don't know is whether Embark is going to hire me for any more promotions."

Luggage, clothing, protein shakes. Whatever. I hadn't had a sponsorship deal come through all week. The month's rent was paid, but there was very little left over at the moment. I wouldn't get any money from the interview until it was done. Ryan's suggestion we move quickly was fine by me. Audrey said she'd hoped for it to be finished in a few weeks. Even with my lack of experience, I was determined to get it done—and get it done *right*—asap.

*If only I could lock him in a room for twenty-four hours and get all the info I need.*

My face ignited. The thought had meant to be focused and professional. But the idea of being locked in a room with Ryan Molloy brought on extremely *un*professional thoughts that I couldn't get a handle on. Especially after skating with him that morning. My god. I never knew I could be so warm on an ice rink.

I adjusted my newly acquired beanie and refocused on the meeting.

Bruce hummed. "Trashing Molloy isn't going to work if he's winning. Are you ready to talk ideas as *equal* partners?"

My shoulders slumped. I needed streams of income. The article alone wouldn't keep me fed. "Yes," I whispered.

"Start a new page. This one for Molloy. Don't show your face—you can't be known for running two platforms so similar—but get all the inside details on this guy that you can. What he likes. What his routines are. What makes him tic. He's clearly a bit of a nerd based on everything he's shown so far. If you spin it right, you'll get people to fall for him."

*I don't think it would be hard to fall for Ryan Molloy.* I frowned. "A fangirl page for him? Come on, Bruce. I thought you were going to suggest something more commercial or—"

"Know your niche, Nica. You found a talent for making people thirst. You can breathe new life into your presence if you lean into it. I'm telling you. Sell this guy, and the cash will roll in."

*You're already writing a story on him. Why not make the photo version? Audrey would love it! You can build buzz around him immediately this way. And that'll make your article even more relevant. Omg, this is genius.*

I looked at Bruce. "Great idea. I'll let you know when we make any money."

At home, I sat down with my phone and culled all the footage I had of Ryan. Not a lot so far, but enough. I had shots from the press conference and video from the ice last night. The best stuff by far was the video from this morning's skate, but I'd need more content soon. Hopefully he wouldn't change his mind about our next meeting. We could get him new clothes. Maybe talk over dinner...

*You are crushing so hard, girl.*

For the millionth time, I shook that thought out of my head. The butterflies just wouldn't go. I knew I was foolish. I knew there was nothing between us. But damn. Between the goalie core and the unrelenting memories of his kiss, Ryan Molloy occupied a lot of mental real estate. Every time he caught my eye with that sly, annoyed-but-not look, I had flashes of the way his lips and tongue could tease me senseless.

*How would that tongue feel on other parts of my body?*

"Ugh, give it a rest," I shouted into my empty apartment.

If anything, my daydreams were a testament to how rare great kisses were. Bruce's kisses were shitty and had always been. I hadn't caved and called him outside of our work meetings in ages. Certainly not after Long Island. Memories and my vibrator were better than sex with a narcissist.

I threw the beanie on the coffee table and went back to work. My vision of how this platform would look had already started to come together. When I launched Mrs. Quentin Paris, I'd randomly posted whatever came to my head. This one would be more polished. I would keep it professional. That meant no pics of Henrik and no personal details. I'd use Irish music on action videos, stuff like "I'm Shipping Up to Boston" except obviously without the lyrics. He had such a Celtic look that it just made sense. For casual footage, there was really only one choice: the *Star Wars* theme song.

I giggled until I was breathless as I spliced a clip of Yoda training Luke with the on-ice footage. Then, I found a Darth Vader clip, added text over that said, "I sense a disturbance in the season," and finished with the press conference where Ryan gave his statement.

Oh, this was fun.

Now, if it worked, things would be just peachy.

I looked around my little apartment. A pile of once-worn dresses lay on the kitchen table, waiting to be shipped. I sold them all online this weekend, along with my pretty peach suitcase and a whole slew of high heels.

*I don't need that stuff. Momma would've hawked it as soon as she got her hands on it. This is different. This is being economically smart. As long as I have a nice dress and something professional, I'm fine.*

My phone vibrated, pulling me out of those thoughts.

AUDREY:

Hey! The guys are back in town. I have a PR stunt scheduled for tomorrow after their skate. Be at the arena around noon, ok? This is an invite-only thing. It'll be great for your article. ;)

ME:

Absolutely!

I launched my new page with the victory lap video from his shutout and got busy interacting with other hockey fans to build momentum. If I did this right, this would be great for me *and* Audrey.

The next morning, I wore black trousers and a sweater and made sure my hair was sleek. Since I wouldn't be on camera,

I toned down the makeup a little. My stomach rolled at the thought of other journalists side-eyeing me, but screw them. If I kept faking it in this new position, someday I'd probably actually make it.

I texted Vinny.

ME:

> Press event at the arena. Palms sweating. They're gonna see right through me.

He didn't reply until I was nearly to Seacrest. Then again, he was always busy at the garage he ran with his partner. Taking time to reply at all meant I was a VIP in his life.

VINNY:

> See right through you? U mean see what a badass you are.

I replied with a string of hearts and shut off the engine. I sucked in a deep breath and got out of the car. *Show them you're a badass.*

Joey escorted me to the media room. I walked in to find three women and three photographers hanging out. The women stopped talking when they saw me. *Great.*

But one of them smiled and walked forward. "I'm Sandy from *Puck Drop Daily*."

I shook her hand. "Nica. I'm—"

Her smile lifted higher on one side. "I know. And now I hear you're doing a freelance piece for us. How did you get that gig?"

There was no malice in her tone. The others gathered around us. I kept my shoulders square and shrugged. "Audrey decided I might be an asset. Or she wanted to keep an eye on me."

They laughed lightly like I'd wanted. Sandy looked me

over again. "Your copy is strong. I'm excited to read your article."

"Thanks."

She smiled briefly. "Real question is, do you know what this is all about?"

I didn't. But the fact that we were the only ones here made me very curious indeed. We hung out for several more minutes before Audrey walked in wearing a cheeky smile. "Ladies. I've put together an exclusive photo op that I hope your readers enjoy. Let's join the guys on the ice first."

We followed her to the rink to find the team practicing. As soon as they were in range, the photographers aimed their cameras and began shooting rapidly. Audrey handed the four of us headsets.

"Channel one is Dustin's mic. Channel two is Ryan."

It took a lot of muscle control to casually slip that headset on instead of snatching it from her like a fiend. I told myself this was professional and nothing more while I flipped the channel to two.

"Nope... Not today, Captain..." His voice was a soft mutter, but then he was talking to himself. And even with the mic on, there were long stretches where he didn't talk at all.

I wandered to find a good angle to shoot from and pulled out my phone. Because this was a content goldmine, I made sure to capture as many of the guys as I could. But, of course, Ryan was my main focus. I set the video to record and watched him.

"Gotcha!" His singsong exclamation hit my ears when he blocked a shot by Dustin Simmons from the blue line. I laughed.

Simmons and Ethan Rivera passed the puck back and forth and raced in on him together. Rivera stopped short just in front of Ryan, hitting him with a little spray of ice while Simmons took another shot. This one squeaked in through his legs.

"Interference! That's goalie interference if I ever saw it!"

I could hear Rivera laughing. "Ref says it was a good goal, Sieve."

"Fuck off, Twinkle Toes. That was textbook interference." Ryan's voice had a laugh in it, but I hurried to make notes: *Sieve?? Twinkle Toes???*

The guys skated away, and Ryan dropped to his knees. I made sure to zoom in on him while he pushed the blue snow off to the side of the net and smoothed the ice over with his glove. "Crease maintenance," he muttered, and I added another phrase to my list of questions.

Too soon, which was to say ever, the guys cleared the ice and disappeared into the locker room. But Audrey waved us all to her, still wearing that smile.

"Follow me, ladies."

# 12

# RYAN

I toweled off from the shower with my heart in my ears. Jesus Christ. Just when I thought I'd adjusted to my new role, Audrey hit me with *this*. I'd walked into morning meeting expecting a typical day. Before I could gear up, she'd pulled me, Ethan, and Dustin aside. Her cat-ate-the-canary grin had told me something was coming.

I hadn't imagined *this* would be her request.

"Stop! Dammit, Molls." Ethan's laughed shout spun me around. "You can't towel dry your hair, bro. It makes you look like a poodle."

I threw the towel at him. Nica's gentle teasing came back to me. "What am I supposed to do?"

He handed me a comb. "Comb it out. Simsy, give him your stuff. Give it a light touch and leave it damp for now. You don't have time to blow-dry. Trust me."

Dustin lobbed a jar of sculpting paste at me. I ran it through my hair and yanked the comb until there were no more tangles. My hair was too wet to stay back, but at least it fell straight. When the guys nodded, I stepped into the navy sweatpants Audrey had gifted us this morning and pulled on a black muscle tee. "Can I wear my glasses?" I asked with an eye roll.

"Oh, yeah," Dustin said. "Your new fan page will love that."

"My new what?" I froze mid-stride.

He laughed. "Didn't you know you've got a fan page? Our Boy Molloy. Corny as fuck if you ask me."

"Jesus, this is my nightmare." I reached to ruffle my hair.

Ethan slapped my hand away. "Aww, come on. Audrey hasn't been this excited all year. Let's just have some fun for her sake."

I couldn't argue with that. Certainly not when Audrey beamed as the three of us walked out into the hallway. "I know this is silly, guys, but I think it'll be a huge hit. Thank you so much."

"Anything for you, Auds. Hey. Who let you in?" Ethan winked at his wife, Stella, who stood to the side with Jazzlynne, Dustin's girlfriend.

"Snuck in. We couldn't miss the show," she replied as we all headed toward the gym.

I filed in last. Audrey was already talking to the small crowd assembled there. She was clearly working hard to suppress laughter as she said, "... just wanted you to have a better understanding of our guys' fitness levels."

Stella and Jazzlynne didn't bother to hide their giggles. I swallowed another groan and leaned against the wall. While Dustin and Ethan spread out, I looked around at our audience.

*Fuck. Of fucking course, but still. Fuck!* My stomach hit the floor the second I spotted Nica. She had her attention on Audrey like the rest of the reporters. As soon as Audrey stopped talking, though, those blue-gray eyes swept the room—and caught instantly on me.

I resisted the urge to ruffle my hair while I watched her eyes widen and her lips fall open. Damn my pulse for refusing to chill. Damn the way I couldn't quit replaying her kiss despite vowing it never happened. And damn the way she pinned me with that look.

Well. It was more than a look. Ms. Nica Solance was most definitely checking me out.

I held her gaze and refused to budge from the wall. She looked around and took half a step toward me, but "Push It" began to play through the speakers. Audrey let out an excited yelp, and Dustin started us off with a box jump.

He talked to the reporters while he went through a short workout routine that included burpees and battle rope. Although he ostensibly explained the routine, I paid close attention to the way he smiled and winked at key moments. This was all a flirt. That was the whole point, as Audrey had explained to me. Photo ops showing us being strong, sweaty dudes in the gym.

Dustin and Ethan had laughed at this proposed objectification. I'd not been as keen, but Audrey said it was good for my image. The guys assured me it would be a goof, all good fun. Dustin was clearly enjoying himself, but the whole thing had impostor syndrome wrapping its fingers around my neck again.

*Me? Flirt? Flex? Be in the spotlight? Since when?*

I glanced at Audrey, Stella, and Jazzlynne. They stood holding each other's arms, pink-cheeked and grinning. I thought about Quinn, about all he was going through right now, and I took a deep breath.

*You can do this.*

Dustin finished his set on the floor. He held onto the weight rack above his head, lifted himself off the ground until just his shoulders supported him, and did bicycle crunches without lowering down.

Every female in the room whooped.

He collapsed on his back, laughing. "Thank you, thank you," he said as he jumped to his feet and pointed at Ethan.

The music changed to Usher's "Yeah!". Ethan palmed his face. "I told Audrey to choose whatever song she wanted for this." He picked up the jump rope, listened for a moment, and then began to jump.

Except, of course, that we called him Twinkle Toes for a reason. No one on the team had dance moves like Ethan Rivera. He made jumping rope look like something else entirely with the way he moved to the music. And, again, all the women cheered.

Ethan dropped the rope and accepted a towel from Stella when the song ended. Like Dustin had done for him, it was his turn to pass the spotlight.

Right over to me.

"Pony" started to play. I twisted my lips and sucked in a breath. Both of them had jumped right into their routine with no introduction. I didn't want to jump into anything, but I knew I would just be stalling if I tried to talk. So, I pushed my glasses up my nose and walked out into a plank.

*Pushups. Just do pushups to the music.* I listened for a moment to get the beat and began, but after about five reps, Ethan called out to me. "Come on, Molls. Show us what you got."

At least he didn't call me Sieve.

"Fuck it," I whispered under my breath. "Somebody take these," I shouted over the music as I whipped off the glasses and held them out in front of me. They disappeared from my hand in a blink.

Dropping down to my forearms, I slid backward until

my elbows were nearly extended, then slid forward again and piked my ass in the air to do another pushup. Rolling back to my starting position, I lowered down and slid first to the left, then to the right, in time to the music. From there I did a couple of one-armed pushups, then one-legged reps on each side before returning to plank.

"Am I done?" I shouted, my gaze on the ground. "Or do you want more?"

"More," came the unanimous shout.

I did it all again.

Thank god the music ended. I walked my feet to my hands and stood up slowly. My face was hot from exertion, but I realized I was grinning. I pushed my hair away while they applauded.

Audrey thanked the reporters for coming while Stella and Jazzlynne walked us back to the locker room to get our stuff. The women could not stop laughing and replaying the entire thing.

"Ryan, it's too bad you're single, buddy," Dustin said, pulling Jazzlynne closer to him. "All that work you just put in and no reward?"

"I thought the reward was making Audrey happy."

"Oh, it was. One of them." He kissed Jazzlynne's cheek and made her giggle.

The guys grabbed their stuff and were off quick with their partners. I pulled on a hoodie and shouldered my duffel bag. On the way out, I touched the bridge of my nose and remembered that I had ditched my glasses in the gym. I hurried out of the locker room, wondering where I'd left them and who'd taken them from me.

There was no need to ponder. As soon as I stepped into the hallway, my glasses were waiting for me—perched on Nica's nose. She leaned against the wall, wearing a cheeky smirk. Her dark hair peeked out from under a very familiar-looking beanie.

"Hey. Great road trip. Four in a row. Crushing it."

Her words momentarily distracted me. I felt a pleased smile tug my lips. "Why, thank you."

"Where does Henrik stay when you're gone? Ooh, or does he travel with you?"

"He stays with the neighbor. May I have my glasses back?"

"Maybe. Do they make me look smarter?"

"You are smart. They dwarf your head."

"They're making me dizzy." She pulled them off, blinked hard, and stepped forward to slip them into my hand. "Can you see without them?" she asked while I pushed them on.

"Yeah, but not far away."

"How do you play hockey, then?"

"Contacts, of course. I just don't like them as much. Besides, I think these suit my face."

Her gaze swept over me. "They do."

"Should've known you stole them. Should've known you'd be trespassing again."

"You really should've. On both counts."

"Nice hat."

"Thanks. It's new."

We traded a glance.

Good god, the ache in my chest would not quit. She gave me a buzz without doing a damn thing, and I couldn't sort out why. No logic could explain why I'd wanted to punch the air at the sight of her waiting here. Why I loved the idea of her quietly snatching my glasses, so quick that no one noticed. Why a big-mouthed social media personality made my mouth fucking water.

"Can I ask a few questions? Not a full interview. Just a little?"

I groaned. "More torture? Wasn't that enough for today?"

Her smile stretched wide. The delight on her face made me warm all over. "That was amazing. Content gold."

"It was all Audrey's idea."

"Mm, I figured you weren't the one to suggest it."

I laughed.

"Was it difficult?"

"Nah. Challenging, I guess, but not too draining. Not as draining as the mental load of performing for an audience."

"Oh, such a flex. 'No big deal. Just three straight minutes of hard-as-hell pushups. Day's work, really.'"

"It's not a day's work. A day's work is way more demanding than that. Pushups are easy."

"Can you do the thing Simmons did?"

I nodded.

"Can you jump rope like Rivera?"

"Mm, not with as much rhythm."

"What else can you do, Goalie?"

"I mean, everything? I bench press around a hundred fifty, so... more than you."

Her brows went up. "You can bench press me?"

"Easily. I could do those pushups with you on my back."

Her eyes lit up. "I would pay you to show me that."

The next thing I knew, I was pushing open the gym door and motioning her inside. A small part of my brain asked what the hell I was doing. The rest of me didn't give a fuck.

Nica let out a little squeal and hurried to follow. "Ohmygod, are you really going to?"

"Once." I tugged off my hoodie and walked out to plank. "Hurry up."

But Nica didn't move. "Um, what should I do? Or how do I, um... mount you?"

I laughed so hard, I had to drop to the mat. Her giggles hit my ears, so I looked up to where she stood over me. "Don't make me laugh, please. I said I could do it, but not if I've got a cramp."

"Sorry, sorry."

"Just, I don't know. Sit on my back." I pushed up again.

"Like Yoda on Luke?"

Right back to the floor. "Dammit," I wheezed. "Forget this."

"No! I have to see! I'll be good. I promise."

I took a few deep breaths and resumed plank. She kicked off her shoes and padded toward me. After a moment's hesitation, her hands planted on my shoulders. Nica threw one leg over my back and held me tight as she steadied herself.

"You good?" I grunted.

"Oh, yeah."

I took a deep breath and lowered down. This wasn't easy. She wasn't terribly heavy, but her center of gravity wobbled with my movement. "Oh, shit, I'm gonna fall," she yelped.

"Just hold on," I gritted out.

Suddenly, her arms hugged my neck—like Yoda on Luke. Her breath tickled my ear, and it took every ounce of discipline to push us back up. Nica's feet touched the ground. I held still while she climbed off. My arms shook, breath coming hard.

Breathing wasn't the only thing that was hard.

Her sweet scent lingered in my nose while I jumped to my feet, facing away from her while I cooled off.

"Wow," she whispered behind me.

With a quick glance at my sweats to make sure I was

decent, I turned and strolled as casually as I could for the hoodie. "Satisfied?"

"Impressed is a better word. How much do I owe you?"

"Ten."

"Ten dollars?"

"Ten digits. Please give me your phone number, Nica Solance."

I noticed how she blinked every time I used her name. It told me she was either easily startled or very pleased. And this woman didn't seem startled by much.

"Well, if you insist," she drawled.

"Afraid I do. I'll need it to contact you for our next meeting." I hid a grin that would've told her that was bullshit. It was, of course. I could've had Audrey schedule for us, but I wanted her number in my phone.

Nica winced but hid it fast. "Right. Get ready."

I keyed in the numbers and texted her, "hi." She tapped the screen, typed, and then looked up at me. "Big mistake, buddy. Now I've got yours, too."

"Don't think this means you can text me questions whenever you want."

"Don't think this means I won't try."

I chuckled and held the door open for her. Nica looked at it but hesitated. She toyed with her purse and cut her gaze to me.

"What is it?"

"Can I ask you a personal question?"

Nod.

"Do you hate me, Ryan Molloy? Do you hate that I'm doing this interview?"

I exhaled hard and pushed my hair back, careful not to ruffle it. Slowly, I strode to where she stood and looked down at her. "I hate the interview because I don't like interviews. But I don't hate that you're the one doing it, no. And, no, Nica. I do not hate you."

*I think I like you. Way more than I should. But I can't really tell because there are logistical hurdles between us. Plus, you're so damn guarded that half the time, I feel like I'm talking to a person. The other half feels like I'm talking to a* personality.

*But my god. You are captivating.*

Captivating was the right word. She was beautiful in an unusual way. Almost elfish features that didn't quite work with the glamorous look she usually rocked. Today, she was more subtle—more real. But her appearance wasn't what hooked me. I fucking loved her duality. The way she could flip between riling up thousands of followers and practically hiding in plain sight. She was funny and observant. Confident and cautious. For all those reasons, plus an indescribable animal instinct, she captivated me.

And by captivated, I meant she turned me on something wicked. By captivated, I meant I wanted her to rip my clothes off and mark me with her fucking teeth. By captivated, I meant I wanted to taste every—

"Ryan?"

I blinked. "Hm?"

She made a face. "You're looking at me like you want to eat me—uhh, for dinner. Or lunch. Or whatever people say when they mean eat as in devour—shit, no, I meant like... you know what I meant."

"I do."

Dear god, her face was crimson. "You do? W-want to eat me?"

I laughed despite the *hell yes* my brain shouted in reply. "I know what you meant."

Her lips parted in a perfectly nauseous look. "Oh. Good.

I'm... not at all humiliated right now. It's just really, really hot in here."

"Best get out, then."

I walked her to her car in silence. She opened the driver's door and finally looked up at me. "You promise you don't hate me? It would be fair if you did. A little, at least."

"Why? Because you embarrassed the shit out of me at our first meeting?"

"You were the one ordering sex drinks!"

I shook my head. I didn't want to talk about this, but I needed her to understand. "Not then. When you disappeared."

"I... embarrassed you? You said it was up to me."

"I did, and I meant it. But I didn't expect you to vanish without at least a no. Doesn't stroke the ego to sit with your door open for over an hour, hoping the hot girl you had the balls to hit on wants you, too, only to come to the realization that she didn't. Embarrassed is the right word, yeah."

I shrugged one shoulder and waited for her reply. Nica's brow furrowed. A little frown creased her mouth. "I'm so confused."

"Don't see what's mystifying there."

She held up her fingers to tick items off. "One, I'm not hot. Two, I figured you'd have forgotten about me and moved on by the next day. Three, I'm sick with regret that I made you feel that way. And... and four."

Blue-gray eyes lifted to me. She wet her lips. "I did want you."

But her confession meant nothing in that moment. I ticked off my answers, mirroring her. "One, shut up, you know you are. Two, I told you that wasn't my MO. Three, good. Think about that next time you ghost someone. And four, then you should've come to my room. But you didn't, and fine. It's past. I don't hate you. We're forgetting it and moving on."

Her lips pressed in a thin line. At last, she nodded. "Okay. Text me about the next meeting. Tell Henrik I said hi. Bye, Ryan."

It was another instance of wondering what the hell she was thinking. Of her guard being so high that I couldn't guess what she held back—but I was sure she was holding back. Not that I wasn't. Everything I'd just said sounded sensible and right. Everything I'd just said belied the rush she gave me.

"Bye, Nica," I echoed as she slid into her car and shut the door.

# 13

# NICA

I stared at last night's messages, flipped over to my camera, and picked up the cup in front of me. "Besties, it's Mrs. Q.P. here. What's an autumn day in New England without a pumpkin spice latte from Hartford's own Joe to Go? Whether you're headed to the rink or out to peep some leaves, swing by today. Mention your girl and get ten percent off your order."

I sipped and ended the feed. Then, I got busy filming the tablescape I'd set up at the café. They'd hired me to promote them on my Quentin page. No reason I couldn't do a free plug on my Ryan one, too. I'd just need to give it a day or so before I shared it to keep the connection from being obvious. Hopefully, I could get two endorsement deals going.

When I was done, I sat back in the booth and checked the time. Ryan had said to meet him at ten. I'd arrived at nine to do the videos and had a few minutes still before he arrived. Just enough time to get my head on straight.

Again.

*He doesn't hate you. He also doesn't want you anymore. It's past. We're moving on. Just like he said.*

I looked up when the coffee shop door opened right at ten. Despite my mental pep talk, my breath caught at the sight of him. Dark coat and jeans, two-day scruff on his jaw, those glasses...

And his hair. Sleek, a little wavy, and combed away from his face. Much more like the first time we met. The style made it look darker. So much fucking hotter.

The pushup video had gone viral, and I'd needed to do very little editing. Why would I when his muscles bulged and rippled like that on their own? Why would I, with the way he huffed a little sigh through his lips when he was done? Nope, that porn wrote its damn self. All I had to do was trim it for time and optimal angles.

The wave of thirsty comments that flooded in would've had me dancing across my apartment. Except I was in bed, busy with my vibrator and watching the video on repeat.

Now, I felt the goofy, morning-after grin that wanted to break my face. *Don't you dare swoon at him. He doesn't need to know you came twice last night after he texted you. You're here to do a job. God knows you need the money. Hold it in, girl.*

He slid into the booth opposite me with his usual neutral expression in place. "Hey."

"Hey." I debated teasing him and decided to go for it. "Nice to see you got dressed today."

Green eyes rolled. "Ethan has a nickname for me. Every

time he uses it, I tell him to fuck off. I think I'm going to say the same to you when you make digs about my wardrobe."

"You mean when he calls you Sieve?"

That got his attention. "How did you know that?"

"You were mic'ed up at practice. Oh, speaking of, I have questions." I pulled out my phone and opened voice notes. "Well, after his jump roping, I guess I know why you call him Twinkle Toes. So, um, what does sieve mean?"

"A sieve, like a strainer, right? It's an insulting nickname for a goalie."

"Ohh. I get it. Okay, so what did you mean when you said crease maintenance?"

His gaze darted back and forth, clearly trying to recall. Then, he laughed. "Oh, that was just me being silly. I probably said that when I was smoothing the ice in the crease."

"Crease?"

"That's the blue paint in front of my goal. Goalies stay in the crease. If they come out to play the puck, they're more vulnerable to getting checked—or scored on."

"Interesting." I made a note and set the phone down. "Today, I get to ask about your personal life. Where are we shopping?"

He slid out of the booth and motioned for me to follow. "Boston."

I yelped. "Boston? That's two hours away."

He opened the door to his Tesla for me and nodded. "Ethan gave me his guy. I don't ask questions."

*Okay, cool. No big deal. We'll just spend the day together. I can totally handle this.*

Ryan eased us out of town and onto the interstate. The car hummed like a spaceship as we hit a healthy cruising speed. "Now's a good time for questions, if you must."

I fumbled for my phone and switched it on. "Starting with a few things about hockey. Did you ever play offense?"

"No. Always D."

"Are you married?"

"Nope."

"Kids?"

"Nope."

"Favorite position?"

His head whipped to me before he refocused on the road. I grinned as his ears turned red. "Besides goalie, you mean?" he grumbled.

"I meant to make a save," I said innocently.

His jaw slid back and forth before, "I guess any position where I get the puck is my favorite."

I shut off the camera and howled. "Brilliant answer."

"You're welcome."

The trip flashed by. Before I knew it, we rolled to a stop at a valet stand by an old white townhouse. Inside was a boutique suit shop with an old man who smiled when we walked in. I half expected a secret door to open up that would lead us to some spy organization's headquarters.

But the man didn't show us any weapons or secret rooms. He just nodded and said, "Mr. Molloy, good afternoon. Right this way, sir. Can I get you something to drink?"

"Water, please. You want a champagne?"

The tailor peeked around him to where I was trying to disappear into the jackets. He smiled to see me.

"Sure. Thank you," I murmured.

Ryan gestured. "Pick out... I don't know. Whatever you like. Whatever I should have."

Ryan Molloy had the air of a man who drank cheap beer and shopped at bargain department stores. It was only in that moment that I registered how wrong I was about him.

He was a pro athlete. Even if he wasn't making the most of any Commodore, he had the means to buy out this store if he wanted.

And he wanted me to help him do it.

I bubbled with excitement and champagne while the tailor took him away to do measurements. Wandering up and down each wall, I pulled sample suits in navy, gray-green, and a faint blue plaid. I added dark gray and black just to keep it classic and walked them back to the dressing room.

Ryan stood in his boxer-briefs and t-shirt. If being in his underwear made him self-conscious, he didn't show it. He just looked at the suits and nodded. "Dress shirts?"

I got a lot of those. And shoes. And totally didn't think twice about the cement blocks of muscles that man hid under so much flannel.

When I returned to the back, he was dressed again except for his coat. He looked at the pile in my arms and quirked a brow. "Pink?"

"It's sexy."

"I *am* pink."

I laughed at that. "It'll look good with the navy or green suit. Promise."

"Fine. These, please. Oh, and Ethan said you do jeans, too. Yes?"

The tailor smiled. "We certainly can. I have your measurements. How many would you like?"

Ryan shrugged. "I don't know. Ten? Different color denim, please."

"Absolutely, sir. Everything will be ready a week from today."

"Can it be delivered?"

"Of course, Mr. Molloy."

I waited at the door while Ryan paid. Hearing the total felt too nosy for some reason. But he just smiled and ushered me out and back to the car. He stopped again at a hotel valet on the corner of Newbury Street. We left the car and ambled side by side down the street full of fashionable shops.

"What else do I need?" he asked while we walked, hands stuffed in pockets to keep out the chill.

"Well, you're getting new jeans, so let's find you some flannel that actually fits."

"Fine."

"Save those diva sighs for your momma, Goalie. I'm here to work."

He chuckled. "Yes, ma'am. How about... that one?"

His fingers touched my spine to steer me toward a shop. The loveliest little electric current zipped through me. It took a lot not to lean into it, to turn to him on the sidewalk and tug on that coat, to... *Stop, Nica. Just stop.*

"Now who's sighing?"

My attention jerked to him. "Hm? Oh, well. I was just thinking about your wardrobe. Obviously, I'd sigh over that."

A laugh burst out of him. Ryan palmed his face and shook his head. "Fuck off."

I swatted his arm. "How dare you speak to me like that!"

"I warned you. You want to rag on me like the guys? You're going to get talked to like the guys." His eyes sparkled with teasing humor.

A grin tugged at me. "Hm. One of the guys with the Connecticut Commodores. That's pretty fucking cool. Okay, you can tell me to fuck off as long as you smile like that when you do."

"Deal."

We walked up a small flight of stairs to the shop. The vibe screamed "country gentleman," so it was perfect for him. Within an hour, I'd curated a whole new day-to-day wardrobe that he actually liked.

I stood beside him in the dressing room while he buttoned the last shirt. "Explain how this is different than what I normally wear."

I shooed him off the platform and turned him to face me. Standing on the box closed the height gap, so I didn't need tiptoes to reach his shoulders. "How freaking tall are you, anyway?" I muttered as I fussed with his sleeves.

"Six-two."

"That would explain it." He had nearly a whole foot on me. "Anyway, look at the way this lays your shoulders. See how the cuffs land on your wrist? The fit in the chest? The clothes you have aren't fitted to you. They're too big. They look as if you bought an extra-large and said, eh, it's not too small."

One brow lifted over his glasses. "I definitely probably don't shop like that."

"Riiight. At least you definitely don't now that you have me around."

I fixed my gaze on his sleeve. If I hadn't been crushing on him so hard, my words would've just been more of our back and forth. But as it was, I cringed at how pathetic I sounded. *Look at me! I'm fun and stylish and one of the guys! You loser.*

Ryan cleared his throat. "Nica Allison Solance. Journalist. Troublemaker. Patron saint of fashion challenged nerds."

"What would you do without me?" I asked, heavy on sarcasm.

"Focus on hockey? Shop off the rack? Not worry about having my possessions stolen? Any of those seem accurate."

I gave his hem a final unnecessary tug and made myself smile up at him. "Sounds boring, honestly."

"It does, doesn't it?"

"Can I show you anything else?"

We jumped at the clerk's interrupting question. Ryan shook his head and smoothed the shirt. "I think we've got enough. I'll wear this one out."

The clerk nodded and disappeared again. I hurried to follow him to the register. While Ryan settled up, I wandered around and realized this shop shared a walk-through with a dress boutique. Since he had a mountain of clothes to be folded and boxed, I stared through the arch into a world of sumptuous gowns in every imaginable color, cut, and cloth. Both clerks were busy with other shoppers, so I snuck in and stuck close to the wall.

A red velvet bodycon hung on the rack in front of me. I fingered the sumptuous material and sighed. For just a moment, I closed my eyes and pictured a fairytale Christmas party. Wearing this dress and sipping champagne without feeling out of place. Dancing with a certain goalie who couldn't keep his green eyes off of me...

"You'd look great in that."

My daydream shattered at that goalie's voice in my ear. I glanced behind me and rolled my eyes. "Anyone would look great in this."

"Untrue. I don't even want to picture Yuri in it. Or my mother, for that matter."

I giggled and covered my mouth to avoid the clerk's attention. "Stop that. Let's go."

Ryan's brows knitted. "Try it on if you want. I'm not in a hurry."

Dammit, the clerk spied us. She beamed and hurried over. "Can I get you a dressing room?"

"Oh, ah, no thanks. We were just leaving." I all but dragged Ryan back into the men's shop to the exit.

Out on the street, he turned to me. "What just happened?"

I waved it off. "I have nowhere to wear a dress like that, silly."

"There's the team holiday party. If you want, I could—"

"Ryan. Stop."

He shut his mouth, so I went on. "I can't afford that dress. I can't afford anything in that store."

My face ignited at the baffled look on his face. His jaw slid side-to-side. "If you want the dress, I'll get it."

A sharp laugh burst out of me. "No freaking way."

Ryan didn't move for another long moment. Then, he shrugged and turned to walk us down Newbury Street.

"Done for the day?" I asked, working to keep my voice light.

"Shopping, yes. Let's go to dinner."

I slid my gaze to him.

Ryan gestured to the bumper-to-bumper traffic. "It's going to be madness if we try to fight traffic right now, which means that either way, we're home late. Might as well pass the time constructively instead of sitting in the car, right?"

The man had a point. Ryan walked us to the hotel where we'd left the car. "The Newbury Hotel. Aptly named," I whispered as I followed him through the revolving doors.

We rode the elevators to the top floor and stepped out into a gorgeous lobby with a host stand. The two women there stopped shuffling menus when Ryan approached. It didn't seem like they recognized him, but I couldn't blame their gaping. He was huge and absolutely dashing today.

"Yes, ah, I was told to ask for Austin Faron's usual table, please." His voice was quiet. Subtle.

The women consulted the book and nodded quickly. "Of course," one said. "Right this way."

Ryan touched my back again, and I nearly cursed his name. The floors were shiny marble. They were beautiful but would be a bitch to go sprawling on. A very real threat with the way his fingers jolted me. We wound through one room into another and were seated at a semicircle booth in the corner facing the windows. Below, Boston twinkled in the inky dusk.

Dread twisted my stomach. *You don't belong here. Lay low.* I slid into the booth with my chin tilted down and whispered thanks to the hostess. My gaze stayed on the table's edge while our water glasses were filled.

Ryan leaned closer and kept his voice low. "Are you okay?"

"Hm? Mm-hm." I glanced at him and angled my chin a little higher.

He tried again after several moments' silence. "Do you... not like it?"

"It's lovely."

"Then why do you look like you want to blend into the paint?"

I clenched my jaw and reached for a water glass. "Uh, I guess because I do. This place is super fancy. And who the heck is Austin Faron?"

"I thought it would be nice. Austin is Ethan's father-in-law. He's a CEO or something here in town. Ethan said I could use his name to get a good table."

"It worked. This is the best view in the house."

"And yet you look like you want to run away."

I twisted my lips. "Let's just say... forget it. It's fine."

Should've known that wouldn't land. He scoffed. "Come

on, Nica. You've touched my Yoda. There are no secrets between us."

Damn him for making me laugh. I clapped a hand over my mouth to keep from drawing more attention. "Shut up, Goalie," I hissed.

Oh, but it was impossible to be mad when he gave me that sly grin. The one that said he was pleased with himself. I'd seen it after his shutout, when he'd done the pushups—and every freaking time he'd made me laugh.

I gestured vaguely. "I'm more comfortable in the background, okay? People watched us walk through this place. How do I explain myself here? I don't belong."

"Why?"

He looked so adorably lost that I wanted to laugh. Except I wanted to cry more. "Ryan. You don't get it."

He blew out a breath. "I certainly get feeling like you don't belong in a situation. I understand preferring to be in the background. What I don't understand is why someone like you would feel that way."

I tilted my head. "Why do you hate the spotlight?"

"Is this part of the interview?"

"I won't quote you. Can't promise it won't color my narrative, though."

He shrugged. "I'm not comfortable with attention. I prefer to be the numbers guy. Backing up Quinn works well for me. I get to play and practice, which I love, without being a big name. I get to help the guys with their technique and don't have to be under constant scrutiny by commentators—and social media personalities."

I laughed at his playful glare. "So we're just a couple of dorks with impostor syndrome. Is that why we get along so well?"

"Maybe," he murmured, not blinking from me. "But you've yet to explain yourself."

We paused to order drinks and appetizers, but his attention snapped right back once the waitress left. I took a long drink of water. I knew when I opened my mouth that I was going to share more with this man than I ever did, and I was in no hurry for that to happen.

He waited me out until we clinked cocktail glasses. Then, he nudged my knee and gave me a Look.

"Fine. Fine! I, uh, well. I grew up... things weren't easy. Momma had... addiction issues. And addiction issues always lead to money issues. She raised my brother and me as best she could. Tried to hold jobs but usually did gig work, stuff she didn't have to show up to like a nine-to-five. Anyway. I was raised to, I don't know. Stay out of the way. Not only because of how she could get when she got too high. Also because it was how she taught me to make my way in the world. She taught me to steal, too. Food, mostly. I left home when she tried to teach me to lift other shit. I know I swiped your beanie, but I swear to god I'm not a thief. But I am good at going unnoticed. I was a good waitress because I was always there when needed, but patrons barely noticed me.

"Being an influencer is fucking wild, honestly. I feel like such a fake, but I've learned how to make it work. This look?" I gestured to my hair and face. "That plus the filters give me a mask. Let me move through posts and places as someone else. Besides, whether it be a fan post or a product placement, the goal is to put attention on someone or something other than me.

"Mostly, I've learned to go with it. But at certain moments, I still feel like everyone can see right through me. Can see how obviously I don't belong."

I buried my face in my hands and groaned. "And I cannot believe I just told you all that."

## 14

## RYAN

Her face stayed hidden while I sorted through all the data she'd just given me. The waitress dropped off our appetizer, but one look told her it wasn't time to ask for our order.

"Where's your mom now?"

"I don't know," she said through her hands. The pain in her voice was obvious.

"And your brother?"

"He lives in Seacrest. I tried to tell you that he's a regular at The Pub. That's why I was there that night. We're super close."

"So, why did you share all this now?"

Her fingertips slid down so that her eyes peeked out. "I don't fucking know," she whispered. "Maybe so you'd know why I was acting like a street urchin in this fancy-ass restaurant?"

I breathed a laugh and gently pulled her hands away from her face. "You can find other ways to get out of trouble than the truth. I think you told me because you wanted someone to finally understand what it's like to be in your shoes. And now, I definitely see what you mean."

"Yeah. I'm an impostor."

"Try a self-made woman."

Her blue eyes glittered. "I'm trying," she whispered.

I drew in a deep breath and sat back in the booth. Gesturing for the server, I glanced back at Nica. "Try harder. Look like you belong here—because you do."

She shook herself from her shoulders to her head and tapped her cheeks. "Right. Okay. I can do it. I belong here."

And with that, her cool, coy demeanor slid back into place. It was impressive as hell. I had no problem admitting that. I grinned as I watched her make eye contact with the server to order a steak, then sit back and sip her cocktail.

Dinner blurred past. She told me about growing up watching the Commodores. I told her about getting scouted from my travel team in high school. We split dessert discussing the team.

"Okay, but is Quentin *nice*?"

I laughed. "Yes. Well. Yes."

Her eyes crinkled with an ah-ha look.

"Wait. I'll explain. He's Quinn. He's fiercely loyal to the team and intense. He also has a great sense of humor. It's just that when it's game day, the guy's a brick wall, literally and emotionally. You can't talk to him. And he's superstitious as hell."

"Mm, speaking of! What are *your* superstitions?"

I quirked a brow. "Is this on record or off?"

Her eyes cut up and to the side, thinking. "Probably definitely on."

"Fine. Well, you know about Yoda, which I would prefer to remain private. But stuff you can publish... I shave the morning of a game at eleven-eleven a.m. Think of it like a Zamboni making fresh ice."

"Crease maintenance?"

"Something like that. And, uh, oh. I have a four-leaf clover taped on the inside of my helmet."

That made her jaw drop. "Oh, em, gee, you are *so* Irish."

I laughed at her delighted giggles. "I was born in Ireland, goofball. My mom is from there."

"Do the accent then!"

"No fucking way. Your ears would bleed, and I'd make a fool of myself."

She pouted, but her cheeks were pink from laughing.

"Your turn for the spotlight." I stole the bite of Boston cream pie she was angling for.

"Ugh. What now?"

"Why Quinn? What is it about him that made you launch the page?"

"Oh. Well, it started as a goof. My friends and I were out drinking and watching the game a couple years ago. The commentators started highlighting the Commodores' new goalie. I took one look at him and thought, *damn*. We all did. So we started googling him. Before I knew it, I'd made the profile on a dare. I kept at it because..."

"Because?"

"Well, one, because it was a hit. Two, because it's the Commodores—my team. Three, he *is* easy to fangirl over."

"But you could've profiled any player. That was Dustin's rookie season. Why not him?"

She sucked on her spoon and looked me up and down. "I have a thing for goalies."

*Oh, really?* My lips snagged in a smirk. "Is that right?"

Her cheeks turned pink again. "Uh-huh."

"Elaborate."

She huffed and swiped the last bite of dessert. "Basically everything you said in our first interview. They're like the spinal cord of the team. They're integral, but they stand alone. They spend the whole game in the crease, as you say, and yet you carry the team. Win, and you're a hero. Lose and it doesn't matter how the offense played. It's on your shoulders. I admire the personality that lets you stand up to that kind of intensity. And, ha. I like how it makes you quirky AF, too."

*I* liked how she went from "they" to "you" during that explanation. "Well, gosh. When you put it that way, we are pretty badass."

She gave me those eyes again. "Mm-hm."

A corner of my brain tried to remember that this woman had rejected me. But in that booth, in the low light with her gaze holding me, it was hard to remember why the hell I couldn't lean in and kiss her. And everything about the look she was giving said I wasn't crazy to want to.

"Anything else for you two?"

I swallowed a groan as the waitress reached to take the plate. We shook our heads, and I paid the bill. At least Nica didn't skulk her way to the exit.

We hurried out to the car. She gave me her address, and we took off. When I was on the highway, she rummaged in her purse. "Do you realize that I've barely asked you anything on record today?"

"Ugh. I was hoping you'd not noticed."

She opened her phone and tapped record. "No such luck. Okay, so. You said not married, no kids. Tell your fans, Ryan Molloy. Are you *available*?"

"I guess so."

"You guess so?"

I shrugged. "My fiancée left over a year ago. She said she needed time. After a while, I had to assume that was a permanent situation."

"Damn. That sucks."

"It's just life. But I'd appreciate that not going on the internet."

The phone aimed at me again. Her voice cleared. "Well, don't leave us any thirstier than we already are, Goalie. What's your type? I bet you like nice girls. Dainty little darlings."

"Mm, nah."

"Nah?"

"Nah. I prefer women who know what they want and aren't afraid to get it for themselves."

"Does he like *bossy* girls?"

I chuckled. "I don't think bossy gets very far with me, no. I like brave women."

"Sounds like trouble to me."

I glanced at her. "Doesn't it, though?"

The phone went back into her bag. "So then. What *is* your favorite position?"

The air grew opaque with tension. My pulse thudded in my neck. I tightened my hands on the steering wheel and said, "No way am I okay with that being published."

"The phone's away, Goalie." Nica's throaty pitch damn near stole my breath.

"Fine. My face between her legs. It lets me collect the most data about what she likes."

"I see."

"Do you?"

She breathed a low laugh. "Fair point. I guess I don't."

"And you? If this is off the record and all, what's your answer?"

"Damn. Uh, can I say it doesn't matter?"

I cut my gaze to her and didn't speak.

Nica huffed. "It doesn't matter. That's my answer. It's all fine or not fine depending on how he is in bed."

"*Fine*? What a descriptive term."

"I said what I said."

She'd said a lot. Whether she knew it or not, Ms. Nica Solance had just told me that she was sorely in need of an attentive lover. A data point my lizard brain gleefully picked up and ran with, no matter how the civilized part of me wanted to stay neutral.

Nica leaned her seat back and hummed. "Enough talking. I'm sleepy after that meal."

"Close your eyes. I'll have you back in no time."

The car got peaceful. Traffic was light at that time of night, and I pulled up in front of her building in less than two hours.

"Nica? You're home."

She stirred and blinked up at me. "Hm? Oh. Okay."

I jumped out and walked her to the entrance of the old prewar building. She climbed two steps and faced me, hugging herself tightly. "Thank you. This was a blast."

"It was the least torturous shopping trip I could picture. Goodnight, Trouble."

"Hey, Goalie?" she called when I'd turned for my car.

I spun back around, and she crooked a finger to bring me closer. We were nearly face-to-face with her on the stair, but she kept her arms crossed.

Nica wet her lips. "I want you to know how sorry I am about our first meeting."

I shook my head and stepped back, ready to run from this topic forever. "Forget it. We've discussed it and—"

But she grabbed my jacket and held me in place. "Listen to me, please."

I shut my mouth.

"I didn't turn you down. I left because... I didn't have a

room there, and I didn't want you to know that. So instead I, uh. I slept in my car."

That took a long moment to sink in. "You did what?"

She rolled her eyes. "Not a big deal. I just waited for the ferry overnight. But I couldn't bring myself to use you like that. I would've had to explain in the morning why I couldn't go to my own room. Why I didn't have any other clothes. Why my hair was different."

"Your hair?"

She flipped a long strand over her shoulder. "It's not mine. I can't sleep in this."

My gaze flickered back to her face. "So you either presumed that I'd let you sleep over or that we wouldn't be done until morning."

"I... I didn't... I guess I thought you'd let me sleep there."

I let out a tsk. "You always have underestimated me."

"You'd have kicked me out?"

Knowing I should ask first and not able to give a damn, I reached out and held her chin. Nica's hands floated from my shoulders to my arms as she swayed into me. With her breath on my lips, I whispered, "I'd have kept you up all night, Trouble. Well into the morning if you could take it. I know you think I'm a nerdy goalie, but trust me. The way I wanted you that night? The way you kissed me? No way would you have been on the early ferry."

Her breath came in ragged gasps. "Ryan. I'm sorry. I wanted you so much. I just knew it would be trouble."

"Wanted. Past tense?"

"I'm supposed to be interviewing..."

"Past tense, Nica?"

She swallowed hard. Her elbows locked, putting distance between us. I could see her working for an enigmatic smile, but the storm in her eyes wouldn't abate. "If I say yes, I'm a goddamn liar. But if I say no, not past tense... If I invite you upstairs now... If, for fucking once, I let myself be reckless... Then there is no way in hell I don't catch feels. There is no way I can be cool about this one."

*Good. Don't be cool. Just let us be whatever we want to be.*

She sucked in a deep breath. "So yes, Ryan. Past tense."

"You goddamn liar."

"Bet your ass."

And then she gripped my coat and yanked me to her. My eyes barely had time to close before we were a tangle of lips and hands. Her kiss was different this time. Rough and damn near panicked in a way I couldn't understand. I didn't like this frenzy that swirled between us, but I knew I was part of it. Knew that I wanted to kiss her so fucking bad. That I wanted my hands all over her. I wanted to slow us down, to make this real.

I wanted more. But if this was all I got, then dammit, it would have to be enough.

When my hands snuck into her jacket to glide up her waist, Nica ripped her mouth from mine. A strangled cry slipped out of her.

"That never happened. Understand?"

"Nica, I—" I started.

But she turned and ran inside.

# 15

# NICA

As soon as the apartment door shut, I sank to the floor in a blubbery mess of hormones and frustration. Tears soaked my palms until I curled into a ball and used my jacket as a tissue.

"Liar, liar, liar," I wept, so fucking mad at myself for being such a coward. If only I had it in me to be cool. My alter-ego was cool as hell. To the world, I was a flirt and a good time. Underneath, I was a scaredy-cat who couldn't keep her feels in check. Not even to get laid by a super-hot goalie, for crying out loud. Too afraid of the heartbreak when he inevitably realized how completely out of his league plain old Nica was.

I fell asleep on the floor. In the middle of the night, I hobbled to my bed and slept until late morning. When I woke up, I showered, made coffee, and sat down at my computer.

With a blank document open in front of me and all my notes at the ready, I rubbed my hands together. I didn't need the third interview. I had more than enough so long as I did it right.

"Do not fuck this up, girlie. Make it damn good."

"Nica! This is so damn good!"

I nearly dropped the phone at Audrey's shout. Sticky notes fluttered from my forehead and my shirt. My mouth tasted like days-old coffee, and my teeth had sweaters fit for a New England winter on them. My back ached from sitting at the desk for so long.

"It's... yeah?" I rubbed my eyes. Audrey had to have called several times in a row because my phone had been on do not disturb for five days straight. Since that bleak morning after a nearly perfect day in Boston, I'd done nothing but write, sleep, and drink coffee. Late last night, I sent her my final draft. According to the computer, it was seven a.m.

Audrey was clearly a morning person. "It's everything I could ask for. You captured Ryan's personality perfectly. The way you talk about his style of play and how it works with the Commodores... *Puck Drop Daily* is going to lose their minds. I absolutely love it."

My foggy brain struggled to absorb all this praise. Even at my sharpest, such effusive compliments would've been a challenge. Now, my throat closed. For some weird reason, I realized I was blushing.

"I'm so glad, Audrey. Thanks again for letting me have this shot. Of course, I'll change anything they want, but um. Thanks. Just... thanks."

"Thank *you*. And you got it done so fast! I'm amazed at how much you got from him. Ryan's not exactly an open book." She laughed.

I croaked a laugh to keep from crying. Damn, I needed

sleep. Before I could say goodbye, though, Audrey blurted, "Um, sorry but I have to ask. Are you guys dating?"

"What? No. Why?"

"Figured you'd seen it. One of the Boston dailies ran a photo of you two leaving a hotel last weekend."

"What?" I hissed, suddenly wide awake. My stomach hit the floor. "Oh, god. That's bad. I'll—I'll talk to you later, Auds. Bye."

Shaking fingers ended the call and opened my phone. I had a fuckton of texts and notifications. I started with the texts. Six of them were from Bruce. The other six were all Ryan. *I can't deal with you right now, Goalie.* I left those unread and opened Bruce's.

> BRUCE:
>
> WHAT THE HELL DID YOU DO
>
> Are you really fucking him?
>
> You have shot your platform to hell. I hope you know that.
>
> Good thing *I* suggested the other profile. Maybe that'll save your ass.
>
> Really, Nica. I know you've always been a fangirl, but star fucking the backup goalie?? I'm so disappointed.
>
> I should've asked for a bigger cut. We've got work to do to fix this. Text me ASAP. Stop hiding from the mess you made.

Coffee turned to bile in the back of my throat. I didn't give a shit about Bruce's anger, but I almost couldn't bear to open social media. With a hard swallow, I faced the music.

Flamed. Roasted. Absolutely massacred.

I'd stirred up controversy before, usually on purpose.

But nothing could've prepared me for the thousands of comments on my page. The slut-shaming. The accusations of betrayal.

Again, the fucking slut shaming.

I was a hypocrite. A cheater. A whore. A lying cunt/tart/bitch/etc./etc./etc. A filthy whore. An opportunistic whore. A slut—with so many adjectives in front of it that I lost track. Pick a mean thing to call a woman, and it appeared at least once on my profile.

On the other hand, my Molloy page had surged in followers. His fans *loved* the gossip that their guy was skulking around swanky hotels with Paris's superfan. They loved the irony, and while they still thought of me as an opportunistic sleaze, at least they didn't seem to mind. I hadn't betrayed them.

I put the phone face down on the desk and sat with my hands in my lap. The trolls had hit me hard, no doubt. I'd been in the game far too long to take it personally, but damn. Harsh was harsh, and that shit was *harsh*.

Plus, there was the bully in the back of my mind saying, *You are worse than all that. You're a* wannabe *star fucker. You're a pathetic slut from nowhere who's fool enough to care about a rich and famous athlete.*

With a deep sigh, I stood up and went to run a bath. I brushed and flossed while the tub filled and then soaked in the bubbles until I was sleepy again. Showering and washing my hair perked me up, so I dressed and went back to the phone.

The first thing to do was to delete my profile. I got to the confirmation page and paused. A sad smile tugged at my lips. Mrs. Quentin Paris had been one of the most successful things I'd ever done. I built something out of literally nothing. I learned the tricks of the algorithms well enough to quit my job and work for myself. Plus, it had been fun. Without this profile, I'd have never gone to so many awesome events. Certainly not a Hamptons wedding like Quinn and Audrey's.

Which meant I'd not have kissed a stranger at a bar.

And, obviously, would therefore not have fucked it all up with a sloppy kiss and a hopeless crush.

"Goodbye, Mrs. Paris." I hit delete.

Gone were hundreds of posts, stitches, and reels. But that meant the trolls vanished, too. Nica Solance didn't have a social media presence. As soon as the handle had taken off, I deleted every other profile I'd ever made for exactly this reason. Mrs. Quentin Paris was known only by that name. I used filters to change the shape of my face and eyes—not well enough, apparently. Not enough to keep the internet from figuring out who I was from one photo. I'd probably be forgotten quickly, but in the meantime, was there a way to avoid recognition?

I twined my finger around my hair, pondering that bit. Abruptly, I leapt up from the chair and ran back to the bathroom to stare in the mirror. The easy solution literally stared me in the face.

Nica Solance had a choppy, layered long bob. My straight, fine hair didn't have the volume for anything fancy. I'd been wearing the clip-in extensions in public as a default forever, all the way back to waitressing days. They gave me long, sexy curls that I absolutely adored. But they supported the look I'd cultivated, and so they had to go.

I trailed my fingers along the makeup that littered the counter. "Maybe no more cat-eye for a while." I sighed and picked up my eyeshadow pencils. After a few minutes of messing around, I'd managed a cool, smoky-but-subtler look that gave my eyes the pop I wanted. Without makeup, I always thought my eyes looked too small in my face. Washed out by my pale skin and dark hair.

The girl in the mirror wasn't Mrs. Quentin Paris, that was for damn sure. Nica was toned down and a lot less glamorous.

But she wasn't the target of hockey fandom's ire.

Plain old Nica would have to do.

I wandered back to my desk and sat down with a melancholy huff. In a way, deleting the profile was a relief. Something I'd wanted to do for ages. But I missed my alter ego already. I missed having a sassy persona who stirred things up instead of skulking in the shadows. I liked playing that part. For once in my life, I was a diva. A big mouth. A tease. Damn one little photograph for taking that away.

Okay. One little photograph that captured one little moment that meant a hell of a lot to plain old Nica.

I gave myself the day to sulk and sigh. I watched trash TV and ordered takeout even though I couldn't really afford it. Audrey had promised to pay me at the top of next week, so I put my dinner on a credit card and let that be Future Nica's problem.

I also left the phone on do not disturb. There would be time to talk to Bruce. There would be follow-up with Audrey and the magazine. But for today, I just wanted to wallow.

Well. Wallow and watch the Commodores' game. Which, I guess, was just a different form of wallowing. Especially when Ryan made the sickest save to keep Phoenix from tying. He blocked a shot on his right that rebounded straight to an attacker. I gasped and jumped onto the couch, sure it was a goal. But no. Ryan launched himself across the crease, glove extended, and nabbed it right out of the air.

He got a standing ovation even though they were on the road.

I gave him one from my apartment, too.

In bed later, I finally let myself open his messages. I didn't want to read them, but there was more music to face. Probably the *Imperial Death March*. So I burrowed under the covers and opened up.

> RYAN:
>
> I'm so sorry. I shouldn't have pushed the subject. Please tell me you're okay.
>
> Take your time.
>
> We won tonight.
>
> If you, idk, need anything for your story, tell me. (Cringing & well aware of how awkward I sound right now)
>
> L today. :/ I have to work on my glove save.
>
> Right. Okay. Hint taken. I'll leave you alone. Take care, Nica.

Tears slid down my smiling face. I threw the phone on the bed and smothered myself with a pillow to drown out my groan. "Why do you have to be so damn *kind*?" I shouted into the pillowcase. Really, though. This guy was unbelievable. What man cared that much? What person was that considerate? Yes, he could be salty and sullen when he felt awkward. Yes, there had been almost as many weird moments between us as there had been sweet ones. None of that undermined his decency. The way he brought me coffee, warmed my seat in his car, and put up with my teasing.

The way he thought of me enough to message even after that messy, fumbling night.

I debated with myself for about two minutes before snatching the phone again.

ME:

Why the hell are you so nice to me?

My phone has been on dnd. I wasn't ignoring you specifically.

I saw your glove save tonight. Looks like your practice paid off.

I can't stop thinking about you.

I stared at that last message with my finger hovering over send. After a long moment, I deleted it. Instead, I sent:

ME:

Article is done. You're off the hook.

My phone lit up with a call the moment I hit send. I yelped and went to throw it away again, but in my panic, I hit accept.

"Hold on," I said. Reaching to my nightstand, I jammed headphones in and tried to keep my voice from sounding like I'd run a marathon. "Hello?"

"Hey, Trouble."

Tears pricked my eyes again. "It's weird you have a nickname for me, Goalie."

His breathy laugh absolutely lacerated my heart. "Back atcha."

"You *are* a goalie."

"You *are* trouble. And you use goalie as a nickname."

My face hurt from grinning, but those tears blurred my

vision. "Rude of you to sneak attack a phone call. Etiquette dictates a preliminary text."

"Mm. You know I'm bad with stuff like that. You were texting. I figured I had a narrow window of time to catch you."

*You caught me, Goalie. I am so caught by you.* I wiped my eyes and cleared my throat. "What do you want?"

"It's hard to know where to begin. There's a *lot*. But—no, of course. First, are you okay?"

"Of course. Why wouldn't I be?"

"You've been silent for nearly a week after that, uh, awkward encounter. Seemed right to ask."

"I was silent because I was writing the article. I told you, Ryan. It never happened."

"I feel like I pushed you too far," he said softly. "I'm sorry."

"You have nothing to be sorry about. I'm totally fine."

"Are you *good*, though?"

*Good enough.* I didn't know how to answer him without making this worse.

He blew out a breath when I didn't speak. "Anyway, I guess you know about the photo. I mean, if I know about it, then you likely got wind the second it dropped."

I rasped a hateful laugh. "Oh, yeah, I'm aware. Didn't find out until today, though. That gave the internet plenty of time to descend. I deleted Mrs. Quentin Paris once I saw the comments."

Ryan hissed. "Wait. What? What happened?"

"Trolls, of course. Brutal."

"About us? How can they talk shit about a simple—"

"About *me*, sweetie. Of course they did. As soon as there's a whiff of gossip, the trolls come out of the woodwork. That's how it goes."

"You? Why just you?"

"I want you to think for a second about that question. Tell me you don't know the answer."

He sighed. "I hate that. I hate the cruelty for *nothing*. The double standards. It's all fucking bullshit. You did nothing wrong. *We* didn't. And yet you get trolled? I don't understand this world."

"I know. It's unfair as hell. But it's the risk you take if you're someone like me. I knew it when I started. Guess I just got lazy."

"This conversation is creating more and more questions." From his tone, I imagined him rubbing his eyes under his glasses.

"None of which need answering. I'm fine. You're in Phoenix, making sick saves. We leave each other alone, and the interest dies. Headlines move on. We all do."

Ryan was silent for a long time. Finally, he sighed. "Yeah. Okay. We move on. Amnesia, just like in a game. Dammit, Trouble. You're asking me to forget a hell of a lot."

"Last time. Promise," I croaked. "No more accidental run-ins."

"We'll see."

He hung up, and I cried myself to sleep.

# 16

# RYAN

I banged open the door to The Pub and looked around. "Who's Solance?"

Tony pointed down the bar to a guy who'd just jerked to attention. The moment my gaze landed on him, I knew he was Nica's brother. They could've been twins.

The guy gaped at me while I strode to him. "Tony, get this guy a drink. We need to talk."

"Um, hey man. I'm Vinny." He glanced around at the other patrons, who weren't even trying to hide their curiosity.

"Ryan. Come with me."

He followed me to a table out of earshot. I pushed a beer his way. "Tell me about your sister."

Vinny's shoulders dropped several inches. "Nica? What do you want to know?"

"Everything." I sipped my beer and didn't offer more.

He gulped a drink. "I mean, she's Nica. She's tough as hell but doesn't give herself credit. She's a wizard at making something out of nothing. Always has been. She's been running that damn Paris profile for years and still doesn't feel like people take her seriously. I guess you could say she's always sure she's the last in line for, I don't know. Everything. So she makes her own way."

"That... makes sense."

Vinny took another drink. "You got a thing for my sister, man?"

I snapped out of my thoughts and stared at him. "I... yeah. You could say that."

He nodded slowly. "It would be a miracle if she let herself go for it."

"Why?"

"You're fucking famous, dude. Nica's not one to let herself aim that high. That's why she still hangs out with that dickhead who told her to do your profile."

I coughed on my beer. Vinny reached over and thumped my back while I wheezed. "Say what?"

Vinny's expression said he knew he'd messed up. "Uh, I don't know all the details. Just that he calls himself her manager. It was his idea to do your fan page... You didn't know you had a fan page."

I scrubbed my face with both hands. "I'd heard as much. Is she with him?"

"Not that I know of. Hey, I'm sorry if I said the wrong thing. I, ha, wasn't expecting this."

"You didn't. Thanks, man. Tell Tony to put your bill on my tab."

We shook hands. Vinny went back to the bar. I drifted to a booth in the corner and stared at my dark phone for a long moment. *You didn't. Nica, tell me you didn't.*

Oh, but she had. As soon as I found the page, there was no question it was her.

Red with fury. Green with regret. And the bluest fucking balls of my life. All brought on by this one enigmatic, audacious woman. I rubbed my eyes and tried to figure out what the hell came next.

The Pub's door opened, effectively answering my question. Even through all my muddled mess of emotions, my gaze tracked her like a puck on the ice while she stormed in and made her way to her brother. She didn't look left or right, just marched up to him with her arms crossed.

I leaned forward, curious where we were going.

## 17

## NICA

Vinny's eyes widened to see me. Fair enough, as I'd not texted a warning. "Nica. Hey. Uh, I just had a—"

"In a minute. I need you to be my bestie right now."

He cut his gaze around the bar. "Nica."

I spotted a table a few feet away and all but dragged him to it. "Ew. This table needs to be wiped," I said as my palm pressed into a ring of condensation.

"Uh, it was recently vacated," he muttered, yet again glancing around.

"Forget it. Okay, so. I have to say something. And I need you to not be a boy about it. This is the downside of me having no girlfriends anymore, but too bad. Got me?"

Vinny blew out a breath and nodded. "Sure. Assuming this is about a guy?"

"Bingo."

He arched a dark eyebrow. "How's the article going?"

My face was already hot. "Audrey says it's gold," I whispered.

Vinny beamed. "That's my sis. Never doubted for a second."

"Are you going to let me get this out?"

His grin turned sly. "I suspected the two things were related."

I felt like a tea kettle ready to sing. The words and angsty emotions bubbled deep in my chest as my face got hotter. Finally, it all spilled out in a breathless rush.

"I'm fucking crazy about Ryan Molloy. I can't stop... I can't help it. He has me on *fire*. I want that man to do terrible things to me. Terrible, Vincent. Illegal in several states kind of terrible."

My brother cringed. "Fuck, sis," he muttered into his beer.

I punched the table. "Precisely! And before you jump to where I know you're going to, this is *nothing* like my goalie crush on Paris. That was fangirling. Silliness. This? This is *worse*. It's *him*. I have the biggest, messiest crush on *him*. Okay, fine, he's a fucking brilliant goalie—you were right, I admit it—but that's not what this is about. I just... I can't stop caring about him."

I hung my head and took a shaky breath. "And I know I'm a fool. He's so far out of my league, Vinny. I don't know how to stop it, though."

When I looked up, Vinny's gaze was over my shoulder. He looked at me quickly and scrunched his face. "Uh, well."

"Anyway, it doesn't matter. I just had to say it."

"I think it matters, sis."

I shook my head. "No. I'll handle it. It'll go away. I just needed to get it off my chest."

His gaze cut again. With a huff, I spun in my chair to see what he was looking at. Just as I did, a blur of green plaid flannel flashed by me. My stomach hit the floor at the all-too-familiar profile walking out the door. I whipped my head behind me, to the door, and behind me again before staring at Vinny, horrified.

"Did he hear me?" I wheezed.

Vinny shrugged. But it was a shrug that screamed *hell yeah, he did.* My brother sipped his beer. "He likes you."

The "pfft" I made was so loud that three guys at the bar turned to look at me. I ducked my head and hid behind my hands.

Vinny laughed softly. "Classy. Nicely done."

"Your fault for talking nonsense."

Another sip, this time holding my gaze. "He talked to me. Ryan Molloy walked into this bar looking for *me.* All over you."

My fingertips had gone numb. I gaped at him, waiting for more.

But Vinny shrugged. "I told him you'd never go for it."

"Y-you... because of what I said before?"

His eyes rolled. "No. Because you don't let yourself enjoy life. You work your way through this world and reject the idea that anyone would gift you anything without strings attached. So no way could you let yourself go for someone 'so far out of your league'—as you just said."

My brother sat forward and grasped my wrists. "He's not out of your league, Nica. *Any* man would be lucky to have you fall for them. Just because he's famous doesn't mean shit about what *you* are worth. Molloy knows how great you are. But neither him knowing that nor my words mean shit here. What matters is what you believe."

Damn the tears that threatened again. I sucked on my lip as my vision went blurry. "If he liked me, then why did he leave just now?"

Vinny released me and gave me a guilty look. "Might be

a little pissed about the fan page and the douchebag you hang out with."

"You told him?"

He winced. "I thought he knew."

"Of course he didn't know, Vincent Solance!"

"Well, sis, he does now."

My forehead hit the table. Sucking in a ragged breath, I snapped upright, jumped to my feet, and grabbed my bag. "I've gotta go. See you later."

The cold night air hit my face, giving me a little relief from all the bubbly emotions. I hurried off the porch—and nearly collapsed in terror at the six-foot-two figure leaning against the stairs' railing. My feet tangled, pitching me off the last step. I stuck my hands out to prepare to meet the gravel. Instead, my fingers wrapped around thick forearms covered in green flannel. My cheek crashed against his chest, but he held me upright.

"In a hurry?" he asked, still holding me.

"How did you move that fast?"

My cheek vibrated with his laugh. "I'm a goalie."

Ryan steadied me, but I didn't release his arms. I gazed up at him and wished on the moon, the stars, and every paycheck I'd ever gotten that he didn't hate my guts.

No such luck. He lasered me with a glare. "Fucking really, Nica? 'Our Boy Molloy?' What kind of corny-ass name is that? How could you?"

"How could I what? It's just a fan page."

He stepped back and crossed his arms. "Just tell me the truth. What am I to you? A paycheck?"

*Ouch.* I kept my chin high. "How fucking dare you."

"How fucking dare *you!* Are you using me or what?"

I rasped a laugh. "Using you. Yeah, okay. Sure. That's clearly what I've got going on here. A masterminded scheme to get behind-the-scenes footage of the Commodores' starting goalie. Look at the goldmine of dirt I've shared about you. Did you see where I described what it feels like to kiss you? Or how about the post sharing juicy details about your imposter syndrome? And then there are the screenshots of your messages that I shared with the world.

"Oh, *wait*. None of that shit is anywhere to be found, now is it? Look at the page, Ryan. It's Star Wars jokes and action shots. Not even a mention of Henrik. Everything to do with... with... us isn't part of the job."

His jaw slid side to side. "All you want is sound bites and photo ops."

"All I fucking want is *you*!" Tears hit my eyes. I couldn't take this anymore. Not after dumping my feelings in Vinny's lap just minutes ago. "Don't act like you didn't hear me. Don't test me like this. I know who I am. I know I *should* just want those things. But... but I... I mean, this. This is... this."

I gestured between us as if my words made any sort of sense.

But Ryan nodded. "Yeah. This is this."

I sighed. "Look, I'm sorry, okay? I'm *sorry*. I'll close the page. I'll figure out how to make a living. But I damn sure won't bother you again. I'm out of here."

"Nica."

"Fucking what now?"

With the same superhuman speed he'd used to catch me —the same speed that he'd used to make that insane save just two nights ago—Ryan's hands held my face. Our bodies brushed together as he angled me up.

"This," he whispered just before his lips found mine.

*Oh, dear god.* That night after Boston, so much fear coursed through my system. Fear of not deserving him. Fear of not being able to keep my messy feels in check. It had changed the way I kissed him and totally robbed me of the pleasure of the moment.

But now, I had no fight left in me. The feels were unchecked, reason and safety were long gone, and I didn't want to deserve him.

I wanted *him*.

So instead of setting my jaw and kissing him like I was angry at the world, I melted. Fucking melted into him. My arms slipped around his neck to keep me from puddling on the steps. I swooned into him, letting his lips and tongue tease the ever-loving hell out of me. Every lick, every suck on my lips seemed intentional, as if daring me to resist.

I didn't want to resist anymore. So I kissed him back with everything I had.

"Nica?" Ryan murmured, pulling back half an inch.

"Hm?"

He rubbed his nose against mine. "Come home with me. You can tell me about which states we'd get arrested in."

It took me a second to recall what I'd said to Vinny. I groaned as it sank in, and he laughed. We eyed each other— just before falling back into another long kiss. At last, I broke away and swallowed hard. "I'll follow you."

He cupped my face, searching my eyes. "Yeah? You can say no."

"I don't want to say no."

Ryan's fingers slid into my hair. I winced as he toyed with the ends. "You look different."

"This is what I really look like. Plain old Nica."

A low, rumbly laugh vibrated from him. "Stop joking. You know you're gorgeous."

"I truly do not. Especially without my pretty hair." I pouted.

His look was nearly feral. Ryan bent his head and

scraped his teeth on my lip. He licked where his teeth had just been, and I sucked in a shaky breath. "Don't give me that pout unless you want it to be kissed."

I almost collapsed when he released me and spun toward the parking lot. But he caught my hand without even looking, guiding me to follow. I forced my knees to do their job and hurried to my car. Ryan gave me a single nod and shut the door for me. I swung out of the space, waited for his Tesla to appear, and then followed him onto the road.

My phone lit up right away.

"Yes?" I drawled.

"Henrik is staying with the neighbors tonight."

"I'm very sad to hear that."

"Sorry. Seemed most practical. More bad news regarding practicality. We have a huge game tomorrow night. I have to be at the rink at ten tomorrow. So, ah, I can't stay up until dawn. Figure I'll have to crash around midnight."

I glanced at the dash clock. "It's eight. Pretty sure we can be done by then."

"As usual, you're underestimating me." His gravelly voice had a gentle chiding that made me cringe.

"Never gonna let me live it down, are you?"

"No. 'Better on the bench.' I will hold that over you until we're old and gray."

My heart glowed at the idea of knowing him that long, but I groaned. "Fine. Fine! I was wrong. Just like I was wrong not to go to your room. Happy now?"

He laughed. "Slightly mollified."

Silence filled the line. We took a few more turns on back roads and pulled into a wide driveway. I killed the engine and sat with my heart in my throat. Never in my life had I been this nervous over a guy.

But this wasn't a guy. This wasn't a goalie. This was *Ryan*.

I closed my eyes and recalled standing on that beach at the wedding. *Let life be a little sweeter. You'll figure everything out, girlie. You always do. For tonight, give yourself permission to just... be caught by someone.*

"Nica?" Ryan's voice came through the car speaker.

With a deep breath, I ended the call and got out of the car. He emerged from his as I strolled around to him.

"You look good, Goalie. Much more put together these days."

He touched his hair. "Got tired of being teased."

I stepped toe-to-toe with him and gazed up. My voice was husky, giving away every bit of my thirst. "Did you really?"

"No," he whispered. "But I can't have my hot-as-fuck interviewer, slash shopping buddy, slash the girl I can't stop thinking about, calling me a mess."

I gripped his shirt and tugged. "Stop calling me hot. I'm not."

He bent to me. "Trouble? If I have any say in the matter, you're going to be hot as hell for the next four hours. I'm about to fucking worship your body. You got me?"

# 18

# RYAN

If someone had asked me to put odds on Nica Solance standing in my driveway tonight, I'd have said less than zero. I'd still have bet hard against it, all the way up to six little words.

*All I fucking want is you.*

That was the last of my fight against reason. The kill shot to any doubts or hold-outs I had about falling for her. Damn her job, and fuck what anyone else thought. Fuck what *I* thought about all this media bullshit. There were questions to answer and boundaries to set around all that.

But Nica Solance wanted me. And, good god, did I want her.

She glared at my question. "*Worship* me? You're pushing my boundaries. I'm not good at being the center of attention."

I turned toward the house. "Is that a yes or a no?"

She heaved a dramatic sigh. "That's a hell yes."

I laughed. I'd never have put a bet on Nica Solance walking through my door that night. But when I stepped over the threshold, turned, and crooked my finger for her to follow, I knew one thing for sure.

I didn't want her walking out anytime soon. Maybe ever.

## 19

## NICA

The second the door clicked shut, Ryan lunged for me. I gripped his arms as he lifted me off my feet and pinned me to the wall. "Put your legs around my back," he whispered before his lips found mine.

Broad palms held my thighs just below my ass. He squeezed, pressing his thumbs dangerously close to the crotch of my jeans. I moaned into his mouth and slid my fingers into his hair for that. Our kisses were deep and urgent but sweet at the same time.

Ryan kept one hand on my ass. The other reached for my chin, turning me so he could burn kisses along my jaw and down my neck. "So sweet... can't get your scent out of my head... going to taste every fucking inch of your body tonight..."

He muttered promises and compliments between licks and sucks on my skin. Words that made my head spin. Words that seemed too sweet to be true—and yet I believed all of them. Knew without question that he meant it. Knew that he meant it about *me*. Knew, too, that not every girlie got to hear Ryan Molloy praise her like a fucking goddess. This wasn't a man to utter empty words.

*Lucky girl. Lucky, lucky girl.*

I dipped my head to kiss his cheek, which made him find my lips again. Fine by me. My head bumped the wall as he thrust up and kissed me deep. The hand on my cheek trailed downward. His fingertips tickled my neck and danced over my chest. Down, up a little, and back down. Teasing me.

"Hold on." I broke the kiss to yank my sweater off.

But Ryan didn't pull back. Didn't glance down at my bra even once. He kept his lips hovering near mine and smiled. "Make yourself at home."

My shoulders stiffened. "Should I not have?"

His palm splayed over my heart. Long fingers dipped into the satin bra cup, shooting tingly pleasure through my body. Still his gaze stayed on my face. "You should let me know exactly what pleases you. Does this?"

He stroked again, and my head hit the wall. "Mm-hm."

"Come on, Nica. Tell me what you want."

"Um... um. Oh, fuck it. I want you to touch my tits. Lick them. Play with them. Do whatever you like." My face flamed, but a wave of wet heat hit me between the legs, too.

Ryan sucked in a breath. The next moment, my back slid up the wall. He hitched me higher and buried his face in my cleavage. His lips and teeth teased, but after a moment, Ryan paused.

Those green eyes peeked up at me. "This isn't working."

My heart stuttered. "It's not? Okay. I mean, we don't—"

"Your bra and my glasses have to go."

"Oh. Oh, you meant—"

But before I could bumble out anything more, Ryan

lifted me off the wall. He carried me, never once looking around to see where he was going. We left the foyer and stopped in the living room, where he dropped to his knees and lay me on the rug.

"Arch your back," he whispered. I did, and he slipped his hand between me and the ground to unclasp my bra. I squirmed around to toss it aside.

He caught my bottom lip in his teeth. "And don't you ever, *ever* again wonder if this is working for me. Understand, Trouble? This is *all* I want to do right now. Let go of any doubt—or let me prove it."

I grinned, but my throat tightened with affection. "Prove it."

I pulled off his glasses with one hand. With the other, I pushed his head down. He didn't waste time. Ryan sucked one nipple into his mouth while his fingers went to work on the other.

My back arched involuntarily. "Oh, fuck. Fuck, I like that."

He nodded but didn't stop. I could tell he was testing me, learning what I liked, so I let him know. I liked the feathery stuff best. The little licks and the way he rubbed his nose against my ultra-sensitive skin. The way his fingers danced lightly. It was so airy, so gentle, and so wicked all at once.

My goalie was a fast learner. In no time, he had me writhing and digging my hands into his hair in an attempt to hold still. Wet heat pooled between my legs. It was torture that I never wanted to end. I tried to breathe, to not squirm away from the pleasure.

"Ryan, Ryan, please. I need... I don't know. Please," I babbled at last. This man was edging me already, and he was still fully dressed.

"You are so sensitive," he murmured against my nipple. "Where else can I touch you that will make you squirm for me?"

"I don't know." My fingers tightened in his hair while he kissed down my ribcage to my belly. I felt him unbutton my pants before his warm, strong hand slid along my hip, over my panties. His fingers wrapped around my upper thigh, easing the pants down as he touched me.

I finally lifted my hips and let him slide them off. Ryan sat back on his heels and gazed down at me. "Goddamn," he whispered. "You are so beautiful."

Foolish, inconvenient tears pricked my eyes. "Don't lie to me," I muttered, turning my face away.

Without my extensions, makeup, pushup bra—without all the stuff I used to show myself to the world—I felt so fucking plain. So ordinary. My short, fine hair. My elfish face. My b-cup boobs. The belly pooch I inherited from Momma that no amount of crunches would absolve.

And, of course, the fact that I'd not planned to be naked in front of someone tonight. I hadn't shaved in two days, and my panties were plain cotton bikinis with butterflies on them.

Two fat teardrops leaked out and rolled down my cheeks. I sniffled. And then I yelped because Ryan grabbed my hands and pulled me to my feet. Without a word, he walked us up the staircase and into his gorgeous bedroom. My feet slowed, but he guided me past the bed.

Into a walk-in closet the size of my bedroom.

I gaped at the setup, but he spun around and stepped behind me, leaving me facing a full-length mirror.

"Tell me I'm lying again." His whisper matched the way his fingers ran over my body, sending chills all over my skin. "Look at yourself. How do you not see it?"

"I look like an elf in cheap underwear."

His caress froze. Ryan's head hit my shoulder with a rumble of deep laughter. "Jesus, Nica. Is that what you'd have said to me at the inn?"

That brought a faint smile to my face. "No. But I was in a designer dress and had all my, uh, enhancements in place."

Ryan's lips moved along my shoulder. He shoved one hand into my hair to tilt my neck, giving him more to kiss. I hissed and watched, mesmerized by the sight of his mouth against me. My lips fell open over ragged breaths when his other hand teased across my breasts again.

Okay, that sight was pretty hot. Butterfly panties or no.

But it wasn't just the image that was hot. The closet amplified sounds. The sound of his breath. My ragged gasps. His kisses.

His. Kisses.

Every little pop hit my ears and drove me wild. A luscious, wet noise that fit perfectly with his flushed cheeks and shiny lips. I moaned as I watched him kiss my neck. When I moaned again, he dipped two fingers into my mouth.

"Shh."

My gaze caught in the mirror on my lips. Puffy, wet, and now full of him. I swirled my tongue around and between those fingers, pleased when it made him bite down on my shoulder. He teased me back until I was fellating his hand. His gaze lifted to watch, too.

"Look at you," he whispered at last as he pumped his fingers gently. "Tell me that's not fucking *hot*."

"It's fucking hot," I mumbled around him. But I let out a high-pitched whine when he pulled out, leaving a trail of spit down my chin. He drew that line straight down my chest to my belly button and then stepped in front of me to drop to his knees.

"Why did you stop?" I whined. "I liked it."

"Yeah? You want my cock in your mouth like that? You want to watch in this mirror while I feed you my dick?"

I nearly passed out. "Yes. Fuck. Yes."

He smirked. "Then you have to come first. And you have to watch that, too."

"Oh Ryan, I..."

But he shook his head once and leaned in with his teeth bared. I shivered as he hooked my panties in his mouth and dragged them down without once using his hands. My gaze bounced between staring down at him and watching in the mirror. I slid my hands into that strawberry-blond hair when he pushed my thighs apart and skimmed his tongue along my lips.

"*Nica.*" My name came out on an exhale. It sounded a lot like a prayer.

He licked again and glanced up at me. A wicked, satisfied smile flashed on his handsome face. "I'm gonna lie down. I want you to ride my face as long as you need. I could taste you for *hours*, Trouble. So don't rush, please."

Somehow, in a short span of minutes, this man had taken me from tears of self-consciousness to damn near tears of desire. The back corner of my mind gave him a round of applause for whatever "data points" he used to pull that off.

But who was I kidding? My focus was on what was about to happen.

Ryan lay down, still holding my thighs, and guided me to kneel over him. I could see the top of his head in the mirror between my legs—which meant I could see when he lifted up to lick me again. This time, his tongue slid between my lips.

Which meant I had to watch my head loll with a moan.

He tested me. Figured out what I liked best. And, yet again, my goalie was a fast learner. My mind whirled with sensory overload. Sounds, sights, and, my god. The feeling. The *feeling*. They way he held me in place. His tongue moved in an unreal rhythm of long, lazy slides and unrelenting flicks. I couldn't help the way my hips bucked in reply.

Finally, he tugged on my legs, urging me to get lower. I spread my knees, and he let go of one thigh. That free hand immediately slid between us, giving me no time to brace for the searing pleasure of two fingers buried in my pussy. I felt him draw circles, almost daring me to keep a slow tempo.

But those fingers made me think of fucking. Made me want something wilder and deeper. I gripped his hair with one hand and touched my breasts with the other. "Please don't stop," I hissed.

"Please don't worry," he mumbled.

My hips moved faster, and he answered. His tongue focused in on my clit while his hand pumped steadily. I wound up, tighter and tighter, ultimately releasing his hair to attend to my nipples. The girl in the mirror wore a dark red blush on her cheeks and neck. Her lips fell open in desperate gasps. Eyes glassy. Hair wild and stuck to her temples with the sweat of exertion.

*Okay, fine. Right now, I'm fucking hot.* I breathed a little laugh just before my eyes fell shut. Closer and closer until— "Ryan, I'm..."

"Mm-hm."

His thumb reached back and pressed against my ass. My

hips jolted at the sudden, intense pleasure. He pressed again just as his lips closed on my clit.

I fucking detonated.

I couldn't watch myself come. Not because I didn't want to. Because my eyes couldn't stay open under the tidal wave of orgasm that he gave me. My whole body quaked with unending pleasure. I knew I called his name, but my ears didn't register sound for a long moment.

Just before I went slack, I managed to peek at my reflection. The woman in the mirror, flaws and shortcomings and all, personified sex. Looked like a wrecked, satisfied goddess.

I went limp with a shy smile on my face. My arms shot out to keep me from crashing down on him, but Ryan held my waist. He gently moved my hips down until they were over his stomach, and I could fall onto his chest. Strong arms wrapped me in warm flannel as he kissed the top of my head. The way he held me and let me snuggle into him felt so safe. So exactly what I'd expect from my Ryan.

*I want so bad for you to be mine.* I swallowed the thought and looked at him.

"Damn, this shirt needs washing." He sat up underneath me until I was in his lap. I groaned to realize his collar—and now also his shirttails—were soaked from me. But Ryan just laughed and said, "Take it off for me, please."

And just like that, my post-orgasmic feels became kindling for even more fire. I had those buttons open right away. Ryan eased me off so he could stand, but I stayed on the carpet, gazing up reverently. He kept his eyes on me while he shrugged out of the flannel and tugged his undershirt over his head. I reached a hesitant hand for his jeans. With a cheeky quirked brow, he undid them and let me slide them off.

Dear. God.

I'd seen Ryan Molloy in various stages of undress. The muscle tee and baggy sweats for the pushup thing had let me admire those massive biceps plenty. Then I'd seen him in an undershirt and boxer-briefs at the clothing shop. I'd thought I understood what all he was packing.

No, ma'am, I did not. His muscles had muscles. Abs for days. Legs like tree trunks—if tree trunks were made of concrete. Everything. He was fucking *chiseled*.

And his cock strained his underwear. Teasing me. Daring me to rush this moment. As if I could.

I swallowed some of the drool. "Can I touch you?"

"I want nothing more."

I took a shaky breath and reached up to peel those boxers off. Ryan gripped his cock while I tossed the fabric aside, but I hurried to take over. I held his base and let my free hand run over his legs. Immediately, my clit tingled again. I'd never seen a body so perfect. And yet, that feeling of sexiness stayed with me. I didn't feel inadequate or self-conscious. All I felt was *thirsty*.

It might've been the fire in his eyes as I touched him. Or possibly having ridden his face for the past half hour.

"Nica?" he asked after letting me explore. "Can you see the mirror?"

I tore my gaze away from him to watch us. My heart fluttered. This was like some sort of voyeur porn. I never thought a mirror could be this naughty.

"Yes," I whispered.

"Then open your mouth, baby."

I watched as he removed my hand from his cock. I watched myself sit up higher and tilt my head up. And then, fuck, I watched him trace my lips with his head. Watched the moisture he left behind and watched me lick it like an eager little fiend. The butterflies in my chest went wild with anticipation. Ryan was easily the largest man I'd ever seen in every aspect of the term. But when he pressed his cock against my tongue, I opened up and took him as deep as I could go.

Turned out that was a long fucking way.

He hit the back of my throat with a moan. I gagged briefly but managed to calm my reflexes with a deep breath through my nose. Ryan looked up at the ceiling. "Nica," he sighed. "Fuck, Nica, I—"

I hummed, slid my tongue along his shaft, and shut him up quickly. I wanted him to take charge so I could watch us. He blew out a breath and pulled out, and my gaze went back to the mirror. I watched him trace my mouth again before feeding me, just like he'd promised. Unconsciously, my hand drifted between my legs.

"Oh, god yes. Touch yourself while you suck me. I would love to see you come again with my cock in your mouth."

*That's definitely about to happen.* My eyelids were heavy, but I couldn't turn away. Couldn't get enough of the way he looked. Of the way *I* looked. My whole body burned. Every-thing—tonight, him, me, us—was hotter than real life ever was supposed to be. There was sex, there was passion, and then there was *this.*

*This is this.*

My bumbled line from earlier made my heart surge even more. I could taste Ryan on my tongue, could tell that he was close. I dragged my gaze from the mirror up to his face. He wet his lips and crooked a tiny smile, and I was done again. With a loud moan, I came hard on my fingers, taking him deeper even while I convulsed. Ryan's roared *yes* hit my ears as he unloaded down my throat. We rode out our plea-sure together until the last shivers. Then, I released him and fell back on the carpet to catch my breath.

Ryan dropped to sit beside me. He threaded his hands into his hair. His shoulders rose and fell with a deep sigh. "Holy shit."

My head lolled to him. I'd have asked what that meant to him, but my throat was dust, and my brain cells had been eradicated from orgasms. So instead, I just stared.

## 20

# RYAN

I looked over to see her wide blue eyes on me. Her flushed cheeks made those eyes sparkle even more. And her lips. My god. Puffed, shiny, and so fucking perfect. I hadn't meant to fuck that mouth so thoroughly, but she had taken me deep and kept me there for so long. I didn't know I could come that hard.

But then, I hadn't anticipated how hot the whole mirror thing would be. It was an impulse move to get her out of her head. Turned into the sexiest thing I'd ever done.

Given the dopey look of satisfaction on Nica's face, I'd guess it was a winner for her, too. Her hair curled on her forehand from sweat. I could feel my own hair slicked on my neck. I didn't want to leave this moment, but I had to take care of her.

"Are you cold?"

She shook her head, still gazing at me.

"Are you sweaty?"

Nod.

"What are you thinking?"

Her eyes shone in the low light. Her tongue skimmed her lips before the shiest smile appeared. "This."

I blew out a long breath and leaned over to kiss her mouth. "This is this."

She nudged little kisses against my lips and sighed. "This is *so* this."

My dick stirred again as our kisses grew deeper. "You better stop kissing me, or we're never gonna leave this closet."

"Fine by me. I live here now. Here, I'm the sexy girl in the mirror." Her tongue traced my lips and then dipped into my mouth as she palmed the back of my head.

At last, I pulled back and got to my feet, bringing her up with me. "Yeah, but I want you to be the sexy girl in my bed. Come on, Trouble. I'm going to dehydrate if we stay in here."

We stumbled out of the closet and barely made it to the bed. I pushed her onto the mattress before I could give in to the desire to kneel in front of her again. She gazed up at me while I stared down at her, aching to bury myself inside of her and—

*Shit.*

"What's wrong?" she asked at the look on my face.

"I don't have condoms."

Nica groaned, voicing the sound in my head. "I'm not on birth control. My tests are clear, but, uh, yeah. Not a good moment in the month to leave to chance."

While my blissed brain could easily foresee a long-term relationship with this woman, such a risk on our first night together held too many downsides in my estimation. I crawled over her and lowered down for another kiss. "Then I guess we'll have to wait on that for a night. In the meantime, I'll just have to lick your pussy until you come again."

Nica let out another one of those adorable whines.

"Ryan, please. I need a break after all that. And it's—oh, no! It's already midnight! How did that happen?" She whipped her head from the wall clock back to me.

"I don't care. I'll just be tired tomorrow."

I leaned to kiss her, but Nica pushed my chest. "No way, buster. I will be damned if I'm responsible for our goalie being tired and sluggish against freaking *Atlanta*. You go to sleep right now."

She pushed me again, and I crashed onto my back with a dramatic moan. Inwardly, though, I fucking loved that she cared enough about the team that much. That she knew without me saying that we faced our biggest rival tomorrow. That this wild, demanding job made sense to her.

"You're ice-cold, Trouble. You know that?"

She climbed on top of me and pinned me to the bed. "Sure do. And you knew it before you brought me here, Goalie. So save your pouting for your momma."

"Yeah, fine. But I'm saving this for *you*." I gripped her hips and shifted her lower until her pussy rubbed over my cock.

Huge error. Massive, throbbing, and now soaked error.

My head hit the mattress. Nica's whimpered surprise hit my ears. "Fuck," we whispered together.

I forced my eyes open to stare at her. "I want to take you right now," I gritted out.

She nodded quickly and then winced. "But we can't. It's so late."

My dramatic groan was genuine this time. Nica sighed and slid off me. "Oh, god. That was the hardest thing I've ever done," she whispered.

"Baby, you just said a mouthful."

Her gaze snapped to me. I grinned, and she giggled. "Oh em gee, I can't believe you."

"Felt accurate."

"Too accurate. Now, help me find my clothes so I can go home."

My humor died. Nica's smile disappeared as I stared at her.

"Or," I said at last.

"Or... you'd rather I stay? What if that's bad luck?"

I rolled my eyes and got off the bed. "What if it's the best luck? We can't know unless we try it, right?"

"Against *Atlanta*?"

"Who better than our fiercest rivals to test it?" I rummaged in my dresser and tossed her a t-shirt.

Nica set the shirt in her lap. "You want me to spend the night. Even though we have to sleep."

No more shoulds. No more holding back. "I want you to spend the night. Then I want you to come to the game tomorrow and come home with me so we can finish what we started. Which," I added as I knelt in front of her, "is only the beginning of *this* in my mind."

The look in her eyes told me I was right to say it. She needed to hear that this wasn't a one-off for me. I could hardly fathom how a woman this audacious and beautiful could be so insecure and self-conscious. But my girl was an enigma wrapped in a mystery in some ways. And if she needed me to tell her every damn day that I wanted her, then so be it. I'd do it as long as she could stand me.

*Now who's insecure? Just let the thing be what it is. You don't have to plan your future around her.*

Nica wet her lips. It seemed like she wanted to say more, but at last she nodded. "Okay."

"Okay to... which part? All of it?"

Her smile curved. "Yeah. I... don't want to say no."

"Not the same as a yes."

"No, I mean... I want to say yes. Yes. Now, sleep, silly."

Good enough for now. I nodded and went to brush my teeth. She followed, so I showed her the stash of disposable toothbrushes in the drawer.

Nica quirked her brow. "Smooth move. Keep your lovers minty fresh."

I laughed around the toothbrush. "My housekeeper stocked them ages ago in all the bathrooms. For guests, sure. I've not had a guest since my mother visited last Christmas, though."

We looked at each other in the mirror. "Not since your fiancée left, huh?" she asked softly. I shook my head, and she flipped her hand. "Yeah, well. Whenever I'm a guest in a gorgeous house like this, I expect my own toothbrush, organic lavender soap *and* bubble bath, and a purple silk robe."

"Standard requirements to keep you as a lover, huh?"

"Bare minimum, really." She spat into the sink and blew me a kiss, but her sly smile died fast. "Obviously, I'm teasing. I, uh..."

I set my toothbrush down and pulled her close. "Shush. I know that. And I know how weird you're trying to be about this. You don't have to say it, Nica. Just let it be this."

Her arms circled me. I felt her nod against my chest.

We climbed into the bed together. She flipped to her side, facing away from me, so I hooked her waist and pulled her into a spoon. I knew I was supposed to sleep about half an hour ago, but I couldn't drift off. Not before I heard her breathing go shallow.

Not before I appreciated the hell out of the woman in my arms.

## 21

## NICA

I woke with my head on a plushy pillow and my body wrapped in strong arms. Daylight tried to peek in around blackout curtains, but this room was perfect for sleeping.

Well. Sleeping and crazy hot sexytimes. Definitely those, too.

I smiled just as he stirred. A soft kiss landed on my shoulder. "You awake?" His voice was thick with sleep and absolutely delicious. I nodded.

Ryan's hand splayed wide on my belly. My heart skipped as his fingers inched down. His cock stirred against my backside. "Open your legs, baby."

Every time he called me baby, I wanted to cry or come. Or both. The idea that this man wanted me blew my mind.

But also, it didn't.

On paper, I'd never assume he'd go for me. In theory, the only reason I'd go for him was as a fangirl crush. Theory be damned. The *this* between us was obvious, real, and hot. So while I'd never in my life imagined waking up in a house this fancy with a man this wonderful, it also made perfect sense. Him calling me baby made my emotions surge. But it also made perfect sense in its own weird way.

I opened my legs.

The next thing I knew, I was face down in the pillow and crying out in pleasure. Ryan fingered me from behind, kissing my neck and shoulder and whispering lovely, filthy words in my ear. "You're soaking wet... I'm gonna fill this pussy with my cock tonight. Are you ready for that?... Good girl, Nica. Good fucking girl. Come for me, baby. Come all over my hand."

He slapped his palm against my clit and pumped steadily, and yeah. I came all over his fucking hand.

When I quit twitching, he pulled away and kissed my cheek. "What time is it?" he asked with a yawn and then called the question to the home automation.

"The time is nine-fifteen."

We both sat bolt upright.

"Shit," I whispered.

"*Shit*. I gotta hurry. Uh, go—breakfast. Food in the kitchen. I need to shower and eat, but you have whatever you want."

Downstairs was frigid. I shivered in just his t-shirt as I scurried around, trying to find my clothes. They were littered from the foyer to the living room, so it was a bit of effort to get it all together. Even then, I realized my silly panties were still in the closet. "Screw it," I whispered to myself as I hopped into my jeans.

I was breaking off a chunk of banana when Ryan skidded into the kitchen. Bless him, his hair was a wild mop. He ruffled it and shook his head. "Don't start. I had no time."

I grinned. "I wasn't going to say a word."

He pulled a chicken breast out of the fridge and tore pieces off. "No time for coffee. Green juice..."

I gaped, horrified, while he mixed a green powder in a bottle of water. "Boiled chicken for breakfast?"

He nodded as he swilled the juice. "Protein, baby. Pass me a banana. I'll eat that on the way."

"Wow. Food is like science for you, huh?"

Nod. "Optimal performance. Thirty grams of protein plus a carb. I'll do it all again later. Hopefully, that meal will be a bit more tasty."

"Is this how it is with you? No fun foods?"

Ryan rolled his eyes. "No. I love good food, as I believe I demonstrated at the restaurant. We'll have waffles and coffee tomorrow morning, I promise. But game day is different." He glanced at the clock and winced. "I've got to go *now*. You can stay as long as you like. Just use code three-four-three-four on the pin pad to lock when you leave."

But I trashed the banana peel and slid off the stool. "Nope, I'm out."

We power-walked to our cars. Just before I slid in, Ryan pulled me into a kiss. Green eyes gazed down at me, full of the sweetest, sexiest light I'd ever seen. "I'll see you tonight."

"I'll see you first." I booped his nose, and he released me.

The drive to Hartford was definitely not the most focused I'd ever been on the road. Traffic was still slow, so I inched along, replaying everything from last night.

A phone call crashed me out of my reverie. I saw the name and sighed. "Yeah?"

"How long did you think you could avoid me?"

"As long as I needed," I snapped. "I've been *busy*, Bruce. Working. What is it?"

"Are you fucking him?"

"Absolutely none of your business. That silly photo came out over a week ago. And I deleted the Paris profile. All old news."

"Are you fucking him, Nica?"

My jaw slid side to side. "I believe I just answered that question, Bruce."

He growled. "That little photo cost us thousands of dollars. I think I get to know when my client is sabotaging our business."

"Well, consider it sabotaged. Matter of fact, let me buy you out. The Molloy profile is generating about three thousand a month currently. That's thirty-six in a year. Half of which is eighteen. If I can pay you twenty grand before the end of the month, how about we dissolve the partnership and finally move on?"

Bruce was silent for a long moment. Finally, he sighed. "I should protect my assets, and you've become a liability. Fine. Twenty, and we'll call it dissolved. I'll write up an agreement."

My heart beat in my ears. *What the hell have you just done? How are you going to get that money?* "Fine. I'll be in touch."

I disconnected the call and swallowed hard. *You've got a little stashed in savings. That's a start. If you don't spend a single dime and can push for more sponsorships...*

*You're going to have to wait tables. Or ask Vinny for a loan.*

My chin wobbled. The lovely morning was long gone, and I wanted to go running back to it faster than Ethan Rivera could sprint down the ice.

*Suck it up, babe. You get your little fairytale tonight. Ryan's girl at the Atlanta game. Your very own version of Cinderella. Then, you'll figure the rest out. You always do.*

*Tomorrow, you'll sell everything you own. But first, you've got to buy a Molloy jersey.*

## 22

# RYAN

"Oh, ho, what's this?" Yuri's wicked laugh hit my ears. "Molls is *late*? What have you been doing with your morning, Sieve?"

"Fuck off," I muttered as I pocketed my phone. My ears burned.

Max crossed his arms. "You've never been less than fifteen minutes early, even when you're sick. And here it is, right at ten, and you're running in at the bell? Yuri's right. What *have* you been up to?"

I arched a brow and opened my mouth, but a grin broke on my face. "Exactly what you wish you were."

They howled and high-fived me just as Coach walked in. "Sit down, fellas. You know what day it is."

Morning meeting was every bit as tense as I'd predicted. Every year, gearing up for Atlanta meant grim faces and relentless shots on goal in warmup. Coach Delgato had a suit just for this matchup. Gene wore the same socks he'd worn at our last win. Dustin and a few of the younger guys had started following his lead, so the locker room smelled before this game.

For the past two years, my job on Atlanta days had been to offer last-minute tips and fist-bumps. This year, my shoulders were tight along with the rest of them. Saves and stats flipped through my brain to keep me focused. Lyrical music would distract me, so I walked around with my headphones in and the *Lord of the Rings* soundtrack playing on loop.

I could not let myself think about lying in bed with her this morning. After that early bullshit with the guys, no one mentioned it again. We all knew today was for focus.

After morning skate and meeting, we convened at the diner for a late breakfast. Gene and Dustin hung back to do a short interview while the rest of us went on. The waitresses pushed tables together and got busy filling coffee and taking orders like they always did. This was the one moment in the day when everyone could relax a bit.

"Coffee?"

I looked up at the blushing server and nodded.

She beamed and poured for me. "Um, I hope you have a good game tonight. I love your fan page, by the way. It's so cute."

"Thanks?"

Her blush deepened before the head waitress called for her to stop flirting. With an embarrassed groan, she hurried away. Around me, the guys laughed.

"Look at Molls suddenly becoming the ladies' man," Yuri said with a grin. "Give that man a comb and some hair gel, and he's suddenly double-oh-seven."

I rolled my eyes and shoved my hair away. It was still a little damp from the post-workout shower, but at least it wasn't fluffy anymore. "Got tired of getting shit all the time from you divas."

Ethan clapped my shoulder. "You look good. Much more

put together than before. If I didn't know better, I'd say you were getting laid."

"Why would you know better about my personal life?" I asked at the same moment Yuri said, "Oh, he is."

Ethan's attention bounced between us. "Hold on. Hold *on*. Who's the lucky lady? How did I miss this?"

"You should've seen him before morning meeting. Total walk of shame," Max said.

Ethan's jaw dropped. "*Whoa*. The photo from last week? Molls, are you and Mrs.—"

"Don't call her that." My voice was soft. Calm. It shut them the hell up.

For about two seconds.

Then Ethan smirked. "What's her name?"

"Nica." I rubbed my eyes under my glasses.

"What's wrong with Molls?" Dustin asked as he slid into a chair beside Gene.

"Situationship," Ethan whispered dramatically.

"Ohh. The, uh, influencer from the Boston photo? What's her name?" Dustin asked. At least he had the decency not to use her former handle.

"Nica," I repeated. "And I told you last week. We were having dinner."

"In a hotel." Gene gave me a wicked smirk when I gaped at him. Traitorous captain.

Ethan raised his hand. "To be fair, it is a great restaurant. The point isn't the dinner. The point is—is she your girl or not, Sieve?"

I didn't bother with the fuck off that I always gave to that name. "Not officially. But."

The whole table gave me a knowing hum.

Ethan's thumb slid across his phone. After a moment, he looked up and grinned. "Well, Stella just confirmed that she'll be at the game. Audrey's invited her to the box tonight."

Yuri snorted. "There's definitely a joke there about Molls wanting an invitation to the box tonight."

Even I laughed at that.

Gene raised his coffee cup. The rest hurried to follow. "Here's to... things going like they should. Us beating Atlanta. Nica and Molls. And, of course, Simsy finally fucking proposing to Jazzlynne."

We drew more attention than usual with the round of cheers and applause that followed.

Dustin's face turned maroon. "Dammit, Cap. Why you gotta blow me up?"

Gene laughed. "Figured you could use a little motivation." To the table, he said, "He wants to ask her tonight *if*."

None of us needed the end of that thought. If we won. Bad luck to put an *if* in front of it on game day, though.

Ethan tapped his hand to his heart. "That's motivation for all of us. We got you, kid." He and Dustin bumped fists across the table.

Hours later, we marched in a line out to the ice. "Bad Blood" by Taylor Swift thundered from the speakers as the spotlights swirled around the arena. I glove-bumped Jimmy, my backup goalie, and jumped over the boards to skate with the guys. Once we got our legs under us, Jimmy and I drifted over near the benches to stretch.

"How are you feeling?" he shouted over the fans and the music.

"Ask me that in a few hours."

He gave me a pat on the shoulder and went to his spot

on the bench. I stood up and leaned over the ledge for a mouthful of Gatorade. My helmet was cutting into my forehead, so I waited while Coach Bowman adjusted it for me.

"Hey, goalie."

I looked to my left. One of the Atlanta players smirked at me. I caught sight of the number on his sleeve—92—and whipped my attention back to Coach. He handed me the helmet, and I snapped it in place.

But Ninety-Two shouted again. "Goalie. I've got a question for you. I saw the picture of you the other day with that chick. First Paris, then you? Is she a pass-around girl or what? We're staying in Hartford tonight. Think you could send her my way?"

Under my helmet, my ears caught fire with rage. Coach Delgato snapped at him to shut up and leave me alone, so I did what any self-respecting goalie would. I skated to my net without a backward glance.

If Atlanta was our rival, Ninety-Two was our villain. No other member of the whole damn league stirred up as much shit as that one guy did. It wasn't just with us, of course. He was a legendary goon. His defensive skills were okay, but Atlanta kept him around for one main reason: to piss people off. Start fights, draw penalties, distract players—this dude was a master of chaos. I knew all about him, of course. But I'd assumed he'd put his attention on Ethan after last year's brawl between them.

Apparently, I had misjudged the situation. Not only had that asshole fucked with me, he'd hit me in the one place I actually felt sensitive. Any other insult would've rolled off my back. But as I skated side to side, getting comfortable in my crease, I had to run through stats in my head to let it go.

*Don't let it go. Let it make you mad. And let anger make you fucking unstoppable. For Quinn. For her. For the team.*

*For me.*

The puck dropped, and the game began. I blocked an easy shot or two early in the first period, but mostly things were quiet. After a commercial break, though, Yuri put a hit on an Atlanta wing that sent the guy to the ground. Whistles blew as shit-talking began, but the fans read the room. The arena's noise increased. Feet stomped. Fans cheered. And it fueled the players.

Speed picked up. My guys battled hard in their offensive zone for a long time without burying one. Suddenly, the puck slid past the line, and I dropped into a crouch. Two Atlanta skaters rushed toward me, but Yuri and Ethan were in stride with them before they entered my zone. The guy with the puck dumped it around the boards and behind my net.

Ninety-two raced in to play it.

My jaw clenched. As he flew toward the puck, stick out, head down, I skated around the back of the net and threw my shoulder at the right moment. Asshole didn't see it coming. I checked him flat on his back.

Standing over him, I stared down, watching as he blinked in confusion. "What the..."

I didn't say a word. I didn't need to. The stare I pinned on him said enough. His face contorted with anger while a flurry of players and linesmen surrounded us. The crowd kept up a constant *ooh* until another Atlanta player hauled him to his feet.

"Holy shit, Molls," Gene shouted. "What was that?"

I shrugged and skated back to my net. "Just playing the puck."

The linesman pointed at me. "Two-minute minor, Molloy. You know better than that. Shape up." He skated to center ice and said to the camera, "Connecticut number thirty-four. Two minutes for roughing."

One of our fourth-line guys went to serve my penalty, and I snapped back to focus. *Use the Force. Don't drop a goal now.*

Atlanta was pissed, and they let me know with a string of wicked shots. Two minutes felt eternal as I blocked shot after shot, diving from one side to the other and using my stick to keep each attempt out. But finally, the penalty ended. Dustin raced from the bench and stole the puck out of our end. He flew down the ice, wristed a one-timer, and buried it in the net.

Period one ended with screaming fans and blowing horns.

In the locker room, I sat down while the guys talked.

"Molls. You okay, man?" Gene asked at last.

I looked up. "He was talking shit about my girl."

The guys gave me a collective wince that said they were ready to tear him apart, too. "Fuck that fucking guy. He so much as looks sideways at Molloy, and we're gonna light him up. Understood?" Gene said to the group. He got a resounding grunt in affirmation.

Dustin cleared his throat. "Guys. I'm gonna go do it. We're up. I feel good about this. I... wish me luck."

Jazzlynne would be on the ice right now. She had been an ice dancer for the team for years. We all cheered him on as he grabbed a velvet box from his locker, nearly forgot his helmet, and then raced out of the room.

No more strategy talk for the moment. We watched the TV in the corner as he skated out, stopping the ice dancers' routine. Jazzlynne cocked her head. Her hands flew to her mouth as he skated to her down on one knee. The camera zoomed in on her teary eyes. She dropped to her knees, too, nodding like crazy. We all cheered again while they kissed.

"It is about damn time," Gene chuckled, but then he looked around at us. "We can't fuck this up for him. Got it?"

"Aye, Cap!"

Period two began fast and wild. No surprise there. Atlanta was out for blood. We didn't always beat them, although our record had improved over the years since Quinn joined the team. But this matchup was far from a sure outcome. The first half of the period had me sweating buckets as they went on the attack. There were plenty of shots on goal, but the mental game was just as harsh. So many passes. So many dekes, faking shots just to make me flinch. I forgot all about the first period drama. The noisy arena faded away the more I focused until it was just me and the puck in my mind. No matter how many bodies were in front of me, I had one target. And I followed it relentlessly.

Finally, my guys took possession and went on offense. I stood up from my crouch and hydrated while they battled unsuccessfully for a goal. Soon enough, the action flipped again, and I was on. I dropped down into a butterfly and passed the puck to a Connecticut sweater in my periphery— Yuri, it turned out to be. Meanwhile, plenty of Atlanta players hovered around. Yuri fought one-on-one for possession just to the left of my net. He sent the puck to the boards, and it rolled behind the net and out of my sight. I stood up to move right in case Atlanta picked it up. My eyes tracked the puck, but from my left periphery, I saw an Atlanta jersey flying toward me—

The next thing I knew, my ears were ringing, my helmet was off, and I was flat on my back. A wicked pain shot up my neck, like when you turn your head too fast. My lungs felt like I was under a boulder.

From a few inches to my right, I heard a muffled voice say, "How do you like it, goalie?"

"Mother *fucker*!" That was Ethan, screaming from at least the blue line. "Get to your goddamn feet, you son of a fucking—"

Whistles blew. Fans roared. Blades scraped. Pretty soon, I heard the thumps and clatters of gear hitting the ice.

I just lay there, doing my best impression of a snow angel.

Coach Bowman and Doc peered over me. "Molloy? Can you hear me?"

"Yeah, Doc. What, uh, what's happening?"

Doc shined a light in my eyes. I winced. "Got the wind knocked out of you. Gonna have to go check you out. Can you stand?"

The pain had subsided. Breathing wasn't so hard. I nodded and let them help me sit up, noticing suddenly that the arena had gone silent. Coach and Doc braced me, and I got to my feet. As I skated off between them, applause and cheers started up. I looked to my left to see Ethan with a busted lip. He grinned.

"I gotchu, Molls. Hurry up and get back out here!"

I nodded once and followed Coach to the locker room. As I skated off, Jimmy passed me, headed to the net. "Shake it off, buddy!" he called.

# 23

## NICA

"Audrey! You know what to do."

"Already on it. Joey's headed to the press box. I'm gone. Hopefully back in a few."

Audrey's conversation with her father played dimly in the back of my awareness. I stood at the front of the box, staring down at the scene below me. My hands covered my mouth while Ryan coasted off the ice and disappeared.

Stella walked up beside me. "Hey. I'm sure he's fine."

I flashed a worried smile as some of the other women gathered around, touching my shoulders in support. *Is this really happening? Any of it? Am I in the owner's box with all the WAGs? Is Ryan... oh, god. Is he okay?*

I'd texted Audrey this morning for a ticket, but she blew that off and invited me to the owner's box again. When I arrived, she had opened the door with a knowing smile. "Hey! Join the party."

The Cathcart box was full. Stella Rivera said hello right away. She and I had met a few times thanks to Audrey. I also met Ana Valentine, Tonya Ivanov, and other long-term Commodores WAGs.

While everyone mingled and nibbled from the snack spread, I slid up to Audrey and raised my eyebrow. "You could've just given me a press pass."

She shrugged, but her cheeks went pink. "Uh, Ryan texted me this morning before practice saying you'd be in touch. So I thought you should hang with us. Plus, Atlanta is always an event. You might as well meet a few new people."

"I told you. We're not dating!" I hissed. My lips twitched at her transparency.

"Well, that was several days ago! And I notice you've got a new jersey tonight. Cute beanie, by the way. They, uh, don't sell that one at the gift shop, though." Her eyes sparkled with delight as she gave me an arched eyebrow.

I wrinkled my nose and touched the black knit hat. "That doesn't mean that... that... ugh. Fine. Maybe it's a little more of a situation."

She squealed. "I love that for him! And you. He's so great, Nica. You two would be awesome together."

"Thanks. So are these ladies going to vet me or something?"

She blinked. "No. What? Not at all. Ugh, go drink some champagne and stop making me feel awkward."

I laughed and wandered over to the bar. Try as I might to hide in the shadows, the women made a point to pull me into conversations. They all knew I was connected to Ryan, which I guess my MOLLOY 34 jersey didn't hide, although no one asked me about him. And not a single person mentioned my now-defunct social media handle.

It was... lovely. Shockingly fun.

Ryan made us gasp when he knocked that guy down early in the game. I listened while they speculated over why he did it. Mostly what I understood was that the Atlanta player was Enemy Number One in Connecticut. I followed the team, but I hadn't put together that he was such a problem. Play resumed, and we watched while our guys killed a penalty—and then ended the period with a goal!

That cheering was nothing compared to intermission. As soon as Dustin Simmons skated out on the ice, Ana coughed on her champagne. "Oh, he's going to do it!" she gasped.

"About time!" Audrey laughed, but then she lunged for her phone. "Shit. I've got to call Joey and tell him to—"

Stella plucked the phone out of her hand. She gestured to the jumbotron and then to the press box, where we could see cameras following every move. "Joey's on it, hun. Chill."

So Audrey skipped down the aisle to join the women at the window. She grabbed my hand along the way, pulling me out of my chair. I wound up squished between her and Stella. They both held my hands, and I realized we'd made a chain. As soon as Jazzlynne nodded, the room erupted in excited shrieks. Champagne appeared for everyone while Ana, as the captain's wife, made a toast.

Lovely. Shockingly lovely. Even more shocking was how *not* awkward it was to be among them.

Just when I was allowing myself to relax into the evening, shit really went sideways.

Players had been battling for possession at the side of Ryan's crease. The puck slipped around the back of the net, and most of the players went after it—except Ninety-Two. I think I yelped when he threw himself through the air, leading with his elbow aimed at Ryan's throat. They both crashed to the ground. I jumped to my feet along with several others in the box, Hunter included.

Ryan lay flat on his back. His helmet wobbled on the ice beside him, but he didn't move. For a long moment, it was as if someone had pressed pause on the whole arena—and on my heart.

"Jesus Christ. Don't tell me he's hurt too," Hunter whispered in the tense silence.

Ninety-Two rolled to his side and sat up. As soon as he did, Ethan Rivera fucking *stormed* from the sidelines. His gloves and helmet hit the ice as he motioned Ninety-Two to his feet, but Stella's husband wasn't going to wait. He crashed down on that bastard, sending him sprawling as he threw punches with both hands.

Stella gasped. The pause ended.

The arena shook with energy. Rivera beat the ever-loving shit out of Ninety-Two. Meanwhile, players faced off all over the ice. Gear was everywhere. Punches flew, jerseys got yanked over heads—it was wild. I'd never been at an Atlanta game before, but *holy shit*, I suddenly understood the bad blood.

But I noticed all of this as an afterthought because Ryan was still on his back. I registered the frenetic action while my gaze stayed on the man lying in the blue paint. Two official-looking dudes shuffled out to check on him.

"That's Doc and Coach Bowman, the goalie coach," Audrey said from beside me.

I couldn't look at her. I could barely blink. My heart beat in my throat.

After a few moments, Ryan sat up. The fighting died down, and the fans quieted again. They cheered when he got to his feet and skated off without help. I watched him nod at Rivera and the backup goalie.

And then he was gone.

I barely moved when Audrey tugged my sleeve. "Nica. Come on."

"Huh?" At last, I tore my eyes from the window.

She jerked her head toward the door. "Come with me."

"Where? What's going on? Is he—"

But she grasped my wrist to guide me through the sea of concerned faces and out of the box.

Dumbly, I followed her down the hallway and to an elevator. She didn't offer any explanation, and I didn't know what to ask. Panic wrapped around my throat, making me want to hide away from this entire scene.

We emptied out into a very familiar hallway. The media room was just behind us. Blue and navy stripes lined the walls. My feet followed her down to the T, knowing we were going to turn left. But my brain wouldn't accept that we were really headed to the locker room until I was standing in it. I kept my gaze on the back of Audrey's head as a very different kind of panic battled for control. Damn imposter syndrome for the way it screamed how utterly wrong I was to be here.

Oh, but then.

"Nica?"

The *hope* in that man's voice. He was raspy and softer than usual, but the sound of my name filled my head and made tears sting my eyes.

Audrey stepped aside, motioning me forward. I made myself move toward where he sat, still in his gear. His pads made him *huge*. It was like a wall surrounded him.

A wall that I wanted to tear down so I could climb in his damn lap.

Gear aside, he looked like Ryan. His hair was wet with sweat and slicked back from his face. He blinked at me. The light in his eyes trickled down and curved his lips.

"Hey, Trouble. I like that jersey you've got on."

I bit my tongue and tried to smile back. "Goalie. What the hell happened out there?"

"Eh, just a little misunderstanding." His tone was light, but something angry flashed on his face.

"What's the status, Doc?" Audrey asked.

"He's fine. No head injury. Knocked the wind out of him for a minute, but I see no reason he can't play."

"But that guy hit his face with his elbow."

It took me a second to realize I'd actually spoken aloud.

The doctor smiled. "Helmets work wonders. Molls lost his breath when he hit the ice. The hit rattled him, but no trauma. If he feels up to returning, he's clear to go."

Everyone looked at Ryan.

He nodded. "I'll start the third."

Audrey's gaze was on her phone. "Good because Jimmy's given up one goal already. No pressure, of course, Molloy."

She put the phone away and looked around. "There are five minutes left in the period. I'm going to go update Joey so he can spread the word. Nica, you want to meet me back in the box at intermission?"

"Uh. Sure?"

She nodded and spun for the door. The coach gave Ryan a pat on the shoulder pad and said something about getting back to the bench. The doctor squinted at his patient.

"There is no pressure to play again tonight if you don't feel up for it. You tell me if anything is off, you hear?"

"Yes, Doc. I'm good to go."

"Good man. Rest for a bit."

And then, he was gone, too.

Ryan and I looked at each other.

He patted the bench beside him. "Sit?"

As soon as I did, I slumped forward and covered my face with both hands. A soul-heavy sigh dumped out of me.

"Wow. You okay?"

"Sorry. I should be asking you that. It's just... god, that scared me."

"Aw. Don't be scared. If we lose, we lose. There will be other games."

I snapped my hands away, jaw unhinged. His cheeky smile kept my reply at bay. Instead, I twisted my lips and rolled my eyes.

Ryan turned toward me. "I'm okay, Nica. You don't have to be scared."

"Not sure I'm the good luck you needed tonight."

"Mm, hard disagree." He reached out and traced my jaw, urging me to lean in. Ryan brushed a soft kiss on my mouth and hummed. "*Hard* disagree. Which is about to get really uncomfortable in this jock strap."

A relieved giggle bubbled out of me. "Hush."

Ryan quirked a brow and glanced at the TV in the corner. He winced, and I looked over to see we were now losing 2-1. On top of that, the clock was winding down to end the period.

I jumped up. No way should I be here when the entire freaking team stormed in.

But Ryan snagged my fingers before I could bolt. He gazed up at me and wet his lips. "There'll be a party at Gene's tonight for Dustin and Jazzlynne."

"Oh. Oh, so we won't—"

"Get to go home right away, no." He squeezed and gave me a pointed look. "What do you think, Trouble? Can you handle being my date to a team party?"

*His date. To a team event. Just waltz into the captain of the Commodores' house. Girlie, you are out of your mind.*

"Okay."

He grinned and released me. I hesitated, looked at the door, and spun back to him. Ryan held my waist as I gripped those massive shoulder pads and leaned in. I kissed him again and pulled away all in one breath. Then, I ran for the door. The team was marching down the hall, but I managed to reach the turn back to the elevator just before they got to me.

Gene Valentine totally saw me. He wore a concentrated scowl that deepened when we caught eyes. Just before I ducked away, though, his brows lifted in a knowing smile.

This whole night should've been giving me so many imposter vibes. There I was, striding around the freaking Commodores' arena like a VIP. All the actual VIPs seemed totally accepting of my presence. And Ryan Molloy just kissed me in the locker room. Was this a fever dream?

And why did it all feel so real?

In the elevator, I shared a clip of the surprise proposal and congratulated the happy couple. My Ryan post from tonight was a replay of him knocking that guy flat. Tons of fans had commented in the past few minutes to say they hoped he was okay, but I didn't feel right about giving an update yet. He would be back on the ice in twenty minutes. They could find out then.

I slipped back into the owner's box, trying to go unnoticed. Every single person turned when I walked in, though. "How is he?" hit me from all sides.

"He's good. He's going to play the final period."

Relief washed over the room. Chitchat resumed, so I hung back, unsure what to do with myself. Luckily, intermission didn't last long. Audrey walked in just as the period started. We all turned to the window when a roar went up from the crowd. Ryan waved his stick in the air as he coasted toward the net.

I hovered around Audrey while she spoke with Stella, who tossed her long hair and shook her head. "What a mess. Ethan got a five-minute major for beating the shit out of that dirtbag. Dustin, Max, and even Gene got minors. Poor Jimmy. He didn't stand a chance killing off those penalties."

Audrey sighed. "I remember when Jimmy was our full-time backup. Those were different days, bless him."

"Mm, yeah, he's not up for a team like Atlanta. I hope Ryan's really okay."

"Doc says yes, and Doc's not one to take chances."

That made me feel better.

"How did he seem?" Stella asked.

It took me a beat to realize they were both looking at me.

"He, uh... the same. He seemed like Ryan."

They traded a look. Audrey wiggled her head side to side. "Between those two assessments, I feel good about it."

"Atta boy!" Hunter Cathcart yelled. We spun around to see a replay on the jumbotron of Ryan snatching a puck out of the air.

After that, we quit talking and focused on the game. Ryan nearly missed a save, but Yuri kept it from rolling in. After that, Connecticut went on offense. Gene snuck the puck in the net around the Atlanta goalie's pads. While the fans were still cheering, Ethan delivered a slapshot that whizzed right past the goalie's shoulder and lit up the red light again.

We won 3-2. The window's glass vibrated with horns and cheers while we celebrated right along with them.

Ana Valentine threw up her hands. "Let's go celebrate and toast Dustin and Jazzlynne! Party time, ladies!"

Audrey nudged my shoulder. "You coming?"

I blew out a breath. "Yeah. I'm in."

## 24

# RYAN

We walked out of the locker room as a group, high off the game and talking loudly. I dropped down into my car and took a deep breath before putting it into drive. Holy shit, what a night. What a wild fucking game. Ninety-two didn't return for the third period. We assumed the amount of blood coming from his nose thanks to Ethan had something to do with it. I was exhausted mentally and physically but also wired as hell.

My phone vibrated.

Simsy: Thank your fan page for the shoutout.

He sent a link that made me groan. That whole topic got swept aside last night, but I had to figure out what I could and couldn't accept her sharing with the world. Dread tingled as I scanned the page, but no. The only new posts were of me in the first and then Dustin and Jazzlynne. No inside pics from the locker room, no blast about me returning to the game.

*Okay, be fair. She does keep us off this damn thing. And the Star Wars schtick is pretty funny. She knows you, man. There's value in that.*

The party was in full swing when I walked into Gene's. I gave my best to Ana and made my way to the living room. Right away, I spotted Nica standing with Stella and Ethan.

"... A yard sale. That's when there's a huge brawl and there's gear everywhere," Ethan was saying. He grinned at Nica, but his split lip from the fight looked absolutely wicked.

"Well then, I'd say tonight definitely qualifies," Nica said with a little laugh. She turned when I walked up.

My heart kicked my ribs.

Not because Nica Solance wearing my name and number made me dizzy with inexplicable pride, even though it did. Not because I flashed back to my face between her thighs and the taste of her on my tongue, even though I did.

My heart kicked my ribs because of her smile. Because of the way it softened and brightened all at once when she saw me. Because of the message behind a smile like that. It told me I wasn't alone in these feels. It confirmed everything she'd said to her brother at the bar.

*This is so this.*

I sucked in a quick breath and stepped beside her. My fingers touched her back in greeting. She leaned into it, which made me want to punch the air.

Ethan traded a glance with his wife. "Is Nica going to Boston?"

"Mm, you should," Stella said through a sip of her wine. She grinned at Nica. "We're going Friday since the guys are leaving for a week."

Nica sipped her drink and nodded. I realized the question she wasn't asking, so I said, "Shopping trip, right?"

"Oh, yeah. Holiday party is coming up, so it's a good excuse," Stella replied with a laugh.

"You should go," I said to Nica.

She forced a smile. "Need to check my schedule. I'll let you know tomorrow. Is that alright?"

"Absolutely. Just text me. Here, take my number."

The women got busy trading info. Ethan caught my eye. He nodded at Nica and gave me a thumbs up. I answered with a nod and a middle finger to say I didn't need his approval. We laughed together, drawing our partners' attention.

*My partner. Okay, a little premature, but still. Hell, yes.*

We mingled and chatted our way through an hour or so before Gene toasted Dustin and Jazzlynne. While Gene could be a little metaphoric with his speeches, even I had to admit that this one was perfect. The couple looked so shy and happy as they received our blessings. I found myself smiling harder than usual.

The beautiful woman by my side definitely had something to do with that.

Even better was the way she turned to me once the speech was over. Her lashes fluttered as an expectant smile touched her lips.

"What's that look?"

Shrug. "Nothing."

I chuckled. "Yeah, right. I hear you, Trouble. We can go."

It took a bit to give goodnights and best wishes, but at last, I guided her out the front door. She pointed to her car on the block and hurried away.

I had just put mine into drive when a call came through. "We didn't have to leave," she said in greeting.

"That's not what the look you gave me indicated."

"I was just smiling at you."

"Mm, smiling in a way that said you were tired of wearing clothes."

"No!" she yelped.

I laughed at her. We pulled into my driveway and got out of our cars. Nica strolled to me. Her brows knitted. "That Boston thing was so awkward. Did I seem uncomfortable?"

"Not at all. But why was it awkward? You should go."

A bitter laugh rasped out of her. "Absolutely I can't." She glanced at my confused face and went on. "Money, honey. I've got, uh, some unexpected expenses. And even if not, no way can I go to Boston and shop with them. I doubt they even set foot in the stores I'd go to."

I flipped open my wallet and handed her the Amex. "Yes, you can go. Yes, you can shop in the same stores as them. It's easy."

As expected, she stared at me like I'd lost several marbles. "Ryan. I am not—"

I closed the space between us, sliding the card into her back pocket. My hand stayed on her ass and squeezed while I hooked her chin with my other knuckle. "What aren't you, Nica? Are you not my girl? It's okay if you don't feel it. I just don't want to be a fool and misunderstand the situation."

She groaned. Her forehead pressed to my chest before her gaze was back on me. "Of course I feel it, goofball. I don't know if I'm 'your girl,' but obviously I... ah... well."

"Yesss?" I drawled.

"Obviously, everyone treated me like I was tonight."

"Oh, yeah. They all know."

Another groan. I laughed and encouraged her to look at me again. "So, what aren't you, Nica?"

Her brows ticked up. A wry smile twisted those lovely lips. "Very good at going unnoticed, apparently. But I want to be with you, Ryan Molloy. I couldn't have handled all that attention otherwise. I think any woman would be lucky as hell to be your girl. I know I don't really deserve—"

I shut that down with a kiss. Nica's hands slid to my shoulders, pulling me closer. I hugged her tight but tore away before we could get too crazy. "This is officially this. Are we agreed?"

"Oh yeah."

"Good. So you go to Boston."

"Ryan, that's not why I said that."

"Good. And you still go. Be with the ladies. They're fantastic. You'll have a great time. Choose whatever you want and put it all on my card. That's how this works, Nica. But I don't give a fuck about dresses right now."

"What do you give a fuck about?"

"Fucking."

Her giggle made me hold her tighter. A base sense of pride surged through me. No logic there, but making her laugh made me feel like I'd won something.

Henrik burst out of the house as soon as I nudged the door open. Nica squealed as he sniffed and wiggled around us. "Henrik! You're back!"

My heart kicked my ribs again when she crouched down and hesitantly petted him. "He's so wiggly," she said.

"He's thrilled to see you. That's basically what I did when I saw you in the locker room. In my head, of course."

She laughed so hard, she dropped to sit on the stoop. "You are funny, Goalie."

Henrik climbed into her lap and licked her face. "Henrik, leave her alone. You're overwhelming, buddy." I snapped my fingers to back him away, but he was too busy showing off. At last, I took his collar and guided him out into the yard. Immediately, he ran to sniff and pee, so I held out my hand and pulled Nica to her feet.

"Will he be alright outside?"

"Electric fence. He has a dog door into the kitchen. He'll find us there. Want a drink?"

We walked hand-in-hand into the house and into the kitchen. She chose tea, so I put the kettle on while she sat at the island.

Clutching a steaming mug, she eyed me. "I expected a different entry tonight."

I snorted. "I'll enter you soon enough, Trouble. Enjoy the tea."

Nica coughed on her drink. "Dammit! No jokes when I'm drinking hot beverages."

I stood behind her and planted my hands on the island, effectively caging her in. My brain lit up as I nuzzled her neck and inhaled that sweet smell. "Who's joking?" I whispered in her ear.

Her breath had gone shallow, but she leaned into me and murmured, "You want to be inside me, Goalie?"

*Fuck.* "Mm-hm. And I want to stay there until I feel your pussy squeeze the hell out of me as you come. I might have to feel that twice before I finish."

"It can be hard for me to come during sex. I, uh, I brought my vibrator. If that's okay." She turned to glance back at me, and I grinned.

"That's fucking perfect. Very, very good girl."

A sweet blush colored her cheeks. Her pupils dilated. "Say that again, please."

I brushed a kiss on her ear. "You are a very good girl." My fingers skimmed the lettering on her shoulders. "You are *my* very good girl."

Nica tipped her head back and moaned. "Oh, Ryan."

"Nica. Let's go upstairs."

I pushed off the counter, but Nica spun on her seat and grabbed my shirt. "Wait. Can I ask for something?"

"Literally anything."

She wet her lips. "Don't let me stop tonight. Don't let me get self-conscious or weird. I'm still, uh, overwhelmed by all of this. Being with the team, not as press but as a WAG. The wild game. Seeing you in the locker room—god, I was so worried—and then... well. All of it.

"And us. I know this is real, but I'm still me. Still ready to pinch myself and go back to reality. I'm trying to be more, uh, confident. But it's not easy." She looked down.

I nodded. "So what are you asking for?"

"Don't allow me to say no."

My brows hit my hairline. "Nica. You can always say no. I'd never take that from you."

Blue-gray eyes sparkled when she looked up. "Oh, gosh. Thank you for saying that. But, uh, I want to not say no. I want to do... everything. I'm just worried that my silly over-thinking brain will resist. And, uh, I loved what you did last night. Taking me to the mirror to get me out of those imposter thoughts."

*Oh. I see.* My own imposter syndrome had me certain that Nica would run from this relationship. Sure that I was far too ahead of myself in how I felt for her, and that that was my fatal flaw. I'd fall for her, she'd be disappointed when Quinn took over again as goaltender, and boom. Back to me and my spreadsheets.

But all of that was forecasting based on junk data. All of that was me mapping my previous situation to this one. Not only was Nica her own person, we didn't have to know what came next. Now was enough. It could be enough.

And she wanted me to remind her of what we both wanted.

I sucked in a deep breath and nodded. "I can do that for you," I said softly. "This is our rule. You can say no, whine, try to hide from me all you want. I won't let you. *But,* if you say the words 'crease maintenance,' we stop instantly."

"Crease    maintenance,"    she    whispered,    nodding. "Perfect."

I jerked my head toward the stairs. "Let's go."

But Nica turned around on the stool. "I want to finish my tea first."

My lips twitched, but I reached out and threaded my hands into her hair. She yelped when I made a fist and tugged to tilt her face to the ceiling. Upside-down, I kissed her lips. "No. You want to go upstairs. So go up the fucking stairs, Nica."

Her mouth curved into a sly smile. "Good boy," she whispered just before sliding off the stool and running to the stairs.

Henrik tried to sprint after her, but I caught up and blocked his entrance to the bedroom. "Sorry, buddy. Go sleep in the office. I'll see you in... several hours."

The dog huffed and skulked away. I slammed the door and pulled off my shirt.

# 25

# NICA

He met me in the middle of the room and knelt down. I reached for his shoulders as Ryan undid my jeans and looked up at me. "Lie down. Pants off. Underwear off. My jersey fucking *on*."

I shimmied out of the jeans and ran my hands over the navy and maroon top. "You like seeing me in this?"

He wet his lips and nodded. "It turns me on. Much more than I anticipated it would."

"Didn't realize how hot it would be to see your name on my back?"

"Something like that, yes. Lie down, Trouble."

I inched the bottom of it high enough to reveal my maroon lace panties. "I wore the good stuff tonight."

Ryan's palms wrapped around my hips. His thumbs stroked just below my belly button. "So you did. Shame I need them off so fast."

"Well, we could wait on that."

But he yanked the panties down my legs. "Hush and do as I said."

His smile curled into a smirk. I shivered and dropped to

the carpet. Ryan walked out into a plank, just like he'd done at the gym that day. Except this time, he was planking directly over me.

Just like I'd fantasized about him doing after the gym that day.

Biceps flexed as he lowered down enough to kiss me. My eyes fluttered open when he pulled back. Ryan gazed down at me. He kissed my chin. Inching backward on his forearms, he kissed my throat.

And he kept going.

I stared, mesmerized, as he walked on his arms down my body until his face was over the jersey's hem. Ryan used his nose to inch the fabric up, and then he ducked his head and licked.

"Fuck," I moaned.

"Fuck," he whispered at the same time.

Another lick, this one pushing my lips apart a little more. Green eyes lifted to me. "Take off my glasses." I did, and he nodded. "Now, lay there in my jersey, watch me devour you, and come on my tongue like the good fucking girl you are."

*Holy hell. I didn't know he could be so bossy.* I almost wanted to protest, just to see what sexy thing he said next. But my body was in no mood to argue. I kept my gaze locked with his. He started with teasing licks to make me squirm. Just as his biceps began to shake and my clit started to throb, he dropped out of the plank and onto his stomach. Broad palms pushed my thighs apart.

That man ate me like it was his job.

He must've collected *all* my data last night because I was a quivering mess within moments. Two fingers thrust inside of me. I felt them crook, stroking my front wall while his tongue attended my clit.

"Ryan, god, yes, please. Please, please, please," I wailed as I detonated.

When I stilled, he pulled back. "So fucking good," he whispered. His breath tickled my soaked, sensitive skin.

I squeezed my eyes shut and threaded my fingers in his hair. Ryan lay his head on my belly. His arms rested at my hips, almost like a hug. My heart damn near burst. *I know it's the orgasm and the, okay, everything... but good god, Ryan Molloy. I think I could love you.*

Pure terror gripped me—for a moment. It was the terror of a life spent making do. The fear of never being good enough and always needing to get by. The default assumption that things would fall through, and all I'd ever have to rely on was myself.

But all that was only a moment. For whatever reason, my usual worries and assumptions melted away. I had no idea why or what caused it, but my body rose and fell with a contented sigh. As if this moment were enough and I could trust that that was true.

Ryan stirred and looked up at me. "So."

I bit my lip at his cheeky expression. "So?"

"So that was amazing—"

"Pretty sure I'm the one who's supposed to say that."

He quirked a brow. "You can. But if you think I didn't love it too, you're out of your mind."

*Everything. Everything about you, Goalie.* My cheeks heated. "Well, I'm glad you enjoyed yourself."

"Eating this pussy? Hell yeah, I did." His pupils got bigger as a wicked smirk curved those shiny lips.

His words sent a shiver through me. I crooked my finger, and Ryan crawled over me while I finger-combed his hair. "Do you really not mind how I taste?"

"Mm-mm. You taste like pure trouble."

*Ouch.* I forced a little smile, but my voice was thin. "Do I?"

His smile was the opposite of mine. Broad and unforced. "Not at all."

Three little words. All he needed to tell me a hell of a lot. A potent cocktail of relief, joy, and lust crashed over me. I pulled him down, demanding his kiss. He tasted like me, and I didn't give a damn.

"So that was amazing, but I need your cock inside me," I mumbled between kisses.

"Read my mind," he answered before flipping us so that I was on top.

But I pressed into his chest and sat up. "Not on the floor. Ha, well. Unless it's in front of the mirror."

Ryan's brows flew up. "That's your kink?"

I shrugged. "Seems so."

He urged me off of him and walked into the closet. Moments later, he returned with the mirror, which he set by the bed. "I'll figure out a better solution later. But if you want to watch yourself, then I am here for it."

My heart pounded with excitement. Ryan pulled me up to stand. He reached for the hem of my jersey, but I stepped back. "Can't I wear it? There's nothing to see underneath."

"There's *you.* No, you may not wear it."

I fidgeted. "I want to, though."

He glared at me. Before I knew what happened, he yanked the jersey over my head. Damn goalie reflexes. I struggled, but he wasn't having it. My bra hit the floor a second later.

"Dammit! I wore the pushup for a reason!" I crossed my arms over my chest and stamped my foot.

"Don't be a brat. Unless you want a spanking."

"You're not appreciating my efforts. I'm trying to be pretty and sexy to make up for last—"

Ryan grabbed my shoulders and spun me to face the mirror. "Look at yourself. If you feel good going out with sexy underwear, makeup, or whatever, then great. Good for you. But in my bedroom, Nica Solance, you are always..." His lips touched my shoulder. "So damn sexy."

He turned my chin so that I met his gaze. "So perfectly *you*," he whispered before kissing my mouth.

Tears pricked my eyes, but my heart overflowed with the sweetest sensation. *I could absolutely fall in love with you.*

Deep down, I knew I already had.

*Crack!*

I heard the sound before I registered his palm on my ass. "Ohh," I groaned, breaking the kiss.

"So don't be a brat about it. Understand?" He spanked me again. This time, he squeezed my cheek and slipped his fingers between my thighs. "Goddamn, this pussy is soaked."

His fingers teased between my legs, and I hissed. "Then fuck it hard."

Ryan wrapped one arm around me. His chest vibrated with a low laugh. "Naughty girl. You're ready to get fucked?"

I peeked at the mirror to see him holding me while my hips swiveled over those fingers. Shamelessly needy. More ready than I'd ever been in my life. "You tell me, Goalie."

He released me. I spun around to help him strip. My fingers shook, but I worked quickly. He dropped his pants to the floor. I peeled off his underwear and wrapped my hand around his cock.

"Fuck." My eyes fluttered shut as I stroked him.

"Get on your hands and knees on that bed right now."

My lips curved. "I love it when you boss me."

He gripped my shoulders and damn near tossed me

onto the bed. I scrambled to all fours, facing the mirror while he rolled on a condom. My gaze didn't leave the reflection. I tracked him walking to the bed, crawling on, and kneeling behind me. His fingertips skimmed my hips and back.

I didn't expect the way his face softened and his eyes closed. He took a deep breath and opened his eyes again, meeting mine in the mirror.

"All okay, Goalie?"

"Fucking perfect, Trouble."

Before I could say more, his fingers dug into my hips. Ryan thrust up, and ecstatic pain shot through me. Good lord, he was a lot to take. I'd done well with my mouth last night but feeling him buried inside of me was different. A wail ripped from me as my head hit the bed. "Jesus Christ," I panted.

Ryan didn't move. "Are you okay? Fuck, you're tight."

"Fuck, you're big," I gasped/laughed.

He started to pull out. "We can—"

But I rocked my hips back, chasing him. "We're good. Just bear with me while I get used to you."

He froze again. "You're giving me an inflated ego and making me worried about you all at once."

I lifted my head to look over my shoulder at him. "Think less. Fuck more."

A single laugh slipped out of him before he gripped my hips again. "Fine."

He started slow. I couldn't stop moaning as my body stretched and acclimated to him. My god, between his mouth and his dick, he was ruining me for all future men. How would I ever be satisfied by someone else?

"Ryan," I wailed.

"Nica." My name growled through clenched teeth. My

name as an answer to everything he needed. As a promise that I was enough. That he was as into this as I was.

Or he was just really, really turned on, and I was losing my mind to the pleasure.

I finally opened my eyes to take in the sight of him behind me. My hair fell over my bright-red face, tits swaying with each thrust. Oh, but him. He was huge, he held me fiercely, and the look of bliss on his face was perfect. I thought of him in his gear tonight, how impenetrable those pads and blockers had looked.

*I got through. Lucky, lucky girl.*

Ryan looked up and found me watching him. His eyes flared. Abruptly, he pulled out and lay on his back, motioning me to climb on.

So then I got to watch myself ride him.

"Where is your vibrator?" he growled.

"Downstairs in my purse." I stared at the place where our bodies connected, unable to get enough of the sight of him sliding in and out of me.

"Go get it."

"Oh, Ryan, I—"

He pinched my thigh. "This cock will wait for you, baby. Go get it. I want to use it on you while you ride me."

"I like when you call me baby."

I glanced down, and he gave me a cheeky smile. With a huff, I slid off of him. My legs wobbled, but I hurried to find my purse. Henrik peeked at me but shuffled back to bed when I flew back upstairs.

True to word, Ryan hadn't moved. He stroked himself slowly, gaze tracking my every move as I hurried back to the bed. I pressed the toy into his palm, threw my leg over him, and froze up high on my knees.

"What?" he asked at last.

I smiled. "I like watching you slide into me."

"Hmm, me too, *baby*. Let's see it." He held his cock upright, teasing my lips until I spread my knees and sank down onto him.

When I'd found a good rhythm, I nodded and heard him switch the toy on. He touched it to my clit, and I jolted. It took him a few tries to find the perfect spot.

Oh, but when he did.

Pleasure condensed inside me immediately. My movements got slower, more deliberate. "You like it right there?"

"Right there, baby," I panted.

Ryan hummed.

"Right there. Right there. Right..."

My head tipped back with a howl. Waves of pleasure condensed and pooled around his cock inside of me, drawing out and intensifying the pleasure. I was so full of him, and it was *so* incredible.

"That was perfect," he whispered when I quit moaning.

My head lolled while Ryan put me on my back and fucked me into the mattress. I held his massive shoulders and let him go hard. It didn't take long for sweat to slick his skin. His hips jerked erratically. "Nica, I'm done. I... you. You're—*fuck*."

He came with a long groan. I held on and encouraged him through it. At last, he pitched forward and lay still.

"I love you," I mouthed to the ceiling.

Right after sex wasn't the time to say it, but the more I thought of it, the easier it was to admit.

Yet again, I didn't expect how easy that thought would be. Maybe this wasn't a fairytale. But it was the sweetest thing I'd ever known.

## 26

# RYAN

After a game like that—and two hours of raw, sweaty sex with the sweetest girl I'd ever had—I passed out cold. I barely had the coherency to trash the condom. Nica, bless her, pulled back the sheets before I could fall facedown into the pillow. I felt her snuggle up against me, and I was done. Knowing she was safe and warm beside me was the last thing I needed before I could let sleep claim me.

When I finally woke, Nica was propped up on the pillows, frowning at her phone. She tossed it aside as soon as she noticed me stir. A tight smile flashed on her face that told me something was wrong, but she slid down to snuggle into my chest.

"Hi," she murmured.

"Hi." I forgot about the phone and hugged her tight. My dick stirred, but I was equal parts turned on and content as hell. Good god, she felt so good in my arms. Good god, she was officially my girl.

Good god, I wanted this to last.

*Don't think like that. Just let this be this. It is enough.*

Nica's hips flexed against me. Her breasts grazed my

chest, and my eyes opened. "You keep teasing me like that, Trouble, and you might not like what happens."

Her sassy giggle made me smile. "What the hell makes you think I won't like it, Goalie?"

Before I knew it, we were a tangle of hands, mouths, and bedsheets. She was so small, nearly a foot shorter than me and small-boned, and something about it drove me wild. Because she was so fucking *strong*, too. And she could take my cock in that tight-as-hell pussy like I was made for her.

A point she reconfirmed before we ever left the bed.

When we'd caught our breath, I finally rolled off the mattress and caught her hand. She followed me to the bathroom—and, predictably, stopped dead when she saw the counter.

"I was joking! How did you even have time to—Ryan, I was *joking*." Nica palmed her eyes and groaned.

I laughed. "I had my housekeeper get it yesterday. Is it what you wanted?"

She sniffed the lavender soap and bubble bath, then held up the purple silk robe and sighed. "They're perfect. Dammit, I was—"

"Joking. Yeah, yeah. But you said it was the bare minimum to keep you as a lover. And, for transparency, I'm definitely trying to do just that."

Nica set the robe down and wrapped her arms around me. She tilted her head back to meet my eyes. "I'm in, Goalie. This is officially this. You don't have to do a damn thing."

I bent down and kissed her nose. "Yeah, but it's more fun if I do."

After the shower, we went downstairs to make breakfast and say good morning to Henrik. Nica opened her phone again while we sat drinking coffee. Her sigh drew my attention.

"Something wrong?"

"No," she said in a tone that said the opposite. "I, uh, I'll have to go in a few hours."

"Damn. I was hoping you'd stay until tomorrow."

Another sigh. "I have to... do a thing in Hartford. I could come back, I guess. I think I can, at least."

I wanted to question her, but I could tell I'd not get far. "Okay. In that case, go on and get back as soon as you can."

She kissed me goodbye with a brief smile that didn't reach her eyes. I went to update my spreadsheets and pack for the road trip. It was nearly dark when she texted, asking me to meet her at The Pub in an hour.

I walked in to find her at a table with her brother. They both smiled when they saw me, but again, Nica's eyes were sad. Vinny shook my hand while she said, "Vinny, this is Ryan. My boyfriend."

His smile stretched wide. "That's awesome. Congrats, you two."

I kissed her cheek. "Thanks, man. Round on me."

We had a beer, chitchatting about the season, the weather, whatever. Nica was quiet, but she jumped in when we recapped the Atlanta game. When the beers were gone, she nodded to her brother, who got the message. We wished him goodnight and headed outside.

"Hungry?" I asked.

"Very. I haven't eaten all day."

"Tacos? It's just down the block."

She hesitated. "People will see us. Expect to wind up in the local news."

I shrugged. "Fine by me if you're okay with it."

We walked there together. She came to life a little while

we ate. When her phone lit up at the end of the meal, though, she really smiled. "Okay, that's done."

I cocked my head, but she shook me off. We went back to The Pub's parking lot. I looked around for her car, but Nica followed me to the Tesla.

"Hang on. Where's yours?"

She shook her head and dropped into my passenger's seat.

"Nica?" I asked when our doors were shut.

She bit her lips into a line. "I sold my car today. I took the bus from Hartford here."

"What? Why?"

"Can we please go back to yours?"

"Of course. But I'm not going to let you hide from this."

She smirked. "Unless I use my safe word."

I shut up and drove us back to my house. Nica slipped inside and went to the kitchen. I watched her start the kettle and drop a tea bag into the same mug she'd used last night while Henrik danced around her. I loved the way she already seemed comfortable in my home, and she was clearly enamored of my dog. But I had to understand her more.

"Okay, then. Why did you sell your car?"

She sighed again and sat on the barstool, motioning me to sit with her. "I needed money fast. I, uh, wanted to get it over with. The car was the most valuable thing I had, so I sold it."

"You wanted to get what over with? Are you in trouble?"

Headshake.

"Nica," I warned. "Did you do something? What's this about?"

Her lips curved in a humorless smile. "I know I told you all about my upbringing, so it's fair for you to be suspicious.

But, no, Ryan. I'm in no trouble, and I didn't do something wrong. I, uh... the guy Vinny mentioned? My 'manager' who suggested I do your profile?"

I nodded.

"I can still close the page if you want. But I didn't want to deal with him anymore, so I bought him out. Except I didn't have the cash to do it, so I sold my car."

My jaw unhinged. "That car couldn't have been worth more than fifteen grand."

She pulled a face. "Dammit, you're good. That plus what I made from the article let me settle up."

"Do you have anything left over?"

"Enough for rent and food, yeah." Nica's gaze dropped to her lap. "This is really embarrassing to tell you. Twenty thousand isn't a big deal to you, but it is to me. This is why I can't go to Boston with the WAGs. I just don't have the means."

I eased her hand off the mug and laced it with mine. "You don't have to be embarrassed. You work hard and make your own way. What's embarrassing about that?"

She shrugged. I hooked her barstool and dragged it closer to me until she glanced up. "Nica Solance, you are an enigma wrapped in a mystery in so many ways. But if you're with me, you can stop worrying about money. You'll take my card and ride with Stella tomorrow. And if you need cash, you can ask."

Blue-gray eyes flashed. "I could *never* ask you for cash to pay off a debt like that. Don't be silly. It's hard enough trying to fathom shopping on your card. I don't take charity."

I laughed. "It's not charity, Trouble. It's love."

Everything paused. My brain reeled. Good god, I'd blurted that out with absolutely no calculation. Nica's eyes went wide, but she didn't make a sound. Our hands stayed motionless on the counter.

The scene unfroze when two tears rolled down her cheeks. "Love?"

Her voice was barely audible, but I didn't miss it. I blew out a breath. "Sorry. A little premature of me, maybe?"

She pressed her lips into a line, but her smile broke through. "Definitely probably."

"I'll do better. I promise."

She laughed and held my face in both hands. "Maybe you could say it again. Premature though it might be."

My pulse raced, but I leaned my forehead against hers. Surely, this was thin ice. Surely, it was too soon to know it, much less say it.

Fuck calculations. I tested the words again. "I think I might love you."

Nica's face lit with the most beautiful smile I'd ever seen. "Good boy."

"It's far too soon."

She nodded.

"It might all fall apart."

Another nod, still with that lovely smile.

"I'm afraid it will."

"Me too," she whispered.

"But it's okay if it does."

"Yes."

The anxious knots in my stomach started to unwind. "Yes?"

"Yes. It will be okay if it ends. It'll hurt, but this is worth the hurt. Because I, ah, think I might love you, too, Goalie."

Nica clapped a hand over her mouth. Her shining eyes went wide. Meanwhile, my heart went into freefall.

"Oh, you've done it now," I murmured when I could take a full breath.

She didn't take her hand from her mouth. "I have, haven't I? It was worth it."

"What was?"

"The trouble," she whispered before throwing herself into my arms.

I groaned and lifted her onto the island, unwilling to break the kiss as I fumbled with her pants. In no time, I'd stripped her to nothing but her bra. My pants and underwear hit the floor. I eyed the counter. She was just a few inches too high for this to work.

Nica spread her knees and sucked on two of her fingers. I forgot about logistics as I watched her trail those fingers down her body to tease her clit. "Fuck," I sighed.

"Mm, I'm ready for you, Goalie."

"I can see that from here, Trouble. I—Henrik, *go lie down!*" My lust paused briefly when my dog began to sniff the clothes pooled at my feet. He glared up at me and then strode away with a loud huff.

Nica and I traded a smile that turned into a kiss. I sucked on her lip and then stepped back, nodding at her to proceed. She played with herself. A little gasp slipped from her that drove me absolutely wild. I gripped my cock and stroked slowly, enjoying the show. "Good girl. Touch yourself for me."

Her cheeks blushed bright red, but she continued. My mouth damn well watered. I was dying to touch her, taste her, fuck her. But, hell. How could I stop a sight like this?

"Ryan," she whimpered at last. Her eyes met mine. "I'm close. Should I keep going?"

"Oh, yeah." I rasped a little laugh.

"Can I have your fingers inside me?"

As if she needed to ask. I reached out and thrust two deep into that soaked pussy. Right away, her walls squeezed around me. I groaned and pulsed. Nica's fingers switched over her swollen clit, faster now. I leaned forward and breathed in her ear.

"I think I love you, Trouble."

Her wail hit my ears *after* I felt her spasm. I grinned and drew out her orgasm while she pulsed around my hand.

"Goalie, I think I love you, too."

We were playing with fire for sure, but I didn't give a fuck. For once, all the logic that said be careful meant nothing. I felt it. And by the look in her eyes and the force of her orgasm, she felt it, too.

It might hurt later. But it was real.

I couldn't wait anymore. I hauled her off the island and down onto my waiting cock. Nica's legs wrapped around me as she wailed again. "I wasn't ready for more!"

"Mm, yes, you were. You're absolutely soaked."

She clung to me. "Where are we going to do this? You're strong as hell, but standing up is awkward."

I spun and took her to the dining table, lay her down flat on her back, and threw one leg on the table by her hips. Her jaw dropped. "Holy shit, you're flexible."

"Goalie life. But, ah, we forgot a condom."

She shrugged. "Pull out is fine."

Worked for me. I took her hard and slow, not wanting to rush the moment. Not wanting to rush *any* moment between us. We'd been circling this for months, ever since that night on Long Island. Maybe I was surprised we ever got here. Maybe I was surprised it took so long. Either way, I had Nica Solance moaning and sweating on my dining table, and that was a reality I wanted to live in as long as possible.

I made her come again. My fingers did the work this time until she convulsed all over my cock, pushing me closer to the edge. When she melted into the table with a final whimper, I gripped her hips. "Okay to finish?"

She nodded, gazing at me through her lashes.

My orgasm wound up fast after all of that. "I want to come inside of you," I confessed through clenched teeth.

"I want it, too."

"I also want to come all over you."

Her eyes flared. Tongue darted out to wet her lips. "Dirty. Do that one for now, please."

"Do what?"

She smirked. "Come all over me. Mark me. *Claim* me."

*Well, fuck.* I pulled out just as my orgasm barreled over me. Ropes of hot come swirled all over her chest and stomach.

Nica squealed. She threw her head back and grinned. "Yes, yes, good boy. My filthy fucking goalie. God, you're amazing."

"That's you," I panted with what little breath I had. I dropped into the nearest chair and rubbed my face—and realized my glasses were still on. Breathing a laugh, I adjusted them and watched Nica sit up.

She gazed down at her body. "Oh, my. What a mess."

"Good thing someone has fancy soap in the bathroom."

Her lips twisted. "No car, no money, but hand-milled French soap. Just a regular Thursday."

We walked upstairs together to the bathroom. Nica followed me into the shower. She stared at her body as she washed me off of her. "You're a lot sexier than I expected a nerd to be."

I barked a laugh. "Thank you? How dare you? How do I reply to that?"

She smiled up at me. "It's a compliment."

"You're a lot shier than I expected a glamorous influencer to be."

Her eyes rolled. "All part of the smoke screen. I'm, uh, not really... well. I've never felt sexier than I have in the past seventy-two hours."

My laugh was softer this time. "Same, actually."

It was true. She brought out something in me rawer and more open than I'd ever known. She was so much sweeter than I'd expected. The way she put herself in my hands had me stoned on lust.

But then there were moments like this, when she wrapped her arms around me and snuggled into me. All of it combined made *I love you* feel so fucking right.

I kissed her head and shut off the water. "How am I supposed to leave for a week after all this?"

She wrinkled her nose. "Don't remind me."

We went to the bedroom. She'd brought a nightie, so I dressed in underwear and pulled back the sheet. "Two things get resolved right now. Come to bed so we can discuss serious business."

She stared at me when I thumped the pillow. One hand went to her hip. "I've never done anal, but I'm willing to try. Not sure how I feel about a threesome. I guess it depends on who it's with."

For the second time that night, my jaw unhinged. "Fuck," I muttered, instantly semi-hard.

Nica blinked. "Was that not what you meant?"

I swallowed hard. "No, but now it's all I can think of."

She covered her face with her hands and groaned. "Oops."

"No, no. Yours are much more fun."

I recovered myself while she crawled into bed and eyed

my crotch. "Don't tempt me unless you want to go another round."

Her hand skimmed over the half-mast in my underwear. I stared into her eyes and raised one eyebrow. "Willing to try anal, huh?"

She blushed. "I hear it's nice. And I liked that thing you did with your fingers that first night."

I blew out a breath. "Yeah, okay. Talk later." Leaning toward her, I palmed the back of her head and crashed a kiss on that mouth.

We were naked again in no time.

"You mean *that* thing with my fingers?" I panted as I recovered beside her.

"Oh, yeah," she sighed right back.

My head lolled to stare at her. "Two things. One, the profile. Run it if you think it's a good idea. Just don't put anything on it that would make me feel weird, please. It all makes me feel weird, but so far you've done a good job keeping it neutral. Please don't violate my trust with this."

"I never will," she promised.

"Two. Go to Boston. Yes?"

"Ugh. Fine. Yes."

"Good girl. Now, let's get another shower and sleep before I pull my groin and have to sit out a few games."

# 27

# NICA

The next morning, I found myself in the backseat of Stella Rivera's Mercedes. The smell of coffee filled the car, along with excited chatter between her and Audrey. I clutched the travel mug Ryan had given me and listened to them catch up.

"Quinn's ready to get back to it. I think he'll be practicing right after Christmas. No idea when he'll be ready to play, though," Audrey said.

"I'm so glad he's recovering so well," Stella exclaimed.

I forced a smile. A weird ambiguity wrapped around me. On one hand, I was glad for Quinn and Audrey. On the other, well. Quinn's return would put Ryan back on the bench. And, in my opinion, my guy deserved to start.

Stella glanced at me in the rearview. "My real question is, can we please get the whole story on Nica and Ryan? How did *Mrs. Quentin Paris* become Ryan Molloy's paramour?"

Audrey squealed and turned to grin at me. "Yes! Tell us everything."

My cheeks heated. "I don't know how you met Quinn or you met Ethan."

"The team, duh." Audrey shrugged.

"We were seventh-grade enemies. Stop deflecting, woman," Stella said with a laugh.

"Fine. Your wedding, actually," I said with a nod to Audrey. A giggle slipped out of me. "He, uh, had to order all these goofy drinks with sex names. I was at the bar. He was so embarrassed."

They were both grinning. "That is so cute," Stella said.

"It was cute. I didn't know who he was. And then I didn't see him again until Audrey here assigned me the article." I skipped several details there, but it was close enough.

She arched one eyebrow. "Oh, shit. I didn't realize I was helping fate along."

"Yeah, me neither. But, um, yeah. That's how it went."

Audrey clapped her fingers together. "I love it! I take full credit for this match."

Stella snorted. "Don't mind her. Point is, you two are adorable together. I've got to admit, Nica, I've had my doubts about you. Auds always knows what she's doing when it comes to PR, but I wasn't a fan of letting you get too close."

I shrugged. "It's fair. I couldn't believe Audrey was so cool with me, either."

"Well, clearly she was right to be. And you are nothing at all like I expected a superfan influencer to be."

Audrey cupped her ear. "Can you say that again, please?"

"I did not expect her to be so cool," Stella shouted. Her grin said she knew what was coming.

"No, no. The first part."

"You were right, Audrey Paris. About this one, at least."

I laughed at their silly back and forth. Clearly, they were old friends. The kind I'd never really had.

The thought tugged my heart, but I wasn't sad. I hadn't grown up going to boarding school or any of the things that they had. But I did have Vinny. And I had myself. *And* they made me feel welcome here. That could be enough.

Audrey turned back to me again. "I'm right about this part, too. Would you be interested in a job with the team?"

I choked on my coffee. "Job?"

"Joey's assistant. Joey took over my job when I became head of public relations. He's handling all of the media on his own. When I was in his position, he was my right hand. He needs someone to help him cover social media and press communication. You'd be perfect."

Bubbles filled my chest. My head filled with the implications. A full-time job *with the freaking Commodores*. A job where I could do what I was good at. No creeps ordering martinis and feeling up my ass. No worrying about sponsorships or where the next paycheck came from.

A job in Seacrest.

*I'll have to get a new car fast. The bus is so slow. Maybe I can get a little place there. No way can I stay with Ryan, but... but maybe a little bit. And I could see him more, at least.*

"Oh, hell yes," I whispered when I realized Audrey was waiting. My throat tightened. "I'd love that, Audrey."

She did a little arm dance in her seat. "Great. You start Monday. Joey's gonna be thrilled."

We parked in Boston and made our way to Newbury Street. Yet again, I found myself in that adorable dress shop. The other WAGs were already there. They waved when they saw Stella and Audrey. I noticed the moment they noticed me. A lot of them smiled and waved.

Jazzlynne Russo, however, tossed her hair and narrowed her gaze. A not-unkind smirk touched her lips. "I cannot believe Quinn's stalker is Ryan's girlfriend. Are you for real, girlie?"

Audrey started to defend me, but I shrugged. "One was a

job. The other is a choice. *You* dated Quinn before Dustin. Was that change for real?"

Her brows arched into upside-down Vs. "Oh, she knows her team gossip."

"About Quinn when he joined the team? Hell yes, I do. Again, it was my job."

That smirk twisted around her mouth and turned into a smile. "Okay, you're legit. I like you. And, yes, the change was *real*. Quinn and I were never serious. Dusty is..."

Her smile turned dreamy as she toyed with her engagement ring. She met my gaze again, and I flashed a smile in return.

"Quinn and I were never anything," I said softly. "But Ryan is... everything."

My cheeks heated. None of them spoke. But I could see by their expressions that I'd just quashed all suspicions about me and my intentions.

After that, the day was all about dress shopping with the girls.

I felt supremely strange about whipping out Ryan's platinum Amex to pay for a gown that cost more than a month's rent. Guilt tingled in my gut amid all of their chatter and last-minute purchases. Finally, it was my turn to pay. I took a quick breath and slid the card to the cashier. Certainly, she was going to read the name, frown, and accuse me of stealing it. She'd call the police, keep me in the stock room until they came to investigate how the hell I'd obtained—

"Thank you, miss. You're all set."

*What? Really?* Robotically, I took the card back from her manicured fingers and dropped it into my purse. My garment bag got tagged with a receipt that had *MOLLOY* scrawled across in Sharpie.

Damn imposter syndrome. Not a convenient moment to

want to fade into the background. I took several deep breaths as I stared at the slip. Just before I could freak out, Tanya slipped her arm through mine and guided me to the exit. Apparently, we were ready for lunch.

Seated in the booth, I whipped out my phone under the table.

ME:

I got a dress. I'm sorry if it's too expensive.

Minutes later, he sent back a string of laughing emojis.

RYAN:

It's not. Did you get shoes, too?

"Shit."

"What's wrong?" Ana asked.

"Oh, uh, I realized I didn't get shoes."

Stella grinned. An oddly wicked light sparked in her eyes. "Shoes are next. I need new boots."

No one else seemed to understand what made her smirk, either, so I ignored it and nodded. My thumb moved under the table.

ME:

We're shoe shopping next.

RYAN:

Good. Stop worrying about the $$. Just have fun.

ME:

Definitely probably not worrying.

He laughed at that. I could picture him adjusting his glasses and shaking his head at me. Somehow, that took the edge off my nerves. I pushed the phone into my purse and joined the conversation.

By the time we left Boston, I'd bought shoes, new sexy underwear, and fresh makeup. I tried not to think about the amount of money I'd spent. Being around the ladies and watching them flash credit cards without blinking helped. We listened to the game as we rode back to Seacrest. All three of us hung on the commentary, squealing and groaning at the plays. In the end, we eked out a 3-2 win that had us all cheering as Stella rolled into town. She dropped me off at Ryan's house. I pulled my stuff out of her trunk and waved goodbye.

It was only then that I remembered I had no car.

"Shit. *Shit.*" I looked around frantically. What the hell should I do? It was freezing, and the bus to Hartford stopped nowhere near here.

After a few minutes of freaking out, I realized I could use his card to call a taxi home. I pulled out my phone just as it lit up with a call.

"We won." His voice was tired but happy.

I grinned. "I know. We listened on the drive back. But, uh, I'm in a jam. I'm at your house. Is it okay to use the card for a taxi home?"

"Of course. Or you can just go inside. Use code three-four-three-four on the pin pad."

My brows knitted. "Go inside and do what?"

He laughed. "Stay? Sleep? Shower? Things one normally does in a house?"

"You... I can't stay in your home while you're gone!"

"Why?"

My mouth opened and shut. I had no good answer to that.

"If you don't want to, don't. But you can stay as long as you want, Trouble."

"You trust me to stay in your house?"

"Should I not? Are you going to steal all of my shit?"

I snorted. "Nope. I've got your credit card. I can buy new shit."

He laughed. "Exactly. Henrik is with the neighbors, so you don't have to worry about a thing."

I went inside. With a sigh, I set my bags on the chair in the living room. The lights came on as if by magic. "Did you do that?"

"Yep. Tell the automation what you want."

"Sheesh. This is wild. Oh, by the way. I have news. Audrey hired me to be Joey's assistant."

"Nica, that's awesome. Congratulations."

I could hear the smile in his voice. It gave me a warm glow in my chest. "Thanks."

He yawned. "Between you, travel, and the game, I'm wiped. Gonna say goodnight now, but I miss you, Trouble. Stay in the house if you want. Use the card for whatever. We'll talk tomorrow."

"Giving me Cinderella vibes, Goalie."

"Hmm. Afraid I'm no Prince Charming. Just a goalie with more house and cash than makes sense for one person."

"Is that all you are?" I murmured.

His tone softened. "No. I'm a goalie who's crazy about you."

I spun around in a little circle. "Oh, good."

He laughed again. "Night, beautiful."

"Goodnight, baby."

We hung up. I looked around, debated with myself once more, and went up to the bedroom to shower and sleep.

On Sunday, I woke early to get the bus to Hartford. When I was there, I packed my suitcase full of trousers and my best sweaters for the week. Since I had no car, it only made sense to stay at Ryan's as I began my new job. There was a shuttle bus that circled Seacrest with a stop not too far from the house. Much easier than the ninety-minute slog from my apartment.

I'd just filled a duffel bag with miscellaneous essentials when my phone vibrated.

BRUCE:

Meeting? Coffeeshop in 30?

ME:

Why?

BRUCE:

Closing biz.

I groaned and tapped a thumbs-up. Thirty minutes later, I walked into the corner coffeeshop to find him already in a booth. He had his gassy face on.

"What's the business?"

"Hello to you, too, Nica."

I ignored that and waited. Bruce huffed. "I'm impressed you got the money so fast. But you failed to mention the revenue for the article you wrote for *Puck Drop Daily*."

"Because that had nothing to do with our agreement."

"We were fifty-fifty partners."

"On the social media accounts. Not on my whole life."

He smirked and opened his phone. "Look, we can play nice, or we can do it another way. I want half of the money from the article, and we'll be done. Or else…"

He laid the phone on the table, facing me. It was a photo of Ryan and me. We faced each other on the porch at The Pub, so clearly it was taken that night I went to see Vinny. I flipped to the next picture. A close-up of us kissing. Ryan held my face. My arms hugged his neck.

"Go back two." Bruce's voice had a wicked smugness to it.

A video of us arguing. The audio was soft, but I could hear myself say *imposter syndrome* and *what it felt like to kiss you.* And I could clearly hear him say, *All you want is a paycheck.*

I glared at Bruce. "What the fuck is this?"

"Collateral. How much did you earn off the article, Nica?"

"A thousand. That's all."

"Hm. In that case, I'll take it all and delete these. Otherwise, I wonder who'd like to know about your boyfriend's imposter syndrome or your *paid* arrangement?"

My jaw slid side to side. I had $1,100 in my account until I got paid again. With a sigh, I whipped out my phone and opened my banking app. "Done. Delete them. I want to watch you do it—*permanently.*"

He showed me the phone while he selected the files, deleted them, and then emptied the trash folder. I nodded and moved to leave.

Bruce shook his head. "You were always so smart, Nica. That's what I liked about you. I'm so disappointed to see you be such a fool over this hockey player. I thought you had your head on straighter than that. We were such a good team. Good luck with your choices."

I didn't rise to the bait. Just stormed out of there, got my shit from my apartment, and got the bus back to Seacrest.

Ryan didn't have a game, so he FaceTimed that night as

expected. Try as I might to fake cheerful, he saw right through it. "Spill it," he commanded.

I sighed—and told him everything. My stomach was cold with dread while I watched him process the story. "He *blackmailed* you? You paid him?"

"Yeah. But he deleted the files."

Ryan snorted. "From his phone. If he's anything more than a fool, he has them backed up somewhere."

Panic brought tears to my eyes. "I'm so sorry. I didn't realize he'd followed me. I never thought he'd be such a prick."

"Didn't you? He was a prick enough to take half your money."

My chin wobbled. "I'm sorry, Ryan."

He did a double-take at the screen. The anger faded from his face. "Hey. I'm not mad at you, silly. I mean, I'm concerned about your life choices hanging around with a bro like that. Don't worry. We'll take care of it. Just, uh, do you have his email address by chance?"

"Yeah, that's how I pay him."

Ryan smirked. "Text it to me."

"Don't email him. Just leave it alone."

His smirk deepened. "I'm not going to email him. I'm going to make sure he gets our message."

I didn't understand, but I sent him the address. The text went through, and Ryan nodded. "Definitely probably not about to do some computer wizard shit that'll have him deleting this account. Talk to you tomorrow, Trouble."

He winked, and the screen went black. I gaped at the phone for another moment, unsure whether I wanted to laugh or groan. In the end, I did both—and then I texted Bruce.

ME:

> Last message you'll get from me. If those files happen to be anywhere else, I want them gone. If they ever appear anywhere, I'll know it's you. Don't be that guy.

BRUCE:

> You never need to worry, Nica. I'm a man of my word.

"And I'm a woman of mine," I whispered to the phone.

The job was a dream from the first hour on. Joey was thrilled to have me on board, and I got to write social posts all day hyping the team. By the time Ryan returned on Friday, I was quickly settling into the job. I was also a little too settled into his house.

And as for Bruce, well. First, I started getting emails from him inviting me to join weird websites and mailing lists. Stuff like iliketowatch.com and "Voyeurs Anonymous." Then, a few days later, Bruce texted me his new address in case I ever needed to contact him. He added a note: "If you get anything saying I'm inviting you to a peep show or something stupid like that, just delete it. Idk what happened, but obviously it's a scam."

I showed it to Ryan when he walked in that afternoon. He smirked and shrugged—and then kissed me and carried me to bed.

"What did you do, Goalie?" I asked on the way upstairs.

"Just looking out for us, Trouble. Nothing too untoward."

I hugged his neck. "I'm not used to someone looking out for me."

"Not used to having someone to look out for. But I think we'll both acclimate quickly."

"Do you mind that I've been camping out at your house?"

His eyes cut to me. "Yeah. It's a real problem. And I'm about to show you just how bothered I've been about it."

The bedroom door slammed behind us. For the next hour, my goalie made it crystal clear just how *bothered* he was to have me around.

# 28

# RYAN

Nica had a single suitcase stashed in the corner of the bedroom. I realized quickly that she was toting her toiletry bag back and forth to the bathroom.

"Is this what camping out looks like?" I asked while she rummaged in her case. We'd washed up from the first round of the night and had decided on takeout for dinner.

She stepped into yoga pants and brushed her hair away from her forehead. "Yeah. I know it's a little bulky, but I've tried to keep it neat."

I huffed a laugh and gestured for her to follow me into the closet. Pointing at one of the twin bureaus, I said, "That one is empty. Use it. Fill it. Or move your stuff into the guestroom if you want privacy. Come on."

We walked into the bathroom, and I pulled out the drawers on the right side of the sink. "Empty. Yours. Go nuts."

Nica sucked on her lip. Her brows knitted. "Thank you."

"But?"

She sighed and leaned on the counter beside me. "I'll start looking for an apartment in Seacrest. And I'll go back to Hartford for now. It's been so helpful being local to start the job. But I'll figure it out. I can keep a few things here, but I don't want you to feel like we started, uh, dating—"

She made a face to tell me that *dating* meant *fucking*. I arched a brow, and she went on.

"Anyway, I don't want you to feel like I'm just barging into your life like that. Which, ha, I realize is exactly what I've done. But we can walk it back a little."

I caught her fingers as they tapped the countertop. "You realize, of course, that I'm the one who's nervous about moving too fast."

"Nope, that would definitely be me."

A little laugh rumbled in my chest. "Exactly. We have some weird shit in common. Imposter syndrome isn't the greatest thing to bond over, but it can be useful. Because if *this is this*, then we can be here to remind each other that it's real. To remind each other not to overthink things. And to tell each other the truth about what is and isn't too much."

Her eyes were brighter than usual. She bit her lips into a line and nodded. "I like that part. All of this feels like a dream. I expect any moment to wake up in my apartment. It'll be the morning after Audrey's wedding, and life will be normal. I'll have a day of posting, hustling, and forgetting about the guy I met the night before.

"But I keep waking up *here*. With a job with the Commodores, no more obligations to Bruce, and... and the guy I met that night. You. You, looking at me like that."

"Like what?"

"Like you might already love me," she whispered.

"Hmm."

"Point is, the way you remind me of all that stuff is helping me believe this little fairytale is real. For now, at least. And that's all that has to be true."

I pulled her close and wrapped my arms around her. That sweet lavender scent hit my nose. "We're way past that morning in September, Trouble. I have almost three months of spreadsheet data to prove it."

Her body vibrated with a laugh.

"And *my* point is, this house wasn't built for one person. There are empty spaces that can be yours if you want them. I don't care if you get an apartment or not. You should if you want to. If you don't, or if you want to take your time, then there is a place for you here."

I tilted her chin up so I could look into her eyes. "This is this. And you are not at all too much. I want you to take up space in my life—if you want."

"I want." She swallowed hard and nodded. "I really want."

My lips dusted hers, but I pulled back to meet her gaze again. "Like you might already love me."

Her eyes glittered. "Like I might."

Before I could kiss her again, the doorbell rang. "That'll be Henrik. I'll be right back."

But Nica's brows went up. "Can I come, too? I want to see him. He's so cute. I kind of wished he was here while you were gone, even though I don't know how to take care of a dog."

"Well, if you stay, you can learn."

"That's a good excuse," she said with a laugh as she beat me to the stairs. "Henrik! Welcome home!"


She unpacked her stuff. She let me fill the Tesla with more clothes than just a week's worth and drive it back from Hartford. She learned how to feed and walk Henrik. She stopped trying to fit into corners and just let us fit together. She even let me rent her a car after a week or so of taking the bus. I promised I wouldn't offer more, but I think we both knew that was bullshit.

It was fast. It was dizzying. But dammit. It was good.

~

The team holiday party rolled around in a blink. I struggled to keep the drool in my mouth at the sight of Nica in her gown. She went to the salon with Stella and Audrey that morning, so her hair was done in a way that kept her from sighing about how short it was.

"You're a vision," I said as I spun her around in the foyer.

"You're sure I shouldn't have gone with long hair?"

I laughed. "You look like Nica. No filters. No alter-ego. I'm very damn sure."

She walked in on my arm. For the first time, Nica's steps didn't lag. She didn't once try to fade into the background. Quite the opposite. Tanya and Ana beamed when they saw her. I glanced down to see her grin light up, too.

Nica didn't lag behind, but my brain did. It wasn't until that moment that I fully felt the thing we'd been saying for weeks.

We were together. This was *this*. Not just in the house. Not just in the bedroom. Everyone knew it. My teammates and their partners all expected to see her with me. Gene and Ana. Yuri and Tanya. Ethan and Stella. Dustin and Jazzlynne. Quinn and Audrey.

Ryan and Nica.

Nica glanced up when I squeezed her arm closer to me. "You good, Goalie?"

My ears were warm, but I grinned down at her. Abruptly,

I swooped in and kissed her cheek. "Great, Trouble. I'll go get you a champagne."

The women aww'ed. I shook my head and strode away. When I glanced back, I saw Nica smiling after me. She wiggled her fingers and turned her attention to Ana.

Max was at the bar. He rolled his eyes as I approached. "You fuckin' traitor."

"Me?"

"Hell yeah, you. You were supposed to be my fellow miserably single bastard."

I laughed. "Sorry to let you down."

We clinked beers, and he said, "Ah, I ain't mad at you, Sieve. You two look good together."

"Thanks, buddy. I'll talk to you in a minute." I lifted the champagne off the bar and took it to Nica.

The night blurred away with food, talk, and even a little dancing. Nica assured me that I danced. I let her drag me to the floor for two slow tunes, but I flat refused to participate in Ethan's holiday flash mob. She stayed on the floor, though, so I got to laugh at her red face while she tried to keep up. When the song ended, I whooped in applause, and she flew to me. Her grin would not quit.

"Oh, my gosh. This is the best night," she said as she gazed up at me. "Thank you, Goalie. This is magical."

"And you fit right in."

Her lips puckered. "What do you know? Seems like I do."

Quinn walked up. He was off crutches and looking much more himself these days. He arched one eyebrow at Nica. "My dear Nica. It has been too long. Apparently, I have missed quite a lot, no?"

She beamed and let him kiss her hand. I tried hard not to mind while she said, "You have. I deleted the profile and work for the team now. And, of course, Ryan and I are..."

Her arms slipped around me in a hug. I caught eyes with Quinn, who grinned. "Somehow, none of this made the team meeting agendas, but Audrey has kept me informed. C'est tiguidou! This is excellent. I am so happy for you both."

We all clinked glasses in a toast. Quinn and I traded a nod. "Happy Christmas, you two. Molls."

"French."

Nica hummed as he strolled away. "Yeah, he's a fox for sure."

I opened my mouth to complain, but she crooked a finger to have me bend to her. "But you're my goalie, Goalie. And I'm looking forward to watching you fuck my mouth in that tuxedo later."

A growl rumbled in my throat. "Only after I devour that pussy. I might even let you watch that, too."

It was a long night. We didn't get out of the party until one, so we didn't sleep until nearly sunrise. But it didn't matter. We spent half of Christmas Eve in bed. The other half, Nica insisted on prepping food for the next day. I'd suggested going out to dinner, but she had other ideas.

Christmas Day, I let her take the lead. We went to the practice rink to skate with Vinny, who couldn't stop thanking me for letting him join. Henrik had the time of his life with so many people sliding pucks for him to chase. After that, Nica went back to Vinny's house to exchange gifts. I'd invited him to dinner, but he had friends he spent the day with. Nica promised she'd not be long even though I told her to take her time.

I took a quick detour to The Pub to drop off a holiday tip for Tony and the wait staff, then headed home to shower. I pulled up to the house thinking about the afternoon. Looking forward to snuggling with my girl in front of the tree and a fire. Picturing the necklace I'd bought her and wondering if she'd like it. If I'd chosen the right thing.

So I nearly had a heart attack when I found someone sitting on the stoop. My jaw unhinged. Henrik sniffed the air and ran toward her. She squealed and knelt down. "Henny! My sweet boy, how are you?"

My jaw clenched. "He's not yours, Amanda. You left him, if you recall."

"Oh, but he's still my little pookie, aren't you baby?" She cooed at the dog. Then, she stood up and strolled toward me. "Hey, honey. How have you been?"

Her arms slid around my neck at the same time tires rolled to a stop behind us. A car door opened and closed. I had to suppress a smirk when Henrik bolted to greet Nica, but that was short-lived in the face of this awkward moment.

"What's going on?" Nica asked softly.

# 29

# NICA

Ryan's face was all hard lines. The blonde hanging off of him wore a placid smile. She leaned in and planted a kiss on his cheek. He ducked away from her grasp. I bristled.

"Get out of here." I sounded like a lioness growling at her prey. It was so fierce that Henrik growled with me.

The woman ignored me and looked at Ryan. "Can we go inside and talk, honey?"

At no point did I consider fading into the background. At no point did I wonder if I had a right to be there. I walked up toe-to-toe with her and crossed my arms. "Take your fangirling, stalker ass back to wherever you came from. It's Christmas Day, for fuck's sake. Have a little self-respect. My man isn't into puck bunnies."

"Woof!" Henrik seconded me.

"I'm well aware of what *my* man is and isn't into."

I rasped a laugh. "Wow. A little of my own medicine, huh? It's clever, I'll give you that. But I'm out of that game for good, so you're a little late. Now, fuck off. We're busy."

I turned to Ryan. "Shall we?"

His brows were at his hairline. "Oh, we definitely shall."

He took my hand and let me punch the code for the lock. Just before he followed me inside, I heard him say, "Good-bye, Amanda. Take care of yourself."

The door clicked shut. The lock whirred back in place. Henrik smiled his Corgi smile up at us.

But I spun to him as my blood ran cold. "Hold on," I hissed. "That was your *ex*?"

Ryan nodded slowly. He seemed to be in a daze. "You just told my ex-fiancée to fuck off."

"I called her a puck bunny!"

His lips twitched. "You did."

"I thought she was a crazy fan!" My hand clapped over my mouth.

Ryan's grin stretched wide. He dropped to his knees in front of me and hugged my waist. His head rested on my stomach. "I definitely love you, Nica Solance."

Confusion and horror went silent in my brain. I let his words wash over me, wrap around me like his arms had done. "Because I'm insane?"

"Because you're *you*. Because you didn't for a second flinch or think you shouldn't speak your mind. But I guess I love you most because you let me. And that feels like a very special, very rare thing."

My hands threaded into his hair. It was hard to talk with so much emotion choking me. "All of that. All of that is why I love you right back, Ryan Molloy."

He lifted his gaze to me. "Good," he whispered.

That green stare went wicked. I held my breath as he popped the button on my jeans. "Do you think she's still standing out there?" he murmured with a kiss on my belly.

"I could look." It would've been hard since I couldn't stop staring at him, but still.

"Mm, no. I will. You go to the bed and wait for me."

I bit my lip and nodded. Ryan spanked me lightly and stood up, turning back to the door. As I headed for the stairs, I heard him speak to her.

"Really, Amanda? Two years, and you think you can just show up? ... Obviously not. Obviously, Henrik and I both don't want you to... Please. Just go. This is embarrassing for you, and I..."

*Ouch for her.* I broke into a little jog as bubbles danced in my chest. I didn't need to hear more of that. All I wanted to hear was—

"You better not have any clothes on."

"Ooft." His voice startled me as I was stripping out of my jeans. I landed on my ass on the floor and watched him walk in.

Ryan breathed a laugh, picked me up, and tossed me on the bed. He tugged my jeans off, stripped himself naked, and climbed over me. Before I could speak, he claimed my kiss. We were both a little sweaty from the skate, and neither of us gave one damn. He was warmth and safety and sex all around me. I melted into the mattress, into the feeling of being sheltered by his body.

Into his love.

Ryan pulled back an inch and gazed down at me. I removed his glasses and set them on the nightstand. "Nica," he whispered.

I nodded, agreeing to everything he didn't say. "Ryan."

This wasn't our usual tempo or style. Ryan lowered down, kissing me. Holding me. We rolled across the bed, unable to stop touching each other. My throat still had that knot of emotion in it. Every time he kissed me somewhere new, that knot kind of glowed.

*How, how, how did I get this lucky? What did I do so right? I come from nothing. I've made do for so long. Somehow, that making do led to... this? A freaking love story? Do I deserve it? I don't know, but, god. I want it. I love it. I'm keeping it.*

"I'd like to keep you, Goalie." My voice was a raspy croak. I opened my eyes and smiled at him even though tears blurred my vision.

He blinked and smiled. "You have me, Trouble. No question there."

We made slow, lazy love forever. Forgetting about showers, dinners, and gifts until inky dusk darkened the house. At last, we shuffled back downstairs in the matching bathrobes he'd come home with last week. White fluffy clouds of fabric with my monogram on the chest. How could I say no? I fussed around in the kitchen but had to admit we were way too late to cook. In the end, it was Chinese takeout in front of the tree.

And a sapphire necklace that made my jaw drop.

After I'd tried to protest it was too much, I let him put it on me. We lay staring at the fire from the sofa, me between his legs with his arms around me from behind. Henrik curled up on our feet. I rested my head on his chest and tipped my gaze up.

"This was the best Christmas ever."

He kissed my forehead. "I quite agree."

"Same time next year?"

"Sounds good to me, Trouble. Sounds damn fine to me."

# 30

# RYAN

This was my first holiday season as a Commodore where I had a plus-one to team events. I'd gotten so used to going stag that I never thought about it. I was the guy at the bar with a beer in his hand, ready to laugh and bullshit with whoever walked up.

Now, for the holiday party and then Yuri's New Year's Eve bash, I was the guy with the new girlfriend. I hated the attention and the knowing smirks. But I fucking loved having her on my arm.

In the house, at the games, and in between—anytime Nica was nearby—things seemed right. She never nagged me like Amanda had. Never seemed frustrated if I was deep in thought. Never drank too much and started talking shit about my teammates' partners.

But screw what she wasn't. More important was who she was.

To me, she was everything. For a woman who'd built a platform out of bold statements and flashy posts, Nica Solance was also subtle as hell. Subtly funny, clever, kind, and sexy beyond words. My first impression of her had been right. She was quiet, but she knew how to enjoy life. And I was the lucky bastard who got to enjoy it with her.

My game was better than it had ever been. The more I played, the more my goalie Force strengthened. We were near the top of our conference, flirting with the number one position. I didn't let myself think of it much, but I'd done what I'd promised in that press conference. I'd been myself and not let the team down.

Quinn was ready to start practicing again. By the all-star break, we would likely be splitting games, with me starting four or five in a row to his one. He had to build up his stamina, but he was coming back. We were all happy for him. Even me. With the way this fall had gone, I felt like my place on the team was stronger than ever. It would be some time before Quinn was full force again. I liked the idea of a more even split of games through this season at least.

Everything seemed in its place like never before. Kissing Nica at midnight on New Year's felt like a harbinger of all good things to come.

January was the typical snowy return to focus. Nica never did find an apartment in Seacrest. This month, she let her lease expire on the place in Hartford. We officially lived together, even though she insisted that "soon" she'd get her own place. I didn't argue, but Henrik whined anytime she mentioned it.

Quinn got a round of applause the first day he laced up for practice. He was slower than normal, which was to be expected. I was impressed at how calm he was about it and told him so in the locker room.

He laughed. "I have been working with a mindset coach. It is the only way I can be patient enough to take my time."

I clapped his shoulder. "Smart move, French. You'll be back to full speed soon enough."

And I was right. The recovery team he employed must've been wizards because Quinn looked stronger day by day. We were on track to have him start right after the all-star break.

Nica and I were having coffee. It was Friday, the day before the week-long break officially began. The day before we left for six days in Turks and Caicos—Nica's first time flying first class. I'd laughed at her when she offered to pay half of the trip and assured her I had reward points to cover it. One day, I hoped she'd stop feeling like she owed me something.

I looked at her over my mug. "Quinn will start the first game back."

She nodded. "As if we haven't been blasting that for a week online."

"I just... Eventually, he'll start again, and I'll be backup."

She tilted her head. "Yeah? So?"

That response was enough, but I went on. "You're okay with dating the backup goalie?"

Nica stared at me for a long moment. And then, she burst out laughing.

She giggled so hard that tears glistened her eyes. "What kind of question is that, goofball?"

I gestured helplessly. "I mean, a valid one, I thought? It's not the status that I have now. I just wanted to make sure you understood it."

Nica slid off her barstool and stood between my legs. She cupped my face in her hands. "I love *you*. I hit on you when I had no idea who you were. I crushed on you when your fashion sense made you look like a mop in a flannel and glasses."

I groaned and palmed my forehead, but she pulled my hand away. Her smile was too bright to resist. "I love you, Ryan Molloy. You are my goalie, no matter how many games you play. If you love what you do, then I love it, too."

"God, I love *you*," I said on an exhale before hauling her into my arms and up onto the island. Her coffee-flavored kiss backed up her claims. *This is this.*

She pulled away with a pop of our mouths and grinned. "Save that for the hotel tomorrow, buster. I gotta get to work now."

"Yeah, I have a meeting today. Coach told me last night."

Nica tilted her head. "Team meeting?"

"Don't think so."

She furrowed her brow but shrugged. "Let me know how it goes. Especially if it's something I can share with your followers."

"Ugh. How big is the profile now?"

That got me a huge smile. "Ten thousand as of Monday. I am *so* good."

I leaned in and nipped her neck. "You are good at many things. Making me look cool is one of them."

Her lips brushed my ear. "Taking your cock is another."

With a groan, I buried my face in her shoulder. "Read my mind and also ruined my concentration."

She giggled and scratched my back. "We'll do plenty of that at the beach. I gotta go now, baby."

"But you could come first."

She shooed me away since we both knew there was no time. I grabbed my jacket and followed her outside. Nica slid into her new Mazda, which she'd bought on a New Year sale. I wanted to buy her a car, but she had insisted on doing it herself. We followed each other to the rink and rode the elevator to the third floor together. She blew me a kiss and slid into her chair while I headed on.

"Morning, Coach," I said with a knock on Delgato's office door.

He flashed a close-lipped smile. "Hey, Molls. Let's go talk to Hunt."

My brows knitted. Coach was clearly tense as he stood and led me back to the elevator. We went one floor up to Hunter's executive suite. The owner gave me the same tight smile when we walked in. He shook my hand and gestured to a chair.

"Everything okay?" I asked, glancing between them.

"Yes, and absolutely not," Hunter said. He clasped his hands on the desk and looked me in the eye. "I'll get right to it, Molloy. I've traded you."

The words bounced around my suddenly hollow chest. I stared at him, trying to absorb the moment.

He went on. "I'm mad as hell to do it, but I have to remove my feelings from business. The new Oregon franchise has struggled with their defense all season. No way are they making the playoffs this year, but they have potential. They're offering me a top-round draft pick in exchange for you. Your contract is up this year, and they've told me they're willing to negotiate generously to keep you.

"They want you as the backbone of the team, Ryan. Now, I could say no. I could turn down fresh talent for our team and keep you on. But that would deny you a chance to be a starting goalie. Quinn is this franchise's star in net. *You* are a fucking star, too, and you should be playing as such. So I said yes. It's gutted me to do it because, hell, you're integral to our team in so many ways. But that's the game."

"Oregon," I echoed.

"Oregon."

Delgato spoke up. "I fucking hate this, Molls. Don't know what I'll do without you and all your notes for the team. And, ha, I'll be nervous as hell to face you in a game eventually. But you deserve to start, kid. You're not meant to ride out your career on the bench."

I cleared my throat and took a massive breath. *This is the life. This is the job. You jumped from Virginia to Connecticut to become a Commodore. You can make this transition, too. It's how it goes.*

"I see. When do I need to report there?"

Hunter wiggled his eyebrows. "Monday. They want to use the break to set you up with the franchise."

I pushed my glasses up and rubbed my eyes hard. "Wow. Alright then. I'll, uh, get my stuff."

They each shook my hand when we stood. Ambivalence gripped me hard. Resentment and anger at being blind-sided. Respect and appreciation that they gave me this shot. All those roiling emotions churned in my gut while I followed Delgato to the elevator.

He punched the third floor and glanced at me. "You going to see Nica?"

*Nica.*

I swallowed hard to keep the bile down. Shaking my head, I punched the bottom floor. Coach didn't press or make chitchat. I appreciated that.

The maroon and navy stripes led me to the locker room for the last time as a Commodore. The next time I was here, I would be in a different uniform, headed to the visitor's door. *I am not a Commodore anymore.*

Grateful as hell that no one was around, I stepped into our locker room—*their* locker room—and sank to the bench. Bittersweet tears stung my eyes that I didn't try to dam. I loved this fucking team. Would die for them. Didn't know how to envision life without them.

And by the end of the season, I'd feel that way about a

whole other group of people. *If you're lucky. If lightning strikes twice and they turn out to be as incredible as the Commodores.*

I wiped my eyes and sniffled hard. Pity party was over. I went to my locker and grabbed Yoda and the few effects I stored there. Then, I reached up and swiped my name plate from its slot as a souvenir.

I did not let myself think about Nica. Not until I got home and saw her mug beside mine on the counter. Only then did another wave of tears hit me.

How the hell was I going to tell her?

My phone jerked me out of my thoughts.

GeneV: The Pub. Now. That's an order.

No way could I go out with red eyes and a mopey expression. I splashed water on my face, combed my hair, and went back to the car. Tires crunched the gravel parking lot, so familiar. So final. It was noon, but cars filled the lot. I jogged up the porch and hauled open the door.

A wall of cheers and applause nearly knocked me off my feet.

The entire team, Tony, and all our regulars formed two lines into the bar. I shook my head and walked in, high-fiving every last one of them. My throat clenched with more emotion. By the looks on their faces, I wasn't the only one holding a lot in.

"Dammit, Molls," Gene shouted to get the mob quiet. "Damn you and your sick skills. Why you gotta be so good, huh? If you were just a little more mid, we could keep you on the bench forever."

I bit my lip. "Sorry, Cap," I rasped at last, drawing a round of laughs.

Gene lifted his glass, and every last person followed.

Ethan pushed a drink into my hand and tapped his iced tea against it.

Gene smiled. "Here's to Ryan 'Molls' Molloy. May his new team bask in the glory of his talents. May his spreadsheets be populated with wins. May he never, ever flinch from a shootout.

"Except when he's playing the Commodores!"

I laughed, and more damn tears blurred my vision. "Here, here!" I shouted.

They went quiet, and I looked around. "Thanks, guys. Fuck, I can't believe I've gotta go. I was ready to wear maroon and navy until I retired. But, uh, I guess this is the game. Still. You goofy, talented jerks are my friends. And I will never forget that. So here's to the game, and here's to teammates for life."

"The Game! Teammates for life!" echoed everyone in the room.

From there, the party quieted down. Everyone took a turn wishing me well and saying goodbye. I promised Dustin I'd be back for his wedding next year. I told Ethan to fuck off one more time. And I held up my glass to Quinn, who snatched it from my hand and instead clapped me in a massive hug. Wiping my eyes again, I turned around.

Face-to-face with Vinny Solance.

My jaw clenched as he nodded once. "Gutted to hear it, man," he muttered.

"Same."

He breathed a dry laugh. "What am I going to do without Nica around?"

My brows knitted. "Dude. I... don't expect her to come with me."

Vinny stared at me like I'd lost several marbles. It was an oddly familiar look, thanks to his sister. At last, he shook his head slowly. "I'd be shocked if she didn't. Why the hell wouldn't she?"

"She's got her life here. I can't ask her to leave that."

"Pretty sure you won't have to, buddy. Just, you know. Let her come home to visit when she can. She's the only family I've got."

I wanted to argue more but then realized he wasn't the one I should be discussing this with. Plus, the pain in his eyes said enough. We clinked glasses, and he drifted away.

There had been so many team gatherings at The Pub where I was the last to leave. The single guy in no hurry to go home. Today, I was the last to leave for a very different reason. I couldn't bear to think about not seeing these guys all the time. Couldn't process that I'd not walk into this bar again anytime soon. But at last, the party was done. I thanked Tony once more and cruised home, so deep in thought that I didn't register her car in the drive.

Reality smacked me straight in the face when I walked in and found her sitting on the floor with Henrik in her lap. Fear and pain dulled her gaze.

"Goalie. What the fuck?" she whispered.

I bit down on my lip, but my eyes leaked anyway. "Sorry, baby. Gonna have to cancel the beach."

# 31

# NICA

My little fairytale was crumbling. *I should've known it was too good to last.* For almost three whole months, I'd been in a dream. Dream job, dream boyfriend, dream life in Seacrest.

And now? Pop! The bubble burst.

Bless Ryan. His clenched jaw did nothing to hide the anguish radiating from him. Green eyes glittered with the tears that slipped down his cheeks. My heart cracked even more to see him like this.

"What are we going to do?" I asked, totally ignoring his beach comment.

Ryan dropped his glasses on the entry table and walked toward me. He wiped his eyes and sat down beside us. Henrik shifted his head from my lap to Ryan's for more pets. I swore the dog knew something was wrong. "We're going to spend the next thirty-six hours or so in bed. And then I'm going to get on a plane to Oregon."

I sat up straight. "Ryan. Wait. *You* are? What about me? What am I supposed to do?"

But my goalie got to his feet and hauled me into his arms. "Questions later, Trouble. I need you now."

*You have thirty-six hours left in the fairytale.* I nearly called a time-out, but that thought hit me as his lips fit against mine. In my brain, I could see a huge hourglass. We could figure everything out later.

We began a marathon fuckfest in the kitchen. Ryan had never seemed restrained or hesitant with me, but he was a new level of unleashed suddenly. His teeth scraped my neck, my nipples, my thighs. His tongue danced across my clit, dipped into my pussy, and then teased my ass until I came, right there on the kitchen island. As soon as I stopped moaning, he hauled me to my feet, directing me to take off his clothes. I lay on the table with my head hanging off, mouth open to receive his cock. While he fucked my mouth, he fingered me. No matter how I squirmed or moaned with my mouth full, he did not stop touching me.

And, oh, the things he said. The filthy, reverent, bossy, wonderful things he said.

My eyes watered while I swallowed his come. I pressed my thighs together around his fingers, and he pulsed just to tease me. But the moment he pulled away from my mouth, I was in his arms again, headed to the bedroom.

To the mirror to watch us. Except this time, it was hard to watch and not want to cry. I turned my head away from my favorite vision. Ryan didn't argue with that. He just kept kissing me, kept driving me into a heartbroken ecstasy.

We forgot about dinner. We fell asleep in each other's arms, woke in the middle of the night, and right away resumed licking every inch of skin we could find. His words were softer then but no less perfect.

Pass out again. Wake up again. Hold each other again.

*For the last time?* I couldn't process the questions yet. Instead, I buried my head into his chest. Very soon, I was straddling him, sliding down onto his cock *again*.

Ryan gripped my hips and helped me ride him. My vibrator was clenched in one of his hands, ready to switch on when he knew I needed it.

"Thank you," he whispered.

"For what?" I panted.

I heard the vibe switch on. "For being exactly who you are."

The toy touched my clit, and I couldn't talk anymore. All I could do was moan and whimper his name until I exploded all over him.

Ryan flipped me to my back and drove into me. "If I come inside you, is it a problem?"

I'd had my period just days before. I shook my head. "Fill me, baby. Come hard for me."

His eyes flashed like a storm at sea. "Yeah? You want me to come in this pussy?"

"I do. I need you to."

*I would totally have your baby, Ryan Molloy. Someday.* The thought didn't have legs. It was just a hazy, lusty knowing deep inside me. Deep down, beyond worry and logistics, I knew I would love this man for a long fucking time.

Ryan grunted. I felt him tense in the way that told me he was close. He sat up on his knees and kept thrusting, so I reached between us and teased my finger just behind his balls. He threw his head back to the ceiling and groaned my name. I felt him pulse inside of me, and a feeling of intense connection wrapped around my heart.

He fell back against the pillows to catch his breath. I lay there until I felt his come leaking out of me, and then I rolled off the bed and hurried to the shower.

He joined me while I washed up. "What time is it?" My voice was husky with sleep and a hell of a lot of pheromones.

"Nearly noon."

"Wow."

"Come back to bed with me. We'll eat in a while."

"Let Henrik come snuggle with us."

He smiled at my request. "Of course."

I shut off the water, wrapped in my robe, and went to let him hold me again. Ryan opened the bedroom door and whistled. Then he lay with his chest to my back and stroked my arm. Neither of us slept.

"Can you refuse the trade?" I asked, knowing the answer thanks to Audrey.

"No."

"Can anything be done?"

"Except relocate? Afraid not."

"Okay." I sighed and closed my eyes.

"Nica?"

"Hm?"

"I'm just going to say this. I don't expect you to come with me."

My eyes opened.

"Expect or want?" I whispered.

He tugged my arm, so I flipped to face him. "Expect, of course. Do I want you to come? Of course I do. But I don't want to take you from your home or the team. I realize that I'm the only variable in your life that isn't ideal suddenly. You have your life here. I respect that."

"But. But. But what would I do without you?"

"Live your life," he said patiently. "There's a lot of it to live. And you can keep this house if you want. And the Tesla. No need for you to go through upheaval like that. Especially not with Vinny so close by."

*Vinny.* My breath caught at the idea of leaving my

brother. How could I go across the country when he was here?

Ryan saw the thought in my eyes. He nodded. "Exactly."

"What if I want to come with you? What happens then?" I asked after a beat.

His fingertips traced my cheek. "Trouble, there's only open doors for you in my life. But I think you should think hard about that. What that would look like. How different it would be to move like that. I'm worried you'd resent me for taking you away from everyone you know and love."

"But I know and love you."

He twisted his lips. "Indeed."

My eyes burned. "And I do not want to lose you."

Those fingertips cupped my face. "You couldn't. We can be long distance. You can date if you want to, of course. But there's summer, and I can fly you out to visit whenever you want."

"I fucking hate that idea."

"Yeah, me too," he sighed.

"What about Henrik? This house? What happens to all that with you leaving *tomorrow*?" A wall of panic threatened to crash down on me. Where would I live? How could I...

Ryan shrugged. "I can take him with me. Or you can keep him. He'll be better off here with you. I can keep this mortgage, so you don't have to move. And my neighbor will help you with Henrik."

For some reason, this broke my heart more than anything else. Tears leaked out. "Ryan. How could you just leave us?"

I didn't want to make it harder on him, but dammit. His eyes glittered. "I have to, baby. It's the job. If I get traded, I gotta go. I don't want to leave either of you. But I can keep you safe and comfortable here. Knowing that's true is a huge comfort to me."

Henrik chose that moment to leap onto the bed. He shuffled up to us with something in his mouth. With the blackout curtains darkening the room, I couldn't see what it was. Ryan reached out and took the cloth from him. He stared at it and began to laugh, then handed it to me.

My butterfly panties from the first night.

"Henrik!" I exploded in weepy giggles. "How long have you had these? Oh my god, I can't believe you, you little thief!"

Henrik tried to reclaim his prize, climbing on top of me to get to my hand. I stuffed them under the pillow and showed him my empty hands. "You'd think the toys I get you would be enough, you little monster."

"Oh no," Ryan chuckled. "They smell like you to him. They're probably his favorite toy, and that's why he's been hiding them."

I groaned. Henrik licked my face. He shoved his head under the pillow and stole the panties, then leapt off the bed and disappeared again.

Ryan wrapped his arms around me and kissed the top of my head. "Take care of him for me, yeah?"

"Of course I will," I sighed. I buried my face in his chest and let him hold me. We had no answers. But I still had that knowing deep in my heart that told me we weren't over.

## 32

## RYAN

I flew to Oregon Sunday morning. The taxi drove me away from the house early, but Nica and Henrik stood on the front stoop even so. She clutched Yoda in her left hand and his leash in her right. Henrik strained to run after me, but she held him tight. Her haunted stare and his barks followed me until the car turned off our road.

We had gotten nowhere with answers. Strategically, I knew it was the right move. Everything happened so suddenly. Trying to make life-altering decisions in a day was foolish. It would almost certainly result in poor choices with doubtful outcomes.

Strategy be damned. I'd have given my entire salary and then some to have them both going to the airport with me.

First thing Monday, I met with the team's new player liaison, the owner, the goalie coach and head coach, and their head of marketing. Everyone welcomed me to the franchise and got busy orienting me to the team, the facilities, etc. The liaison promised to send some real estate listings over that afternoon. I toured the locker room and found my locker. MOLLOY 34 had already been lettered above it. A sky-blue jersey with the same lettering hung on the bar. I touched it and nodded. Something about that helped all this feel more real.

The afternoon was for PR stuff. The head of marketing was a woman named Lauren. She seemed more like a mom than a marketing wizard, but our meeting dispelled that. She asked me about my fan page. Immediately, I gave her Nica's info, which she took with an eager nod and a promise to get in touch with her asap. Meanwhile, we scheduled a branding shoot and an interview for the week.

I went through all the to-dos with focus and agreement. But none of it felt real. Surely, this was a dream. No way had I really been ripped from the bubble of Seacrest in just two days. I floated back to the hotel room that was my temporary home and lay on the bed with my phone open.

ME:

Hey, Trouble.

NICA:

Hey, Goalie.

ME:

I miss the hell out of you.

Bubbles floated on the screen until:

NICA:

Same. How is Portland?

ME:

Don't know yet. The team liaison gave me some places to check out. Seems they have good beer here. And coffee. And bakeries. And restaurants.

Thinly veiled suggestion that you should come check them out very soon.

NICA:

Hahaha, don't think I won't come right now.

I heaved a massive sigh.

ME:

Trouble, you can come whenever you like.
Put a flight on the card at a moment's
notice. I don't care. I'll text you where I'm
staying & put your name on the reservation.
Whenever it feels right, just show up, baby.
You are always welcome with me.

The phone lit up with a call. "Sneak attack," I murmured.

Nica sniffled on the other end of the line. "If I'm welcome, why didn't you let me come with you?"

Dear god, her voice was so small and broken. "I didn't want you to have to make that decision so fast."

Little whimpers filled my ears, making me feel like a total piece of shit. "But I would've."

"I know. And then you would've had to live with that decision. And what if it was the wrong one? Of course you could go back, but... but..."

I trailed off as I realized what I'd done. In "sparing" her the choice, my own doubts had taken control. What if she followed me and it wasn't the life she wanted? What would I do when I came home one day to find her stuff packed? How could I listen to her tell me she needed to take some time? How would I handle the enormous fucking hole Nica Solance would leave in my heart when she left?

The move had given me an excuse to ward off that dread. For as much as I'd told myself that each moment was enough, I'd subconsciously jumped at the chance to escape emptiness. The trade would make it easy for us to enjoy each other—and slowly drift apart eventually. Which is what my fucking imposter syndrome whispered would inevitably happen. No matter what reality indicated.

Nica was quiet while I kicked the shit out of myself for this error. At last, she spoke.

"I've got to go, Ryan."

"Nica, wait. I'm so sorry. I—"

"I know you are, baby," she said gently. Bless her, she sounded exhausted. "We'll talk again soon."

The line went dead. My head hit the pillows.

I had never felt more alone in my life.

Nica didn't call again that week, and I didn't have the nerve to face her disappointment. We texted each day, but it was superficial shit. Updates on Henrik, funny memes, and nothing more. I knew she was in touch with Lauren, though, because my profile page started blasting news of my move. The hockey world had exploded with stories on the trade. Even I was aware of that fact. Connecticut fans bemoaned my departure while Oregon loyals begged me to turn their year around. I tuned out the noise as soon as I heard it, though. No way could I focus on this transition with the pressure of thousands of voices shouting at me.

By Saturday, I had my eye on a couple of houses just outside of the city as potential places to buy. The hotel suite was comfortable enough that I felt no need to rush, but I wanted to settle in as quickly as possible. That morning, I met the team. It was the usual deal, handshakes and nods, and a fairly reserved air. But once we got to our practice skate, things started to loosen up. The guys were funny in a self-deprecating way. It was easy to see where the weaknesses were. I wasn't sure about calling them out, but fuck it. It was how I worked. So, I did. I told the captain to lift his shoulder on his slapshot. He blinked at me and skated away —but the next time he took possession and aimed for my net, that shoulder didn't drop.

"Glove save!" I shouted as the disc hit my palm.

"Dammit," he groaned, drifting toward me.

I lifted my helmet and took a drink. "Better. How did it feel?"

He grinned. "Better. Thanks, Sieve."

"Fuck off."

We stared at each other for a moment. Then, both of us laughed.

"Welcome to the team, Molls."

"Thanks, Cap."

"The wife and I want to welcome you to the team before the first game. My house, four o'clock tomorrow. You free?"

"I am."

"Good. I've already told the other guys. Bring your girl-friend—wife, whatever."

I twisted my lips. "I'll be there."

By the time we got to the locker room, more of the guys were ready to chat with me. All in all, it was a good first meeting. Even better, I had a new spreadsheet to create. Something to do with my too-empty personal time.

I walked through the lobby with my phone in my hand.

ME:

Can we talk tonight? It's been too long.

NICA:

When?

ME:

I'll be in my room in 2 mins. Whenever.

NICA:

Speak soon then. Xoxo

Off the elevator, I couldn't wait any more. I dialed her as I headed for my room at the end of the hall.

"That was like one minute," she said in greeting.

"Couldn't wait to hear your voice. What are you doing?"

"Just sitting here, waiting for you."

There was a tease in her voice like a spring breeze. I grinned and fished my key card out of my wallet. "Wearing what, exactly?"

I pushed the door open as she said, "See for yourself."

Nica's voice hit me in surround sound. Both from the phone's speaker—

And from the middle of the suite.

## 33

## NICA

He froze as the door fell shut behind him. I darkened my phone and watched him gape at me. At last, he set his phone down, but he still didn't move. Henrik danced at his feet, beside himself with joy to see his dad again. At last, Ryan bent down and used both hands to pet the pup.

My heart crawled up my throat. To be fair, it had done that regularly for the past two days.

"Nica?" he whispered at last.

I swallowed hard and tried to remember what I'd planned to say. "You said I could come anytime. So, I did. *We* did."

"I didn't see the flight on the card. How did you get him on the plane?"

"I didn't. I drove."

His jaw fell open. "Why?"

*Just do it. Be bold. Be audacious. Be—oh, just do it.* "Because we had to bring our stuff. Good thing I got a new car. The old one wouldn't have made it cross-country in February."

"Nica, that wasn't safe. You should've—"

"No, Goalie. *You* should've. You should've stopped for a

second to think about what you were doing leaving me behind. How dare you? How dare you force me to drive three thousand miles with nothing but my thoughts and Henrik to keep me company? Do you know how loud the voices in my head were? How many times they screamed at me that this was a huge mistake? Asked what the hell I was doing, having the nerve to come here? As if I had any right to just waltz into your hotel room. As if you would even want to see me."

He swallowed hard. "You have every right. And of course I do."

"You say that. But you didn't send for me. Didn't break down and hop a plane to come get me. You... you were content to leave, Ryan."

Damn the tears that I promised I wouldn't cry. I bit down on my wobbly lip.

Ryan threw himself to his knees in front of me. His hands gripped my waist. Green eyes begged me. "I am nowhere near content. I am a fucking *mess*. And a goddamn fool. I had no choice but to go, Nica. But I know I fucked this up. I know it was all my shit that kept me from strategizing better for us. I just didn't want you to have to choose between me and Seacrest. I didn't want to pull you from your happy life just to follow me. Who am I? How could I ask for that? And what would I do when you—when you regretted it?"

His voice broke in a hoarse rasp that shattered my heart. I sobbed ugly tears. "You are my goalie," I bawled, but my voice was garbled.

He cocked his head. "What did you say?"

I tried to check the mess. "You... you are my goalie. That's who you are. I come from *nothing*, Ryan. From a trailer park in rural Connecticut. Everything I've ever done,

I made happen for myself. I've slept in my car, stashed food in my purse to keep from going hungry, and *made do*. And somehow, some fucking how, all that led me to you. To a life. To the little family you, me, and Henrik were becoming.

"I am sure I don't deserve all the love you've given me. I'm also damn sure *you* don't deserve the way I'm overriding your silly fears and obviously flawed plans."

"I definitely don't."

"But it's not about what we deserve or don't deserve." My tears abated, leaving my voice softer.

Ryan nodded up at me. "It's really not."

"It's about what we choose. And I have chosen to fuck with your plans, just like I fucked with your luck. I came out here to stay, Goalie. I don't want to be without you. I'm scared as hell to leave home. I'll miss everyone so, so badly. But if I'm going to say yes to loving you, then I'm going to be in on the hard parts, too. I'll find my way here. I'll go home to visit sometimes. But I'd very much like to work on our life together. If you want it, too."

His hold on me changed. Ryan's fingers loosened to tickle just under my sweater. "Would it be worth it?"

"The trouble?" I grinned, and he nodded. "You tell me."

"Hell yes, it would."

I gripped his shoulders and fell forward. He held onto me as we tumbled to the ground in a kiss. Immediately, Henrik's tongue and wet nose pressed against both our cheeks. Passion dissolved into laughter as we squirmed at the puppy kisses.

Ryan nudged Henrik back an inch and scratched his head. He grinned up at me with tears in his eyes. "Oh, god. I missed my family."

Another sob spilled out of me. "We missed you, too, Goalie."

# EPILOGUE
## NICA

My husband and I just got married.

I was in a gorgeous knee-length dress with a v-neck and beading. Perfect for a wedding in Turks and Caicos. He wore a gray suit that made him more dashing than ever. Henrik sported a sharp little doggy bowtie and stood as our ringbearer.

We waited a year to officially tie the knot because February in the islands seemed right. Everyone in Oregon knew I was Ryan's partner from the start. The day after I arrived, we pulled ourselves out of bed to make it to the party on time. He stayed close to me as we weaved among so many new but friendly faces. Both of us were a bit over-whelmed to be in such a spotlight, but by the time we left, we had very good vibes about the new team.

A feeling that only got reinforced as the months went on.

It was a long summer since we didn't make the playoffs. That gave Ryan and me time to choose our house, remodel it how we wanted, and decorate it to our liking. He left for training camp for several weeks in August. I missed the hell out of him, but I took one week back in Connecticut and spent the rest of the time with my new friends in Portland. All the while, I ran his social media. The head of marketing for the team, Lauren, offered me a job. I held out until the start of the season, a little superstitious about getting into something just to leave again.

Oh, but the day Ryan came home from contract negotiations.

It was just before the opening preseason games. He staggered in, glassy-eyed, and whispered a number that sounded fake.

"No, Nica. It's *real*."

My mouth opened and closed. "Well. I guess I won't mind when you buy me pretty things with money like that."

He just laughed.

And now, in front of family and old and new friends, I watched my husband pull off his glasses and lean in as the officiant said, "Kiss the bride."

Whoops and cheers floated up and mingled with the shushing waves behind us. We faced all our favorite people hand-in-hand.

"Ladies and gentlemen, may I present Mr. and Mrs. Ryan Molloy!"

∽

**Max is a laid-back defenseman with a mess on his hands. Dani is the matchmaker his momma hired to find him a date.**

*Deked* is fake dating like you've never seen it before. Start it right now.

# DEKED

Dani

I applied a fresh layer of lipstick by using my camera's selfie mode as a mirror. We rolled to a stop in front of a quaint Colonial in the South West neighborhood of Hartford.

With a deep breath, I pushed away the thought that I had no freaking time for this. Mom called yesterday afternoon with a convoluted story that I was still trying to sort out:

Alice hosted Mom's weekly club. She had a teenage granddaughter who told her about... some hockey player. Lana, another club member, had a son. A "nice young man," which told me fuck-all about him, including how old he might be. Could I possibly do Mom a favor and come talk to this nice young man? Help him find a good match?

I hadn't played matchmaker in years. The more the company grew, the further removed I was from our product. But I'd started Hearted after working as a matchmaker in Boston and building a reputation for excellence.

Of course, that was before my personal love life went up in smoke.

And, of course, Mom wouldn't hear any of those protestations. "You're the best, Dani. Max is so sweet. A perfect gentleman. He needs someone good. Do it for me. Please?"

How could I refuse? Mom had let me live with her after Paul and I split in the middle of Hearted's second year. She'd given me shelter and food while I launched a company, and she asked for nothing.

So there I was on a Monday night, out in Hartford, walking into a stranger's house to meet some kid who needed a date. I glanced at the shiny F-150 parked in the drive and pursed my lips. *So he's old enough to drive. What are you hauling with that big ol' truck, Max?*

The house's front door opened before I was halfway up the walk. Mom beamed at me while two other women peered over her shoulders. "Dani!"

"Hey, Mom." I kissed her cheek and stepped inside.

"Dani, this is Alice. And this is Lana, Max's mom."

I shook their hands while Mom made introductions. "So, where is Max?"

"He's in the den. Bless his heart, he's nervous. Sitting there like he's been put on punishment," Lana said, and I immediately noticed her Southern drawl.

Lana looked to be around Mom's age, but I pictured a teenage boy, head hung low, scrawny arms crossed. Dressed in an old graphic tee and ratty jeans, sporting peach fuzz on his cheeks. Glaring at me while I introduced myself. Refusing to give me any information on himself or why I'd been summoned to meet him.

I pursed my lips into a tight smile. "I'll try to make this as painless as possible. Is there a place he and I can talk in private?"

Alice nodded. "Of course. We'll clear out of the den and leave you two there. Once the door's closed, we won't be able to eavesdrop—even though I know we want to."

The other two laughed while I smiled. "Great. Let's dive in. Lead the way."

We walked down a short hallway in a little line, with me at the rear. They stepped through a doorway and fanned out. I followed them in to come face-to-face with two other women. They smiled at me and quickly stepped aside to reveal a round games table and Max seated in the corner.

My thoughts froze. So did my feet.

Not a kid. Not grungy. Not glaring. And *definitely* not scrawny. I could not have been more wrong.

The man in front of me wore a white dress shirt open at the collar. His chocolate-brown hair was combed back from his face in stylish waves. A well-groomed line of stubble edged his square jaw and enhanced his mouth. And... my god. A little tuxedo cat peeked out of the lapels of his gray suit coat. It mewled, so he scratched its head. His palm was so big that the cat almost disappeared.

I stared while he lifted the cat from his jacket and bent beside the table. The sound of a pet carrier's door latching hit my ears. Then, his gaze locked onto me with a guarded but steady stare. Slowly, he rose from his seat.

*My god. He's massive.*

He towered over everyone in the room. His suit was clearly bespoke, but it couldn't hide how broad his shoulders and arms were. He wore matching trousers with a black belt around his slim waist.

*You are a professional matchmaker, Daniela Moon. Act accordingly.*

**Keep reading *Deked***

Thank you for reading *In the Crease*! If you enjoyed it, I'd love so much for you to leave a review on Amazon or BookBub.

~

**More Commodores Action:**
Read Quinn & Audrey's book, *Scoreless*.

Read Stella & Ethan's book, *Scored On*.

Read Max & Dani's book, *Deked*.

Read Lucas & Neve's book, *In the Slot*.

(All of my books are stand-alone stories. Together, they make a world for you to get lost in!)

***Want a free story? Then Get on Skye's Newsletter Now!***

# ACKNOWLEDGMENTS

This book was a tough one. Not because Nica & Ryan didn't belong together. Because I've written this through a period of change that I didn't see coming.

When do we ever see it coming?

But even in the storms of life, I have my people. And for that, I am immensely grateful.

So thank you to the kindred spirits who have been there with and for me in this strange time. Your presence means more than I can put into words.

Thank you to Jarred for again being my technical support as I wrote another goalie story.

And thank you to my readers, who keep shouting GAME ON to the love stories!

# ABOUT THE AUTHOR

Skye McDonald writes books that will make you laugh, cry, and swoon. She believes that falling in love with yourself is the real path to happily ever after.

Skye's first novel, *Not Suitable for Work*, won the Linda Howard Award for Romance in 2019. *Scoreless,* her first hockey romance, was an Amazon Bestseller and #1 New Release. Her co-authored Unlikely Pairings Series have also held bestseller status.

Born in Nashville, Tennessee, Skye spent years teaching English in Brooklyn, New York. Now, she lives in Montclair, New Jersey, where she writes and facilitates a women's group. In her free time, she hikes with her dogs, travels, Scuba dives, bakes killer biscotti. Someday she'll take a break and chill out, preferably on a beach. But not yet. There's so much life to live first.

# MORE BOOKS TO BINGE

## The Connecticut Commodores Series

Book 1: Scoreless

Book 2: Scored On

Book 3: In the Crease

Book 4: Deked

Book 5: In the Slot

## The Anti-Belle Series

Book 1: Not Suitable for Work

Book 2: Off the Record

Book 3: Nemesis

Book 4: Just Your Type

Book 5: What Happens At the Beach

# LOVE & MIXTAPES SERIES

1. Side A: Summer Heart

2. Side B: Summer Hate

3. The Hidden Track

## As Sarah Skye

The Unlikely Pairings Series

www.ingramcontent.com/pod-product-compliance
Lightning Source LLC
Chambersburg PA
CBHW070638260626
47161CB00007B/2748